Christine Merrill lives on a farm in Wisconsin, USA, with her husband, two sons and too many pets—all of whom would like her to get off the computer so they can check their e-mail. She has worked by turns in theatre costuming and as a librarian. Writing historical romance combines her love of good stories and fancy dress with her ability to stare out of the window and make stuff up.

Liz Tyner lives with her husband on an Oklahoma acreage she imagines is similar to the one in the children's book *Where the Wild Things Are*. Her lifestyle is a blend of old and new, and is sometimes comparable to the way people lived long ago. Liz is a member of various writing groups and has been writing since childhood. For more about her, visit liztyner.com.

Elizabeth Beacon has a passion for history and storytelling—and, with the English West Country on her doorstep, she never lacks a glorious setting for her books. Elizabeth tried horticulture, higher education as a mature student, briefly taught English and worked in an office before finally turning her daydreams about dashing piratical heroes and their stubborn and independent heroines into her dream job: writing Regency romances for Mills & Boon.

REGENCY CHRISTMAS WEDDINGS

Christine Merrill,
Liz Tyner
and
Elizabeth Beacon

MILLS & BOON

First published in Great Britain 2024
by Mills & Boon, an imprint of HarperCollins*Publishers* Ltd,
1 London Bridge Street, London, SE1 9GF

www.harpercollins.co.uk

HarperCollins*Publishers*, Macken House, 39/40 Mayor Street Upper,
Dublin 1, D01 C9W8, Ireland

ISBN: 978-0-263-32098-5

11/24

This book contains FSC™ certified paper
and other controlled sources to ensure responsible forest management.

For more information visit www.harpercollins.co.uk/green.

Printed and Bound in the UK using 100% Renewable Electricity
at CPI Group (UK) Ltd, Croydon, CR0 4YY

CONTENTS

A MISTLETOE KISS
FOR THE GOVERNESS

Christine Merrill

To Annie Warren.

Off to a great start.

Chapter One

December 1814

Major Frederick Preston stared out of the window of the hired carriage at the bustle of London, still amazed to be home. It had been five years since he'd been in England, but now that Napoleon had been exiled to Elba, he was confident that the war was over. There was no reason he should not return to see how much his daughters had grown.

'How is the leg?' This comment came from his travelling companion, a captain in the Fusiliers who was sharing the ride into the city.

Frederick flexed his knee, trying not to grimace at the injury that was still not healed, though it had been over six months since he'd taken a ball at Toulouse. 'Fine, thank you.'

In truth, it was beastly. When he had been on the ship from Calais there had been space to walk around and keep the joint limber. But on the ride from Dover, it had grown stiffer and more painful by the mile.

'It will be better once you are home with your family,' the Captain said, ignoring his lie. 'The last time I was in London, I enjoyed dinner and a delightful evening of cards with your daughters. It is most kind of you to open your house to junior officers when you are not there. We are all very grateful for your generosity.'

Frederick smiled and nodded. 'I know how lonely it can be when one is between postings and without the proper time to have a decent meal. The least I can offer is dinner now and then. And in her letters my girls' governess assures me they appreciate the company.'

'Mrs Lewis?' the man said with a smile.

'You have met her then?' he asked, trying not to appear too curious.

'She is never far from the girls when we are there,' the Captain assured him.

'Lewis has been a godsend,' Frederick admitted. 'I hired her through an agency while I was in Portugal and she took everything in hand with barely a word of instruction from me.'

'You have never met her?' the man said, surprised.

Frederick shook his head. 'We correspond frequently, but I have been rather busy these last years…'

The Captain laughed at this assessment of a long and brutal war, then said, 'You will be pleasantly surprised, I am sure. Mrs Lewis is a favourite of the regiment.'

'Like a mother to you all,' he said, for didn't all governesses have a maternal air about them?

There was a strange pause, probably caused as the carriage bounced in a rut. Then the Captain gave a weak nod and said, 'You really have not met her.'

'But I am looking forward to it,' Frederick replied. 'I wish I'd had her on the front lines to teach my Lieutenants how to write reports. Her letters were succinct without missing a detail.'

'A useful skill,' the Captain agreed.

'And the old dear follows orders like a seasoned campaigner. When it comes to the care of my children, I have but to ask and she obeys.'

'The old dear,' the Captain said, smiling into the dark.

The carriage was slowing now and Frederick smiled as it proceeded the last few yards to stop in front of his town house. 'Home at last,' he said, slapping his knees with his hands to pound the blood back into his legs. 'We shall see you at dinner soon, I hope.'

'I welcome the invitation,' the other man said, reaching to open the door for him. 'Give my regards to the girls. And Mrs Lewis, of course.'

'Of course,' Frederick said. While he had missed his children and was eager to come home to them, he felt a similar excitement at the prospect of meeting the woman who had cared for them. After years of correspondence, he viewed her more as a friend than an employee. Her letters had been a source of comfort on some of his most difficult days, giving him little slices of the life he missed to raise his spirits. Even when relaying a domestic crisis, she solved the problem with maturity and wisdom and ended the letter with a happy outcome to assure him that all would be well when he returned.

And now, at last, he was coming home to enjoy the fruits of her governance. He took one last, steadying breath before grabbing his stick and heaving himself out of the carriage with a smile, then limped to the front door.

'Father is here!' Eleanor Preston stood in the little window by the door to the town house, bouncing from side to side with excitement. 'The carriage has stopped. The door is opening.'

'Let me see,' her sister Jane said, pushing her out of the way.

'Ladies,' Charlotte Lewis said with gentle admonition, 'remember your manners. You are no longer children and you do not want your father to think he is coming home to a pair of hoydens.'

The sisters immediately calmed themselves and stepped away from the window to stand side by side and straight ahead like a pair of their father's soldiers.

Charlotte smiled in approval. At sixteen and nineteen respectively, the girls were not quite of age. But they had been children when their father had last seen them and she wanted the Major to be impressed by how much they had changed. They were lovely young women now and a credit to his name.

'I was so afraid he would not be here in time for the

ceremony,' Jane whispered, raising up on the balls of her feet for one last peek through the glass.

'He promised he would come,' Charlotte reminded her. 'It would take more than Napoleon to keep him away from your wedding.' He had assured her of it in his letter, but his homecoming had been delayed several times already and it was hard to believe that their waiting was finally over.

She resisted the urge to peer through the window for a first glimpse to assure herself that he was well. In truth, she was just as excited by this homecoming as the girls were, though it was not her place to be so. She was only a servant. Her happiness did not signify.

All the same, her heart leapt when the door opened and a man in a dashing red coat limped though, shaking snowflakes from his hat before setting it on a side table and turning to accept the embraces of his daughters.

She recognised him instantly, for she had seen his face often enough in the little miniature portrait that Jane kept on her bedside table. That picture had been painted years ago, when he had been younger and war had not taken a toll on him. He was still tall and broad-shouldered, but there were touches of grey in the temples of his brown hair and a small scar slicing though his right eyebrow.

She could see lines around his mouth as well, signs of the barely contained pain that his injury must be causing him. It was bad, she was sure, and she ached for him. But she offered a silent prayer of thanks that he was here and on two legs. For some time after the Battle of Toulouse, they had feared him dead. Even after he had been found and taken to hospital, two months had passed when he'd been too weak from blood loss and fever to write them. It had been months after that before he'd been strong enough to travel.

The wait for news had seemed interminable. She'd been as distraught as the girls during that long silence and rejoiced with them when it had ended. And celebrated again, when alone in her room, hugging herself and smiling at the thought that the meeting she'd longed for would finally occur.

His letters had been so much more to her than mundane correspondence from an employer to an underling. He'd filled them with stories of the places and people that he saw, hinting at the glories and terrors and boredoms of his days in a way that her late husband never had bothered with. Though he'd been away at sea for much of their marriage, his letters had been brief and irregular.

But the Major was a natural storyteller. Perhaps that was why she felt such a connection to him. And now here he was, an arm wrapped around each daughter, staring at them in amazement as they squealed in delight.

'So tall,' he said in an awed voice. 'My dear Jane, you are taller than your mother was when she passed.' He glanced to the other. 'And my little Eleanor. Not so little any more.'

'You are being silly,' Eleanor said with a laugh. 'Jane is to be married and next Season I will be out.'

'You certainly will not,' he said with a mocking smile.

'You are far too young. And you, Jane, cannot mean to leave me just as I have finally come home.'

'We already have your consent,' she reminded him. 'Jeremy saw to that before offering.'

'He is a fine young man,' her father agreed, giving her a peck on the cheek. 'But I still have you for several days and mean to make the most of them.'

The footman was bringing in the luggage and Eleanor broke free to open the nearest valise.

'Here, now,' her father said. 'What are you doing?'

'Searching for presents,' she said, showing no shame.

Charlotte cleared her throat to remind her not to be greedy and the Major glanced up, noticing her for the first time. Then he smiled and she felt the warmth to the tips of her toes. 'Christmas is not for two days, Eleanor. Your gifts will wait until then. For now, you must show your manners and introduce me to your friend.'

'Our friend?' said Eleanor with a laugh.

'You know Mrs Lewis,' Jane said.

'She has been here for ever,' Eleanor agreed.

His smile faded as he stared at her, confused. 'Lewis?' he said, furrowing his brow.

She had been longing to hear that single word for months, for he never called her Mrs Lewis in his letters. This abbreviation of her name had come to feel familiar, rather than dismissive, as if he was speaking to a comrade. It was never, 'Lewis, do this' or 'Lewis, do that' as if commanding an underling. Instead, he might write 'The most interesting thing happened the other day, Lewis…' The name felt like a touch on the shoulder, drawing her into a private conversation, away from the rest of the world.

But now it was spoken with confusion, as if he could not quite place who she might be. Had he really forgotten her, after all the letters they'd exchanged? She hid her disappointment beneath a professional smile and dropped a curtsy, eyes bowed. 'Sir.'

'Lewis,' he said in the same dazed tone, then gave a small shake of his head and said, 'Of course.'

'It is good to have you home, Sir,' she said, for what harm could there be in saying so? 'Tea has been laid in the sitting room, in anticipation of your arrival.'

'Tea,' he repeated in the same dull tone.

'And sandwiches and cakes,' she assured him. 'If you prefer something stronger, you have but to ring.'

'Of course,' he said, still staring at her as if she was a stranger.

If she were a lady, she might have flounced away at this cold greeting. But she was his servant. It was not her place to come and go as she pleased. He needed to dismiss her and she prayed it would be soon, for she could not stand another moment of this unexpected awkwardness between them. 'If there is nothing else,' she prompted, 'I will leave you alone with your family.'

At last, he seemed to remember himself and said, 'That will be all, Lewis.'

'Thank you, Sir.' She turned before he could see her expression of disappointment and hurried up the stairs to her room. What had she been expecting? He was tired after a long journey and she was only a member of the staff.

She would take this time alone to get hold of herself and banish any nonsense she'd imagined about their first meeting, how he would greet her as an old friend, or perhaps, something more. If she did not learn to hide her feelings, it might mean the end of her position here. Her affection for him would be an unwelcome embarrassment.

For now, she would stay away until summoned. The family did not need her to watch their reunion. They had much to talk of and she had no part in it.

Chapter Two

As the girls led him into the sitting room, Frederick cast a confused glance back at the woman retreating up the stairs. In his experience, governesses were old. The lady who had raised him had certainly been.

In the five years since he'd hired her, he'd had ample time to create a similar image of Lewis in his head. His Lewis, his faithful sergeant on the home front, was an elderly woman, still in mourning black for a husband she'd lost long before he'd hired her. Though she was childless, she treated his girls as her own and was as vigilant of their honour as a hawk watching over her chicks.

That image, of a bird of prey, formed much of his picture of her. Her features would be sharp and her gaze as steely as the grey in her hair. Despite her stern appearance, she was not humourless, for her letters revealed a sly wit and an ability to laugh at herself and the antics of her charges. She was tough but fair and the girls loved her like a mother.

How was he to reconcile that with the petite blonde who

had been standing in the hallway just now? That woman…
No. That girl had been rosy cheeked with a halo of curls
that framed her perfect, heart-shaped face. Her eyes were
not steely but wide and blue, full of humour and kindness.

The expression in them as she'd looked at him had been
so warm and gracious that he'd felt irrationally happy just
to be near her. He wanted to bask in that gaze, to bathe in
it like the waters of a healing spring.

He blinked to clear such thoughts from his head. She
was a servant and it would not do to be gawping at her
like a moon calf, especially when he had his own two girls
both eager for his fatherly attention. There would be time
enough later to speak with Lewis and to decide what, if
anything, needed to be done about his misunderstanding.

Several hours had passed and it was clear that his girls
lacked Lewis's reticent nature. They talked without stopping for breath, as if it were possible to tell him the events
of half a decade in a single afternoon. When the housekeeper came to summon them to dinner, he was ready for
a peaceful meal.

But apparently they were not. Eleanor took one look at
the place settings and stopped in the doorway as if refusing to enter. 'This is wrong,' she announced.

'There is no place set for Mrs Lewis,' Jane agreed,
reaching for a bell pull.

'Because staff does not dine with family,' he said automatically, surprised that they did not know the fact.

'Mrs Lewis is not staff,' Eleanor said, puzzled.

'I beg to differ,' he replied, taking his place at the head of the table. 'I distinctly remember hiring her.'

'And she has been eating with us each night since you did,' Jane said.

'But I am home now,' he said shaking his napkin into his lap.

They stared at him in silent disapproval. Apparently, though they had been treating him as if he'd hung the moon for the last three hours, his sole presence now was not enough.

He sighed. 'Call her to dinner, then. It seems that I will have no peace until she joins us and I have been looking forward to a meal at home for longer than you can imagine.'

There was a brief delay as the governess was called for and the table rearranged with a place set a ways down from the family.

'Satisfied?' he asked his daughters.

'She usually sits to the right.' Eleanor pointed to the seat next to him.

Mrs Lewis cleared her throat. 'That is Jane's place, until she marries and leaves the house.'

The single quiet phrase was all it took to secure his daughters' obedience. They sat and the meal began.

It was clear that the cook meant to impress him with a lavish repast though Christmas was only a few days away. The table was crowded with more fish and game than he had seen in ages.

But his mind was not on the food. He could not seem to

pull his attention from the woman sitting in silence down the table from him. 'Lewis,' he said at last. 'It seems you have been presiding at meals in my absence.'

'Necessity dictated,' she said, meeting his eyes with the same pleasant smile she'd worn to greet him in the hall. 'Your daughters are far too old to be eating in the nursery and required instruction in the manners required to eat at the adult table.'

He nodded, not convinced.

'And of course, there were frequent gentlemen guests,' she added. 'Someone had to chaperon, if we were to entertain officers every night of the week.'

'So, this change protocol was of my making?' he asked.

'Since there were no specific instructions, I did what I thought was best,' she said.

'And did not feel it necessary to tell me about it in your letters,' he added. Suddenly, her efficient communication felt suspiciously brief.

'There was not space to tell you everything,' she said, in the same reasonable tone she'd been using.

'I see.'

'She will stay with us in the sitting room after dinner as well,' Eleanor announced.

'That is not up to me,' Lewis informed her, looking down at her plate.

Now both girls were looking at him to affirm that this stranger would be tucked into the midst of the family for the evening.

Of course, she wasn't a stranger. She was Lewis and

he knew her well. But when had he ever, even in the most desperately lonely moments of the last five years, wished to see Lewis wearing a low-cut dinner gown and not the practical buttoned-up uniform of a governess? The Lewis he'd known had been a trusted aide-de-camp. This woman, with her trim figure and inviting smile, was as dangerous to his nerves as a French brigade.

The girls were still staring at him, waiting, and he surrendered with a sigh. 'She will join us at table and in the sitting room after. Because, apparently, that is the way things are done here.'

Then he went back to his meal and did his best to ignore her.

The Major was displeased with her.

Charlotte smiled down into her empty plate, her expression unwavering, for she did not wish the girls to know how much this troubled her, nor would she let her employer see her wilting at his disapproval.

She'd suspected that she had overstepped her authority on more than one occasion. But she'd known nothing about being a governess when she'd taken the job. Though her father had been a gentleman, her family had been poor and her parents had raised and educated her without the help of one.

When she'd accepted the position in the Preston household, there had been no lady of the house to guide her and the Major was away in Portugal. So, she had followed her own judgement in setting rules and hoped for the best.

For the most part, things had gone well. Both girls were sweet tempered and well mannered, and Jane had already found a man that the Major approved of.

She had known that things would change with his return and that one did not cross the master of the house, especially not on his first day home. She had tried not to do so. She had planned to take dinner alone in her room like a proper servant and sit the night by her own fire, not disturbing anyone with her company.

But he had summoned her and she'd had no choice but to obey. The fact that he did not seem happy to have her here was not something she could change. Perhaps, if she were quiet and stayed in the corner of the sitting room when they retired after dinner, he would forget all about her again.

But that was not to be. When she retrieved her work basket from its place by her usual chair and carried it to the back of the room, Jane said, 'Do not be silly. You cannot sew a straight seam in the dark. Come sit by the fire, as you always do.'

The Major, who had taken the large wing chair that they'd always saved for him, looked surprised. 'Lewis, are you in the habit of sitting there?' He pointed to the smaller chair, just across from him.

'I did when you were away,' she said, hoping that he and the girls would drop the subject and let her return to the corner.

'That is the seat for the lady of the house,' he said, still staring at her.

'But Mama has been gone even longer than you have,' Jane said. 'And it seemed foolish for her to sit at the back of the room alone when her job was to watch over us.'

'I see,' he said, giving Charlotte a stern look. 'Well, then, by all means, liberty hall. Take your seat.'

She gathered up her work again and went back to her usual chair, staring down into her mending basket so that she did not have to watch him watch her.

'Would you like to hear me read, Papa?' Eleanor asked, ready to distract him.

'Of course, my dear,' he said, smiling at his daughter and immediately forgetting his irritation.

She reached for the book they had been reading and Charlotte tried not to wince.

'I will catch you up on the plot,' Eleanor said. 'It is called *The Animated Skeleton* and is about the unfortunate Count Richard who is usurped by Albert and Brunchilda. They are terrible, but there is a skeleton that is thwarting all their plans. Let me begin.'

She took a deep breath and intoned, *"'I would this minute kill thee and banish thy vile soul from the earth which thou emcumberest, wert thou not reserved for greater torments.'"* She finished the line with a diabolical laugh that made the Major nearly start out of his chair.

As she read on, describing the lurid tortures in the book, the narrow escapes and improbable horrors with relish, Charlotte could feel the Major staring not at his daughter, but at her.

She stole a glance in his direction and could see him grow redder with each turn of the plot. Perhaps he thought that his daughters had read nothing but sermons and recipe books while he was gone. If so, it was proof that he did not know them very well. Especially not Eleanor, who had a touch of the macabre about her and devoured Gothic novels, the grislier the better.

When the clock struck eleven, the Major leaned forward in his chair and said, 'I think that is enough for the evening. Quite enough, thank you, Eleanor.'

She beamed at him. 'Did you enjoy it, Papa?'

'I found it most illuminating.' He shot another dark look in Charlotte's direction.

'It is my favourite story,' she said with pride. 'We have read it at least three times.'

'And now you are reading it for Christmas,' he said, with a grimace.

'Yes, I suppose we are,' Eleanor replied. 'And Mrs Lewis says, with my Christmas money, I shall be able to buy *The Mad Monk of Montenero*. It is just out and is supposed to be a cracking good story with a weeping ghost and a tiger pit.'

'We shall have to see,' he replied.

'Goodnight, Papa,' she said, giving him a kiss on the cheek.

'And to you, my dear,' he said, managing to smile again.

Jane came to wish him a similar goodnight. While she was doing so, Charlotte folded her work and got up from her chair, hoping she might go to her room unnoticed and put the night behind her.

But before she could make it to the door, she heard the Major's voice, sharp as a rifle shot in the silence of the room.

'Lewis.'

She turned back to him, schooling her face to a neutral mask. 'Sir?'

'May I see you in my study, please?'

'Of course, Sir.' She followed him out of the room and down the hall, where he gestured her through the door and into his study, a room she'd rarely had reason to enter while he was away. Once inside, he shut the door behind them, taking the seat at the desk and indicating, with a sharp flick of his finger, that she take the chair facing him on the opposite side.

She sat, hands folded in her lap, and waited for the explosion.

It did not come, which was almost more terrifying than shouting would have been. Instead, he said in a deceptively quiet voice, 'Well, Lewis, what have you to say for yourself?'

She was unsure how to respond. There was something in his manner that made her want to confess every sin, even those he had not discovered yet. She wet her lips.

For a moment, his face went blank, as it had when he had first looked at her in the hall. Then he focused again, his gaze even sharper than it had been before. 'Don't think you can get around me by stalling. Tell me what you meant by taking the mistress's seat at table and in the sitting room. And what do you mean by permitting my daughters to read garbage?'

'I meant no disrespect,' she said cautiously. 'But when I arrived here, I was under the impression that there had been no mistress in the house for some years already.'

'My wife died when Eleanor was eight,' he affirmed.

'And the governess you had for the first three years was in the habit of locking the children in their rooms for their dinner,' she said, scowling back at him. 'When I met them, they had been left unsupervised and uneducated for the better part of three years, and lacked the skills and graces required of young ladies their age.'

'That is why she was sacked,' he said, giving no quarter.

'The dining room had been given over to entertaining your guests, who behaved as men will when they do not have the moderating influence of ladies,' she said. 'In short, they also lacked the dignity and courtesy one might expect of guests in a decent household.'

He leaned back in his chair, as if surprised that she had dared to suggest his friends were anything less than complete gentlemen.

She pressed on. 'In bringing the girls down to table myself, I solved two problems in one. I took a seat near the top of the table, with the girls, but had the servants set your place and left the chair empty as a silent reminder that you might return at any time and see how they behaved.' She smiled at the memory. 'And the officers who came to dine were so embarrassed by the presence of the girls that they were, thenceforth, on their best behaviour.'

'And the sitting room,' he said, still trying to find fault.

'Is exceptionally draughty. We are all in the habit of sitting close to the fire in winter. But, as with the table, your chair remains empty.'

'And the Gothic rubbish…'

'They may be young ladies, but they are also a soldier's children and have a bloodthirsty streak that even I cannot curb. Eleanor can be particularly ghoulish.' She offered a half shrug. 'During the day, they read French and Latin with their lessons. But I allow them to choose the evening's readings when we are alone together.'

There was a long pause as he digested what she had told him. His expression was still grim, but she could not detect the barely contained fury that she had sensed when they entered the room. She waited nervously for his verdict.

'Very well,' he said at last. 'You have done the best you could under difficult circumstances. Until after the wedding, you may continue to take dinner with the family and join us in the sitting room after. But I would ask that you remember your place and know that these privileges are granted by me and can be taken away just as easily.'

'Of course, Sir,' she said.

'Very good.' He was staring at her again, as if there was something more he wished to say. And, as the seconds ticked by, the room seemed to get smaller and warmer. She stared back at him, thinking that the little portrait she had seen did not do justice to the blue of his eyes. She could stare into them for ever, if he would let her.

Then, with a little shake of his head, the connection was broken. 'You are dismissed, Lewis.'

'Thank you, Sir.'

Frederick watched as she rose and left him, letting out a long, slow breath and hoping it would cool his blood. It had all been so simple when he was in France. The employment agency had promised Charlotte Lewis was 'a woman of good character and widow of a naval officer'. From that, he'd formed his own opinions, filing her neatly in a slot in his mind for 'old governess'.

But now that he could see her, every interaction was complicated by her beauty. At dinner, she had been far enough away so that he could admire her in an academic sort of way, acknowledging that she was lovely while enjoying his meal. But in the sitting room, she'd been closer, sharing the fire with him as a wife might. At least there had been the presence of the girls and Eleanor's horrible story to keep his mind from dwelling on the way the firelight danced in her eyes and turned her hair to gold.

But just now, when he'd been alone with her, the door closed and the house asleep? He could barely think straight. If she'd dissolved into tears over his scolding, it might have been easier to stand. A display of emotion would have annoyed him, perhaps giving him a distaste of her.

Instead, she'd been as coolly logical as she had been in her letters. Except for that moment of hesitation when her tongue had darted along her lower lip. Had she been trying to provoke him? Because, for a moment, he'd been transfixed by that kissable mouth, unable to string two thoughts together. And then, when he'd managed to get all the answers from her that he required, he had not wanted to let her go.

There was only one reason to be locked away with a beautiful woman for any length of time and there was nothing proper about it. If she was to remain in this house, working for him, he must be sure that no more of these private interviews were needed. Though he'd thought himself battle hardened, his nerves were not strong enough for too much time with Charlotte Lewis.

Chapter Three

The next morning was Christmas Eve and, as she always was, Charlotte was the one to supervise the decorating of the house. The footman had stacked the front hall tables with an assortment of fresh greens: pine and bay and hawthorn, holly and ivy. The cook and housekeeper had filled bowls with nuts, apples and oranges, some of which were studded with cloves. The air was filled with the scent of spice and evergreen and she smiled and hummed a carol as she gathered ribbons to add colour to the garlands she was making.

Then she sent the girls from room to room, draping mantels and windowsills, and tying bows on sconces and chandeliers.

When the Major came down to breakfast, they were just finishing the sitting room and she was balancing on a ladder, hanging a kissing bough of mistletoe and velvet streamers at the centre of the doorframe.

'What the devil are you doing?' he said, startling her and making her teeter on the ladder.

He stepped forward automatically and reached out to steady it as she grabbed at the door for support.

'We are decorating for Christmas,' Eleanor said, craning her head around Charlotte to answer her father.

'We have servants for this,' he said, then looked up at Lewis before adding, 'Other servants.'

'Christmas would not be the same if we left it all to the housekeeper,' Jane said, smiling just as brightly. 'When I have a home of my own, I shall decorate it, just like this.'

'With a kissing bough in every doorway,' Eleanor said with a giggle.

'What do you know about such things?' the Major said, frowning at his younger daughter.

Charlotte bit back a smile. It was very naive of him to think that the sixteen-year-old Eleanor would not be curious about kissing, especially with all the handsome Lieutenants that had been passing through the house at supper.

Before she could say anything, Eleanor proved her point. 'It is hardly complicated,' she said. 'You kiss and then pull off a berry.' She pointed to her governess. 'Mrs Lewis is under the mistletoe right now, Papa, as are you.' She held out her hand in a gesture of revelation and smiled expectantly.

Though she knew it was wrong, it was what Charlotte had dreamed of when she'd thought of the Major coming home for Christmas. That there would be a random moment like this one where he realised why she had been so loyal to him all these years.

He was staring up at her now with the puzzled expression he'd worn yesterday, as if she were a problem that he could not manage to solve. And she remembered that one of the possible outcomes was to have her sacked at Christmas. He was her employer, nothing more than that.

She straightened the ball of mistletoe, then jumped from the ladder to be out of his reach just as he said, 'Certainly not.'

Then she gave Eleanor a warning look and said, 'It is a little early in the day for Christmas games. And, in any case, the decorations are not here for me to enjoy.'

'In Portugal and France, we had no time for such nonsense,' the Major said, equally firm.

'But you are back now. We finally have you home again. The war is over and that is reason for celebration,' Eleanor reminded him with a smile. Then she turned to Charlotte. 'And you are not usually so stuffy, Mrs Lewis.'

'I am not being stuffy,' she insisted, though having to scold the girls always made her feel older than thirty-three. 'I am speaking the truth. I shall have all the fun I need on Boxing Day. Until then, it is my job to help you ready the house for the season. That is all.'

The girls were looking at her in surprise, for that was never the way it had been. She'd always taken joy in the Christmas season and celebrated it with the girls as a friend and not a servant, playing games and singing carols with them, before sitting down to a fine dinner on

Christmas Day. With their father gone, she had wanted to make the twelve days of Christmas as merry as possible.

But this year, they had a father to celebrate with and would not need her. The disappointment she felt was sharp and strong and it surprised her. To hide it, she grabbed a sprig of holly from the nearest table and said, 'And now I will go and be sure the cook has this to decorate the puddling.' Then she pushed past the Major without bothering to wait for a dismissal and headed for the kitchen, where the family would not see her should she shed a tear.

Frederick looked after her, then back to the girls, trying not to scowl. He was annoyed with himself and not them, for he must sound like a proper curmudgeon, railing against Christmas as he had. But his leg was paining him and the sight of Charlotte Lewis under the mistletoe had raised thoughts that an honourable man did not have towards a member of the staff. It did not help to have Eleanor suggesting that he act on them and claim it was the spirit of the season.

Now the girls were looking at him with trepidation, as if waiting for another scolding. They had done nothing to deserve it. It was he who was the problem and he had best acknowledge the fact.

He braced himself against the doorway to take the weight off his knee and folded his hands behind his back. 'I am sorry I was so short with you,' he said. 'Sometimes I forget that I am home and do not need to be a mean old soldier all the time.'

The girls gave him a relieved smile and Jane said, 'You do not need to order us about, you know. Our love is sufficient reason for us to obey you.'

'If you do not like the decorations, we will take them down,' Eleanor said, though she did not sound very enthusiastic about the fact.

'Of course not,' he said hurriedly. 'The room looks lovely.' If he was honest, it reminded him of a part of his life that he'd thought dead and buried, when his wife, Anna, was still alive and the girls were small, and he'd had no notion of loss or war. Would it really be so bad to let a little bit of that hope return to comfort him now?

'We usually leave the presents here on the mantel until tomorrow,' Eleanor said, pointing to an empty space among the greens. 'In case you have forgotten,' she said, giving him a sharp look.

'I have not forgotten,' he assured her, thinking of the silk shawls he'd bought in Paris for the girls.

'I have taken care of the Boxing Day packages for the servants,' Jane said in a motherly voice. 'But you must find something for Mrs Lewis. After all, she remembered to give us gifts each year, in case yours did not arrive on time.'

'I…' He had made a special effort to remember their governess. There was a gift in his luggage, right now. But that had been for the Lewis he'd expected to find, an old woman with an old woman's problems. He'd bought her a sensible woollen cap to wear in bed that would keep her poor ears warm all night.

He imagined those gold curls smashed beneath the dowdy thing and winced. She would look and feel a hundred years old in such a cap.

'I have got her a box of lace handkerchiefs and Jane has embroidered her a pair of mitts,' Eleanor said, giving him a look to remind him that, as master of the house, he must do better than either of those.

'I will find something,' he assured them, trying not to grit his teeth as he said it. The last thing he'd wanted to do, on Christmas Eve day, was to go to Bond Street. He'd much rather have braved a battle. When at war, one was allowed to cut down anyone that got in one's way. One did not have to stand patiently behind other people as they dawdled. 'And I suppose you will need me to help prepare for the wedding,' he added, ready to receive his orders from the bride.

'I think Mrs Lewis has taken care of everything,' Jane replied. 'St George's is reserved for ten o'clock on the twenty-eighth. We have set the menu for the breakfast. My dress has come from the modiste...'

'Then you do not need me for anything,' he said.

'You must give me away, of course,' Jane said, sensing his disappointment.

'And what about the flowers?' he asked.

'I had thought, perhaps, some of the greenery from the house,' she said, gesturing at the decorations on the mantel.

He smiled and shook his head. 'I must know someone

with a glasshouse in the country. You shall have roses, my dear. Nothing else will do.'

'Roses at Christmas,' she said, her eyes shining with unshed tears, and threw herself into his arms to kiss him on the cheek.

So he took his breakfast in the study and wrote letters to several of his friends, requesting that they send flowers immediately after Christmas. Then he summoned his carriage and set off for Bond Street.

His first stop was at his bank, to get a stack of shiny gold sovereigns to add to the staff Boxing Day gifts. From there, he went to a jeweller to find something special that the girls might wear to the wedding. He chose a pair of pendant crosses in amber and garnet hanging from fine gold chains and had them wrapped so he might give them at Christmas along with the silk shawls.

Now, he must find something to give to Lewis. The necklines of her gowns were cut too high for a necklace, but perhaps there were some earrings or a cameo here that might suit. Something small and impersonal, but as delicate and feminine as she was.

The proprietor sensed his hesitation and stepped forward to help. 'You are seeking a gift for a special lady, I assume?'

'Yes,' he agreed.

'Diamond bracelets are always a popular choice,' the man said, pointing to an elegant display. 'Or, perhaps, some earrings.' He withdrew a case from a drawer and opened it to reveal a pair so gawdy that they could only be worn by a courtesan.

'No,' Frederick said hurriedly. 'Not that sort of lady.'

'Your wife, perhaps?' the man said, gesturing to some necklaces that were just as expensive, but more tastefully designed.

'I have no wife,' he said, automatically.

'Not as of yet,' the man said, then opened another drawer and pulled out the tray to set it upon the counter.

Frederick stared into the velvet case that the man held, mesmerised. It was full of wedding bands. The ring that the jeweller indicated was set with emeralds and rubies arranged to look like the leaves and berries of a holly sprig. Without thinking, he reached out and touched it. Compared to the tiny circle of gold his hands were large and clumsy. But he could easily imagine this on Charlotte Lewis's slender fingers.

'Perfect for a Christmas wedding,' the jeweller coaxed.

He snatched his hand away. 'Not what I was looking for.' He had only known the woman two days, yet he had known her for years. He had trusted her with his daughters and she had been like a mother to them.

Not only that, she'd been his confidant. When he'd written to her, he'd often said more than he'd meant to about the loneliness and difficulty of his life away from home. At the time, he'd thought of her as a confessor. But perhaps it had been something more than that, all along.

And what had she thought of him?

It did not matter. She was a servant. He was her employer. If she saw him looking at wedding rings, she would think him a fool. He backed away from the case in confusion. 'I think the necklaces will be sufficient, thank you.'

The man looked disappointed at the loss of a sale, but wrapped the gifts he'd chosen. Then Frederick paid for them, dropped the packages into his pocket and went back out on to the street, sucking in a breath of city air to clear his head. Jewels were far too personal for Lewis, too likely to be misinterpreted as meaning something far more than they did.

Just down the way, there was a perfumery which would be much less intimidating. He used to get cologne for his mother, when he was a child, and she had been most happy with it. He would find something like that.

He pushed open the door and was instantly awash in scent, his senses muddled and his mind almost as confused as it had been in the jewellery shop.

'May I help you?' the girl behind the counter said with a sympathetic smile.

'Please,' he said, eyeing the plethora of delicate bottles around him with suspicion. 'I need a gift for a…friend.' That sounded innocent enough.

'A special friend,' she concluded. 'A lady.'

'A lady in every sense of the word,' he assured her, thinking of the gaudy eardrops in the last store.

'I am sure we have something to suit,' she said and turned to scan the shelves behind her. 'Is she young, this friend of yours?'

'Young,' he agreed. 'But not too young.' The agency

had said she'd been a widow for some time when he'd hired her, so she might not be as young as she looked. He was only forty himself, older than her, but not by an improper amount.

He blinked, confused again by the direction of his thoughts.

'She is still beautiful, I am sure,' the woman hinted.

'Very,' he said, for there was no ignoring the fact.

'And her heart,' the woman asked, tapping her own chest. 'What is it like?'

This question was even more confusing than the fragrances clouding his mind. Did he dare to even wonder about that?

When he did not answer, she tried again. 'Does she have hopes? Dreams? What does she want?'

He had not presumed to wonder. He had always assumed that her best years were behind her and that she would look on his children as she might her own grandchildren. But now, after seeing her, what did he know?

'She is a widow,' he admitted. 'A young widow. She has known disappointment, but it has not crushed her. Her heart is true. Her wit is sharp, but her nature is gentle. She is…' What was a word that would fit? 'She is a marvel.'

The woman smiled and nodded, then turned back to the shelf, scanning along the bottles before choosing one. Then she reached beneath the counter and withdrew a handkerchief, touching it to the mouth of the bottle. She wafted the cloth in the air to spread the scent in front of him.

He leaned into it, unable to resist.

It smelled of spring. Of new grass and tiny flowers and something else he could not name, something that drew him in and made him long for a future that was just out of reach.

'It will be different on her skin,' the girl warned. 'When heated by the blood, each perfume becomes unique to the wearer.'

A scent unique to her. He liked the sound of that. It was innocent enough, yet far more personal than a cameo might have been. For a moment, he imagined how small her life must have become, if she could fit all of it in the little room by the nursery that had been allotted to the governess. The scent he was giving her smelled of something much larger than a stuffy back bedroom. It was a whole world in a bottle.

He smiled. 'It is perfect,' he said. 'Wrap it for me and I will take it away.' He put the little package in his pocket and went back to the carriage, ready to go home to dinner.

Chapter Four

When Charlotte returned from her manufactured errand to the kitchen, the Major had left the house and the girls were eating oranges that had not been needed for the decorations. Her mouth watered for a taste, but she had best not join them. If the Major returned, he would think it another example of her taking advantage of her position and acting like a member of the family.

But Eleanor patted a place beside her on the couch. 'Come, Mrs Lewis, you know you want to sit down. It was a long morning and we were all very busy.'

She hesitated a moment longer, then settled into the seat and stole a walnut from the bowl on the table at her side. 'I suppose a few moments' rest will do no harm.'

'You are not usually so proper,' Jane said. 'It is because of Father, isn't it?'

'I would not dare to presume,' she said, immediately regretting it. She might as well have just said yes.

'I don't remember him as being so stuffy,' Eleanor said.

'That was probably because you were little when he left,' Charlotte said gently.

'No,' Jane said, considering. 'He was different, back then. It is probably his injury that has changed him. That, or...' She looked at Charlotte, then shared a smile with Eleanor.

Charlotte looked back at her, waiting for an explanation, but she only shrugged and nibbled on a bit of orange.

From the hall, they heard the front door open and the Major stomping his feet and muttering to the footman. Then, before she could move to a different seat, he was in the doorway, smiling at the three of them.

'Did you finish your errands?' Jane asked with a critical frown.

'Yes, Ma'am, I did,' he said, saluting her.

Charlotte tried to hide her surprise, for it seemed, wherever he had gone, he had found a measure of Christmas spirit on the way. To make sure he remained as happy as she was, she gathered up her nutshells and prepared to move to a different seat.

'At ease, Lewis,' he insisted, taking a chair opposite and helping himself to an orange.

'Yes, Sir,' she said automatically and sat back down.

He took out his penknife and peeled away the rind in an even spiral, then tossed it into the fire where it snapped and sizzled, filling the room with the pleasant smell of orange oil. Then he tasted a segment and made a disapproving face. 'Not bad, I suppose. But not as good as fruit straight from the tree in Spain.' For a moment, his face took on a distant, thoughtful look. 'Not all I experienced while gone was bad. I quite liked the people and the food, when we could get it.' He looked at them and smiled again. 'Perhaps, now that the war is over, we might travel there.'

Charlotte was surprised as his gaze fell on her for a moment, then hurried on to look at Jane.

'That would be nice,' she said with a misty smile. 'Jeremy is not sure where he will be posted, or whether I might come with him. But I should like to see Spain. And Paris, of course.'

'I want to go to Italy,' Eleanor announced. 'Venice seems very mysterious, like something out of a book.' Then she turned to Charlotte. 'And where would you like to go, Mrs Lewis?'

Moments like this showed how little the girl knew about the differences between Charlotte's life and her own. She gave the girl a firm smile and said, 'I go where I'm sent, Eleanor.'

The girl smiled, still oblivious. 'Then, when I go to Venice, you shall come as my chaperon.'

She hadn't the heart to tell the girl that such decisions were up to her father, who seemed to have mixed feelings about her presence in the family.

And then, as if from nowhere, an orange landed in her lap, making her jump.

'Eat up, Lewis,' the Major ordered with a smile. 'You will need strength for that trip.'

She could not help smiling back, for his good mood was as rare a treat as the fruit was.

'And what are we doing tonight?' he asked in a teasing tone. 'It is Christmas Eve, after all. What new family traditions am I unaware of?'

The girls both laughed and Jane said, 'Just a dinner for your friends. I have prepared the seating arrangements, just as Mrs Lewis taught me to. We shall have roast beef tonight, then parlour games, punch and gingerbread.'

'It sounds fine,' he said, leaning on his stick to rise. 'I will be looking forward to it, though you will not catch me playing Blind Man's Bluff with a room full of junior officers.' Then he limped from the room, leaving them alone again.

'Did you invite her?' whispered Eleanor, a worried expression on her face.

'I saw no way to avoid it,' Jane whispered back, her brow creased in a frown. 'This is her first Christmas alone and she hinted most shamefully that she wanted the seat next to Father.'

'Who are you speaking of?' Charlotte said, forgetting any plans she'd made to keep to her place and not meddle in family affairs.

'Major Baker's widow,' Jane said.

'According to Jeremy, Mrs Baker is just out of mourning and ready to return to society.'

'You are matchmaking?' she said numbly, thinking of the Major, still alone after so many years.

'Not as such,' Jane said firmly. 'There are always many officers here. If she is set on remarrying, perhaps she will find someone.'

'And what will your father think of such a plan?' she asked cautiously. It had never occurred to her that he might be seeking a wife, but the thought was troubling. A new mistress in the house might dismiss her out of hand. Then she would lose both the girls and the Major.

'I have no idea,' Jane said with a sigh. 'But it might be good to see him settled with someone. Now that Father is home, we want to keep him here.'

'If left to his own devices, he will wait until his leg is fully healed and will find a reason to go back to France or India or the Americas, and we will never see him again.' At this Eleanor looked truly worried.

'It is time for him to sell his commission and come home,' Jane agreed.

'That decision cannot be made by you,' Charlotte said, though she could not help but agree with it.

'We can at least see to it that his evenings are full of pleasant company,' Jane said with a strained smile that made Charlotte wonder if Mrs Baker was included in that group.

'And one wedding often leads to another,' Eleanor added.

'You make your sister's impending marriage sound like a contagion,' Charlotte said.

'I do not mean to,' Eleanor said. 'I should simply like Father to be as happy as Jane is with Jeremy. And you should be happy, as well,' she said, giving Charlotte a pointed look.

'What does any of this have to do with me?' she said, trying not to blush.

'We both love you and want to keep you with us,' Eleanor assured her.

'But we also want to see you as happy as you can possibly be,' Jane added. 'You are young enough yet that you could marry and have children of your own to care for. Perhaps Mrs Baker is not the only one who should be returning to society.'

'If I wanted such things, I would get them for myself,' she said firmly, then added, 'And it would not just be to any man who asked. He would have to be…'

She thought of the pang she'd felt at the idea of the Major remarrying.

'He would have to be the right man,' she concluded. 'If he was not? Then I should much rather stay just as I am, thank you very much.'

Both girls looked at her with frustration. Then Jane shrugged. 'I suppose we shall just have to try harder to find you the right man, then.'

'Well, do not try this evening,' she said, using the firm tone of a governess. 'I will have enough on my hands chaperoning you during the games without having to disappoint some young gentleman.' Then she rose to signal that it was time for all of them to go upstairs to dress for dinner.

Chapter Five

That night, the dining table was packed with his friends from the regiment, the first wave of officers who had been invited to celebrate Christmas with them. Two of the Captains had brought their wives and it surprised Frederick to see that the women were barely older than Jane. It was no surprise that her fiancé, Lieutenant Jeremy Tucker, was there as well. He would be the only member of tonight's company who would be joining the family again tomorrow at dinner.

Seated beside him was the widow of an old friend. Mark Baker had taken a ball through the heart at San Marcial. Frederick had written a letter of condolence to Phoebe himself. And now here she was in a bright blue dress, chattering away as if nothing had happened.

He knew that a soldier's wife could not be expected to grieve for ever. But neither did he feel comfortable with the way Phoebe was looking at him now, as if he was the answer to her prayers.

He hoped that the girls had not arranged this meeting

as a hint that he should remarry. If he got them a stepmother, it would not be Phoebe Baker, who had annoyed him when she was married and whose personality had not improved with bereavement.

As she prattled in his ear, his gaze strayed down the table to where Charlotte Lewis was sitting. As he had promised her, she was still allowed to dine with the family and was seated near the foot of the table to chaperon and round out the numbers so there were not too many single men. The gown she was wearing was as modest as her day dresses. Unlike the Widow Baker, whose neckline was low to the point of immodesty, Mrs Lewis's was filled with an organza chemisette that left everything to the imagination.

Perhaps it was because he could see nothing of her shoulders and breasts that he was fascinated by them. Did she ever long for the freedom to dress as other women did, in fine muslins and silks that would accent her beauty instead of the more sensible garments that she could afford as a servant?

As Frederick watched her converse with her neighbours, he remembered what the Captain in the coach from Dover had said about her being a favourite of the gentlemen who dined here. He'd thought nothing of it at the time. But then, he'd thought of her as a motherly figure. That officer must have been secretly laughing at his mistake, for there was nothing filial about the gazes of the officers on either side of her as she chatted with them. They looked smitten.

It annoyed him on several levels. If he had followed his

first instincts, she would be eating in her room. But if she was here, guests should not be noticing her in that light. It was not her place to outshine her charges. Next to his daughters, she should be nearly invisible.

As if invisibility could be possible for a woman as lovely as she was. Even he had been imagining her in silks and satins just now, taking a place at the head of the table where the annoying Mrs Baker was still chattering.

Most importantly, he should not be sitting here, guessing at her feelings in response to the attention she was receiving from the Lieutenants beside her. Did she wish to marry and leave her position? Why did the idea bother him so? The dismay at the thought of her leaving was far deeper than he would have expected after such a short acquaintance. But the sight of the men flirting with her made him want to bark orders at them, something that would force them to silence and have her fleeing in terror.

Of course, she did not frighten easily. Nor did she seem flustered by the gentlemen around her. As she turned from one to the other, she glanced up the table at him and their eyes met.

And, as he did each time they looked at each other, he felt a funny little tug on his soul that made him want to hold her gaze until she gave up all her secrets to him. He had no right to feel thus and no reason. He forced himself to look way, refilled his wine glass and deliberately turned to Phoebe Baker, making some offhand comment that he hoped would prove he'd been enraptured by her ramblings and not secretly thinking of someone else.

* * *

The meal went on for some time longer. After a dessert course of sherry-soaked trifle, the women withdrew to the sitting room, leaving the gentlemen to their port. As Frederick poured for his neighbour and passed the decanter, the officer to his right said, 'We cannot thank you enough for opening your home to us so soon after returning.'

'I am most happy to do so,' Frederick replied. 'I understand that you have enjoyed the hospitality here before now.'

'Many of us have,' the Captain replied. 'Your daughters are delightful company and Mrs Lewis is always there to keep us on our best behaviour.'

'You do not find it unusual to have a governess as hostess,' he said cautiously.

'We would not have it any other way,' the Captain said with a smile. 'She is a favourite of the men and I swear some come just so they can see her.'

'More than some,' Jeremy said, sipping his port. 'Half the regiment has offered for her at one time or another.'

'Marriage?' Frederick said, shocked.

'She deserves nothing less,' said one of the men who'd been sitting beside her. It was clear from the look in his eye that she was on the way to making another conquest.

'And what has she done with these offers?' Frederick said, uneasily.

'She has refused them all,' Jeremy replied. 'Graciously, of course, but refusals all the same.'

'She has no favourites?' he asked, trying to contain a rush of something that felt rather like jealousy.

'None that she will admit to. She insists that she is happy where she is, working for you.'

'Although she will not be so for very much longer,' one of the officers said. 'With Miss Preston marrying and Miss Eleanor growing closer to her Season…'

'Eleanor will not be marrying any time soon,' Frederick said, unable to keep the gruffness from his voice. 'And as for Lewis leaving? It might be several years yet.'

'A patient man can wait,' the smitten Lieutenant replied.

The fellow was an insolent puppy and Frederick could not fathom what had possessed him to invite the man to dinner.

As if sensing his displeasure, Jeremy changed the subject. 'But offers to her were not the only ones made. It was Mrs Lewis that put me in mind to go to France and meet with you, Sir.'

'Not orders from the Horse Guard?' Frederick said with a laugh. He'd still been on his sick bed when young Tucker had come to visit him with letters from home and a request that he be allowed to marry Jane.

Jeremy smiled. 'They are always looking for someone to deliver dispatches. I knew that we would need your permission, since Jane is not yet of age. But it was Mrs Lewis who reminded me that you were more likely to respect my request if it was put to you in person and not by letter.'

'So, you volunteered to go to France,' he said, surprised.

'With Napoleon captured, it was hardly as dangerous

as it was during most of your time there,' Jeremy replied modestly. 'And it would not have been right for us to plan a wedding without knowing that you would be well enough to attend. A havey-cavey elopement would not do. I honour Jane too much for that.'

'As well you should,' he said, giving the boy a sharp look to accompany his smile.

When the men joined the ladies in the sitting room, the parlour games began, with a round of 'Jacob, Where Are You?'. Charlotte tied a handkerchief over Eleanor's eyes and Lieutenant Wilkerson was given a bell to help her find him. Then he darted around the room, hiding behind the other guests and ringing it as she stumbled about, calling for him.

While other guests stood ready to take their turn, the Major took a seat by the fire, turning his chair into the room, and announced that he did not intend to play, but would be judge, should one be needed.

Now that her job of starting the game was done, Charlotte took a seat at the back of the room, well out of the way of the activity. Though she always dined with family, she sat out of games like this, reminding the girls with a firm smile that it was never proper to tie a blindfold around the eyes of the chaperon.

As the game progressed, she could not help but watch the Major and notice a slight grimace of pain as he shifted his leg out of the way of the partiers. It made Charlotte wonder if he would be sitting on his dignity if his leg had not pained him and if his daughters had chosen less active games.

The answer presented itself when they decided it was time to play 'I Love My Love'. Then he acquiesced and dragged his chair into the circle, ready to join the fun.

'You must sit here,' Mrs Baker said, pulling him across the circle to sit opposite her. 'The light is better here, I think.'

'If there is anything I must read, I will keep that in mind,' he said, giving her a puzzled look and taking the chair she'd found for him.

'And you must play as well,' Eleanor insisted, taking Charlotte by the hand and leading her to a seat. 'There is no blindfold in this game, so you have no excuse.'

'It is Christmas, after all,' Jane reminded her.

'Christmas Eve,' she replied, but took the chair they offered and waited for her turn.

Mrs Baker began the game, screwing up her face in concentration before beginning. 'I love my love with a letter A because he is ardent. I hate him because he is ambiguous. I took him to Avon to the sign of the Antelope and fed him on apples. His name is Andrew Andrews.'

The room laughed and one of the Captains complained that the surname was far too similar to the Christian name to count. But the room voted to let it stand without her having to pay a forfeit and the turn passed to the next player.

Charlotte watched as the game proceeded through B, C, and D and it grew closer to her turn. She had best come up with words that began with F so she was not embarrassed. Fanciful was good. Faithless could come next. Falmouth at the sign of the Fawn. She would feed him on fennel and his name would be…

She froze, only half listening to the room laugh as the man next to her stumbled through the E's. What name began with F other than Frederick? It was the only thing she could think of, looming large in her mind to block out all the other words. If she said it aloud, she would blush and everyone would know the truth. She was in love with Major Frederick Preston and doubted he even knew her first name.

Perhaps she could pretend to be ill. Or claim that she didn't have an answer. She would be made to pay a forfeit like hopping around the room on one foot, but a moment's embarrassment would be better than total shame.

'Mrs Lewis's turn,' Eleanor sang, leaving her no more time to think.

She took a deep breath and prayed for a miracle. Then she began, reciting the beginning of the script while her mind raced to find an ending. She had no more time. The moment was here. 'His name is…' She paused, searching. 'Francis Ferdinand.' She let out a gasp of air and smiled in relief.

The other players laughed and applauded, and the turn passed to the Captain at her left, with no one the wiser.

The play continued around the circle until it reached Jeremy, who had the letter J. Of course, he announced that his love was Jane, but insisted on giving her the last name

Preston and losing the turn. It made his beloved blush and had the rest of the room calling for a forfeit. He hopped to his feet and surprised everyone in the room by standing on his head.

A little while later, it was the Major's turn and he was tasked with the letter P. Charlotte had wondered why Mrs Baker was so insistent that he take that seat, but now it was clear. She wanted him to say that his love was Phoebe Preston. As he prepared to speak the horrid woman leaned forward in her chair, her breasts nearly falling out of her gown, and gave the Major an encouraging smile.

He stared at the ceiling, as if totally oblivious. Then he recited, 'I love my love with the letter P because she is prim. I hate her because she is parsimonious. I took her to Paris to the sign of the Pigeon and fed her on pomegranates. Her name is Pamela Paul.'

The widow slumped back in her chair and the girls exchanged a look of relief as the rest of the room applauded.

But Charlotte released a held breath, slowly so as not to call attention to her special interest in this turn. Tonight, when she was alone, she would brood on each word he'd said. He could have chosen pickles in Portsmouth, but instead, it had been pomegranates in Paris, a scenario so romantic that it set her heart to fluttering and reminded her of their talk of travel earlier in the day.

She had never tasted a pomegranate, but she could imagine it, just as she did Paris and Florence, and all the other places she had not been. She must seem very boring to a man who had seen so much. Perhaps, some day, he would take Eleanor on a trip abroad and she could go along as a chaperon.

She allowed herself a brief glance in his direction and was surprised to see him staring back at her with the same unreadable expression he often had. She should look away, before anyone noticed. But for a moment, she did not. She willed him to see her for the woman she was and not just another servant. She couldn't parade before him in silks and jewels as the widow did. But she should not have to. After all the times they'd written to each other, he must have formed some idea as to her character.

Or perhaps not. There was something about the set of his mouth that made her think he disapproved. But she could not think of what she might have done to change his mood from this afternoon, when he had been pleasantly joking with her and tossing oranges.

He looked away and so did she.

The games continued until nearly midnight when the guests disbursed, going home to sleep away the first hours of Christmas. And, after seeing the girls off to bed, she walked through the ground floor, snuffing candles and straightening chairs in the sitting room before going to bed herself.

'Lewis, may I speak to you in the study, please.'

Charlotte started, turning to see the Major standing in the hall behind her. There was no trace of Christmas mirth in his expression. He looked quite grim, making her dread whatever was to come.

But what choice did she have? She was his to command. 'Of course, Sir,' she said, giving him her governess smile and following him down the hall, waiting as he shut the door behind them and took a seat behind his desk.

She sat as well, though a part of her wanted to stand so she might be ready to run at a moment's notice—he was quite intimidating when he was quiet like this. What had she done to displease him now?

She perched on the edge of the chair, nervous and waiting.

He stared at her for a moment, considering. Then he said, 'It has come to my attention that, in my absence, you have received offers of marriage from several officers of the regiment.'

'That is true,' she said, annoyed. Had the gentlemen been talking about her over wine and cigars? If so, they were not gentlemen at all.

'How many?' He steepled his fingers and stared over them, his scarred eyebrow raised in accusation.

She considered for a moment, counting, and then said, 'Seven.'

'Seven?' he repeated in a shocked tone.

When stated aloud, it did sound like a lot. 'Seven or eight,' she corrected. 'I do not usually count the last one because the gentleman was rather shy and could not get the words out. Before he could make his offer, I warned him that it was hopeless.'

'And why is that?' he asked. 'You are young enough to marry again.'

'Not so very young,' she replied. 'Three and thirty is quite old enough to know my mind.'

'Seven years younger than me,' he muttered, distracted. Then he focused on her again, frowning. 'As I said, you are young enough to marry and have a family of your own.'

'If I wished to,' she agreed.

'Perhaps you do not like soldiers,' he prodded.

She tried not to blush for she liked one soldier well enough, though he did not seem overly fond of her, at the moment. 'I was married to a naval lieutenant,' she said. 'I am well aware of the sacrifices one must make when wedded to a man in service of the King.'

'But the life you have chosen has sacrifices as well. Surely it cannot be easy to work for your keep,' he said. 'Are you not tempted to wed and have your own house, your own servants and the company of a husband?'

Was he asking her if she missed the marital act? If so, the answer was both yes and none of his business, though a part of her wished he would make it so. She redoubled her neutral smile and replied, 'The happiness of a marriage does not depend on personal comfort alone. And as for the company of a man, I had scant little of that in my last marriage, with a husband who was away at sea more than he was home.'

'So, you were unhappy, then,' he said.

She thought back to her marriage, unsure of how to answer. 'When we wed, I had no idea how alone I would be. My life was happy enough, I suppose. But it was not the shared happiness I expected when I accepted Hiram's offer.'

'And what made you seek employment in your widowhood?'

'I had little choice in the matter,' she said, trying not to frown. 'Hiram Lewis was as unlucky in postings as he was in everything else. His Captains were just as likely to lose their ships as to take prizes. When he died, I was left with a modest widow's pension, nothing more. I did not want to rush into another marriage, but neither did I wish to be alone and without the joy of children. Taking a position as a governess seemed a sensible choice.'

'You would do better if you married into the army,' he said, unable to hide his pride for his own branch of service. 'There are many officers coming home from the Peninsula with full pockets and a desire to sell their commission and find a woman to give them a reason to remain in England.'

'Is that your plan?' she said, then immediately regretted it. It was a question as personal as the ones he'd been asking her, but they were not equals and she had no right to enquire.

He looked surprised and she thought she saw the flicker of a smile before he grew stern again. 'We are not speaking of me, Lewis.'

'Of course not, Sir,' she replied, then added, 'If you are asking about my willingness to remain in my current position, despite what must seem ample temptation to leave it, you need not worry. I am content to stay here for as long as you wish me to.'

'That is good to know,' he said, giving her another of his enigmatic looks.

When he did not say anything more, she braced her hands on the edge of the desk and pushed out of her chair. 'If that is all…'

Without warning, he shot his hand out to grab her by the wrist.

They both froze, shocked by the sudden touch.

Could he feel the pulse racing under her skin? She might lie to him about her happiness and satisfaction here, but the erratic pounding of her blood when he touched her told too much of the truth.

He snatched his hand away just as quickly, as though the contact burned him. 'You have not been dismissed, Lewis,' he said. His voice was soft and warm now, making his words seem far more personal than they were.

'I beg your pardon, Sir,' she said softly, but did not sit.

'Merry Christmas,' he said staring into her eyes.

'And to you, Sir,' she whispered back. And for a moment, it seemed that there was a whole conversation in those few words, something she felt rather than heard.

Then it was gone again as he looked away. 'Goodnight, Lewis.'

'Goodnight, Major Preston,' she said and left him.

Chapter Six

The next morning, Frederick came down to find the girls already waiting in the sitting room, smiling expectantly at the little pile of packages on the mantel.

'Are you really so eager for your gifts?' he said with a smile. 'I have not even had my breakfast yet.'

Eleanor pointed to a little table where a large plate of crumpets was sitting next to toasting forks so they might prepare them over the fire. He could smell the chestnuts roasting on a pan by the hearth beside pots of chocolate and tea. 'We have everything we need, right here.'

'Everything except Mrs Lewis,' Jane replied.

'I will get her,' Eleanor said, rushing out of the room, down the hall and up the stairs to find her.

To disguise his feelings, Frederick went to the fire and stared into it, making a show of shaking the chestnut pan. He had no reason to feel so embarrassed at the thought of seeing Charlotte Lewis again. Nothing had occurred between them last night.

Nothing except for a touch on the wrist. He'd had no

right to take that liberty. But she had been about to leave and, suddenly, he did not want to let her go. But once he had stopped her, he'd had no idea why it was that he'd wanted her to stay. She must think him mad.

When she arrived in the sitting room, she showed no sign of embarrassment or reticence. Perhaps he was reading too much into their interaction and she had not noticed the strangeness at all.

Instead, she walked to the mantel and set two packages with the rest.

'You did not have to give us anything,' Jane scolded.

'But I wanted to,' the governess said with a soft smile. 'You are both as dear to me as my own children, should I have been blessed with them. Part of the joy of Christmas is in giving to others. Allow me to do this small thing for you.'

The girls accepted with gracious hugs and unwrapped the two little packages to find a pair of earrings for each of them, gold flowers for Jane and tiny pearl drops for Eleanor.

As they tried them on and smiled into the mirror, Frederick watched as Lewis touched her own ear, which was pierced but bare. Suddenly, he was sure that she had taken these gifts from whatever remained in her own jewel case, to share with his daughters.

Were they gifts from her late husband, or perhaps something she had received from her parents on some long-ago

Christmas? Either way, it spoke of her generous nature that she was so obviously happy to give them up.

It made him more confident in the gift he had chosen for her. If she was giving her own away, she was obviously not in the habit of wearing jewels, while in her current position. That did not mean he would not like to see her in them. Some day, perhaps, when she'd left this job behind and accepted one of the many offers she'd been given. But this Christmas was not the time and he was not the man.

Now the girls were distributing the gifts they'd got for him and Lewis: an enamelled watch chain from Eleanor and a pair of silver brushes from Jane, and, of course, Lewis's mitts and handkerchiefs. She was properly impressed with the handiwork and smiled as brightly as if she'd been gifted with the jewels he imagined for her.

It was his turn now. He gave the girls their presents and took the last package down from the mantel, shifting it from hand to hand as the girls oohed and ahhed over the shawls he had given them and took turns helping each other fasten the chains of the matching necklaces. He had not felt this awkward in decades, not since he was a green boy unsure of every word and action.

He took a breath and summoned his reserve, reminding himself that it was just a walk across the room and not a frontal assault on the enemy. There was nothing to fear. Charlotte Lewis was a lady, with a lady's manners. Even if she loathed it, she would be as polite as she had been when she'd received those tokens from the girls.

But suddenly he wanted more than weak approval. He

wanted to see her face light up. He wanted a smile full of promise meant specially for him.

Maybe he should have got her jewellery after all.

But it was too late to change his mind now. He was standing like an idiot, leaning against the mantel as if he needed it for support.

Perhaps he did. He should not have left his stick by his chair.

Carefully, he took the few halting steps necessary to carry him across the room, then thrust the gift at her. 'Here, Lewis,' he said. 'In gratitude…' Then he limped back to his chair.

She unwrapped it carefully, setting paper and string aside as if she feared being seen as wasteful. Then she stared down at the little gold box, lifting the lid to reveal the crystal bottle inside.

Her response was everything he could have hoped for. She lifted the bottle out of its satin-lined compartment and held it to the light, watching the glass sparkle before daring to pull the stopper and inhaling deeply of the fragrance. Her polite smile turned to something much warmer, more dreamlike than awake, as if she could imagine whole worlds before even trying it.

Then, slowly, she moved to apply the scent. One hand dipped the stopper back into the bottle, taking up a single drop, the colour of fine brandy, on the tip of the glass applicator. The other hand turned palm-up so that the drop could fall on her wrist in the place he'd touched her last night.

'So lovely,' she whispered, as she closed the bottle and put it carefully back into its box. 'I have never smelled anything like it.' She rubbed her wrists together, making small circles, skin against skin, to spread the scent, stopping to smell it again before looking at him with shining eyes. 'Thank you,' she said in a whisper.

'It was nothing,' he said with a shrug and went to the fireside to skewer a crumpet with a fork. Then he turned his back to her, his smile broadening with satisfaction as he toasted his breakfast.

The morning passed quietly, with the family gathered in the sitting room, admiring their new gifts and snacking by the fire. Jeremy arrived in the afternoon and took a seat on the sofa next to Jane, reaching out to take her hand as they discussed their plans for the wedding, which was to occur two days after Boxing Day.

This meant that she would be gone from this house before Twelfth Night, visiting for dinner on the nights that they did not come to her new home in Mayfair.

'And of course you will visit us for New Year's,' Jane said to Charlotte, after she described the menu she was planning.

Charlotte smiled back at her, trying to ignore the tears which were forming at the thought. The little girl she'd helped raise, who had been so shy and unsure five years ago, was now a fine lady who would have a house and husband to think of. In no time at all, she would forget all about her old governess, as she should, and Charlotte would devote herself to Eleanor, until she grew up and moved away as well.

Each new beginning was an ending of something. But she would not think of that today. She took a deep breath and said with a bright smile, 'I will certainly come to dinner, if your father permits it. You must remember that my time is not my own.'

'You would not forbid her from coming to the house, would you, Father?' Jane said.

'Not on my account, I hope,' Eleanor added hurriedly. 'If we are invited as well, perhaps she shall have to come and chaperon me.'

Charlotte stared at her feet, embarrassed to be the topic of conversation. She particularly did not want to look at the Major to see if he was angry again that she did not know her place. The day had been almost perfect thus far and she did not want to spoil it by remembering who and what she was.

She stole a look at the perfume bottle in its elegant box. It had been the nicest present anyone had ever given her. Even better, it had come from *him*.

She heard him stir in his chair by the fire. She'd thought he was napping, but it seemed he'd had no trouble following the conversation.

'I would not presume to tell Jane who she may and may not invite to her own home,' he said with a sigh. 'And you are right, Eleanor. Lewis may accompany us, if we are dining at your sister's house, if she wishes to.' He gave her a sidelong glance. 'She is dining with us this evening, is she not?'

'And helping with the games and the carolling,' Eleanor said.

'It is almost time to go upstairs and dress for dinner,' Charlotte said, gathering up the wrapping at her feet and making a neat stack of her gifts, with the perfume in a place of honour at the top.

'And who are we to have this evening?' the Major said in a dry voice. 'Not another desperate widow, I hope.'

'Mostly bachelor officers who have no family near,' Jane said. 'And Captain Cummings and his three daughters to round out the table.'

'Very good,' he said as Charlotte left the room. 'Very good indeed.'

As she cleared the doorway and walked down the hall she could not help smiling. He thought Mrs Baker was a desperate widow, did he?

She could not help but agree. She should be more sympathetic, since some might see the same qualities in her own life. If they did, that would be unfair. As she'd told the Major, she'd had more than enough offers and was not the least bit desperate. He had seemed most interested in the fact when they'd been alone in the study.

Then, for no reason, he had grabbed her hand. And today he'd given her perfume. Once she was in her room she closed the door tight and set the tiny crystal bottle on the dressing table, staring at it in fascination. There was nothing exactly improper about it, but it was also a much more intimate gift than she'd expected to receive from the Major.

She opened it again, holding it under her nose for a minute before refreshing the scent on her wrists and adding another drop at the base of her throat. She inhaled again. It was a decadent fragrance, a combination of fruit and flower and spice that promised something she could not name.

It had been years since she'd smelled of anything more than soap. Hers was a practical, clean scent to match her sensible, no-nonsense life. But now she smelled like a lady. Better yet, she smelled like a woman.

She closed her eyes as a shiver went through her, touching a part of her soul that had been ignored for far too long. Wearing this scent, she felt capable of anything. She imagined running wild in a field of spring flowers. Better yet, she could imagine being caught, tumbling to the ground, her skirts raised, her legs spread, and the sweet feel of a lover, his lips at the places the perfume had touched, his body hard and eager. And when she looked into his eyes…

Her own eyes snapped open, blinking away the image of the Major smiling down at her as, with one thrust, he made her his.

She hurried to the wash basin and splashed water over her wrists, trying to rinse the scent away. But it clung to her body, her clothes, her mind. She could not shake the changes it was causing in her, this awkward awakening of the senses.

How was she to sit at table with him, after such a fantasy? It was some consolation that she would be seated far away from him, conversing with the lowest-ranked guests as she kept an eye on the girls. There would be distractions that would keep them from having one of those awkward moments when their eyes met.

But suppose he wished to speak to her alone, as he had last night? Her breath quickened at the thought of being alone with him, even for a brief conversation. But how could she make him see her as anything other than a servant?

She glanced at the wardrobe and the row of practical gowns hanging there. She went to it and pushed them out of the way to reach to the back wall. There, she found a remnant of her old life—a dinner gown that she had not cast off when she'd gone through mourning.

Pale blue silk, cut low, with puffed sleeves and a scalloped hem, it had never been worn. With Hiram Lewis always at sea, what reason had she had to go out? But she had seen it in a shop window and been unable to resist buying it for the moment he returned.

It was too elegant for her current life. Far too bold. But maybe with a tucker in the neckline... It was Christmas, after all. She slipped out of her day dress and pulled it from its peg, shaking the wrinkles from the skirt and stepping into it, doing up the fastenings and arranging her best lace fichu to fill the cleavage.

She stared into the mirror and smiled. There was nothing to be done with her hair, she supposed. She'd cut it short when taking this position so she might style it easily without a maid. But she had some combs and pins that she rarely bothered with.

She allowed herself that luxury tonight, along with tiny diamond studs for her ears. She added one more drop of perfume, spicy sweet, between her breasts, and declared herself ready to go down to see that the punch bowl and game tables were ready for the after-dinner festivities. She might look different tonight. She might feel like her old self. But she must remember that it was only an illusion. Nothing had changed.

Chapter Seven

When Frederick came down to dinner, the first guests were already arriving and his daughters stood in the front hall to greet them. They looked as lovely as they had on the previous evening, with the additions of their Christmas gifts, shawls looped loosely over their arms, necklaces sparkling at their throats. And Lewis's earrings were there, glinting beneath their hair.

Ah, Lewis. She was responsible for the beauty he saw here, the gracious manners and the poise. He had been away and could not claim credit for what his daughters had become. Her letters had assured him of what he would find when he returned home, yet it still surprised him, each time he looked at them.

But at least he was getting used to the sight of their governess and over the shock of his misplaced expectations. Perhaps tonight he would be able to dine down the table from her without staring.

Then she appeared in the hall, chatting with the housekeeper about the arrangements for the games. She floated past him in a cloud of blue silk and perfume and he was smitten all over again. Were those diamonds in her hair? Even if they were paste they sparkled like stars on an angel.

She looked every bit a lady tonight, as beautiful as any of the female guests. The only sign of her role as chaperon was that damned scarf, stuck in the bodice of her dress, obscuring the view of what he was sure were luscious breasts. That scrap of lace was the first thing he would get rid of when...

What was he thinking? He snapped his mind back to his duties as host, accepting the salutations of the pair of officers entering and directing them to the sitting room to wait for the call to dinner. When everyone was assembled, he took Eleanor's arm, allowing Jeremy to escort Jane and they all went to the dining room for a feast of roast turkey, currant chutney and sprouts, followed by a Christmas cake and a flaming pudding.

And, as he had last night, he watched a Lieutenant and a freshly minted Captain flirting with his daughters' governess, who smiled and laughed, sparkling as brightly as the gems in her hair.

At least tonight he didn't have to contend with Phoebe Baker. The ladies on either side of him were properly married and capable of holding a conversation without seeming desperate for male attention. And was it his imagination or was Lewis staring down the table at the two ladies with a look of appraisal? Was she comparing herself to them in some way?

She needn't have bothered. In his opinion, there was no comparison. She was the loveliest woman there. He smiled down to her, giving her an encouraging nod, and she smiled back and offered a playful toast of her wine glass before returning to her conversation with the man next to her.

If he'd had any doubt, he knew why there'd been so many offers for her hand. When she was in a mood like this, what man could resist her?

When dinner had ended and the party reformed in the sitting room, there were tables set for snapdragon and bullet pudding and a bucket to bob for apples. Lewis moved from station to station, attending to the games, replenishing the raisins in the flaming brandy and handing towels to wipe faces dusted with flour or soaking wet.

He wanted no part of it. His leg ached and he was longing for bed. Frederick stared at the chaos and the laughing young people around him, wondering when he'd got so old and staid. Not so staid, perhaps, for he was imagining a warm bed and a welcoming woman, something he'd not had for many Christmases. It could be a cold time of year when all the guests had gone home and he was alone with his thoughts.

Then he stepped to the apple-bobbing bucket and plunged his head into the water, chasing a fruit all the way to the bottom before coming up a dripping mess. The cold water cleared the maudlin dreams from his head, leaving him sensible again.

As she had been for everyone else, Lewis was there at his side, offering him a flannel. As he took it, their fingers brushed and he felt a flash of heat, gone almost as quickly as it had come, but leaving the desire he'd been trying to quell.

He offered her a gruff thanks and took a mug of spiced wine and a place on the far side of the room where he could be alone with his thoughts.

The night ended several hours later, the guests wandering to the door in twos and threes, still laughing and chatting, wishing him a Happy Christmas as he stood at the door to see them out. Jeremy was the last to leave, appearing from the darkened dining room with Jane a step behind. They must have crept away from the crowd to share a private goodnight.

He gave the boy a sharp look before reminding himself that the wedding was only a few days away and there was a limit to how much mischief they could get into in that time. Thank God he'd had Lewis to navigate Jane safely to this point. He had nothing to fear, as long as she watched out for his girls.

Then he walked down the hall towards the sitting room and froze in shock. Eleanor was under the mistletoe with Lieutenant Hargraves. And he was kissing her on the lips.

'What the devil is going on?' He used his best command voice and it had the usual, desired effect. Hargraves jumped back, abandoning his daughter and snapping to attention.

'Where is Lewis?' he demanded. Wasn't her job to prevent situations just like this?

'Here.' When he looked into the room, she was sitting in the corner, her hands folded in her lap. She'd been in full view of what had been happening and had done nothing to stop it.

He turned back to Eleanor to chastise her, since it was clear that Lewis could not be bothered to. But the girl was unimpressed by his anger, which was usually enough to terrify even the most seasoned officer.

'How could you?' she said, fists balled and face red, her voice trembling as though she was on the verge of tears. Then, with a shriek of frustration, she turned and ran down the hall and up the stairs. A moment later they heard the slam of her bedroom door.

Then Jane appeared, looking just as frustrated with him. 'Father,' she said, in a tone that implied he had just ruined Christmas. She glanced at Lewis and it was as if they could share an entire conversation without saying a word. 'I will go after Eleanor,' she said, giving him one last disgusted look before disappearing up the stairs to help her sister.

He turned to the Lieutenant still standing stiff in the doorway. At least this fellow understood the danger of the situation for he was white with fear.

What was he to do with him? It was not as if he wanted to force a marriage between them. Eleanor was far too young and he knew far too little about the Lieutenant to want him as a son-in-law. 'If you know what is good for you, you will say nothing of this incident,' he said, letting his voice drop to a dangerous growl.

'Of course not, Sir,' the Lieutenant said, barely daring to breathe.

'Goodnight, Hargraves,' he snapped.

'Sir,' the man said, snapping a salute and running for the exit. A few moments later he heard the front door open and close as Hargraves departed.

That left him alone with Charlotte Lewis. He stared into the corner where she was still sitting, giving her the same glare that had terrified the Lieutenant. 'Explain yourself, Lewis.'

'What is there to explain?' she said in a patient voice. 'I was chaperoning Eleanor.'

'And a fine job you were making of it,' he said, not bothering to lower his voice. 'She was…' He waved his arms at the wretched kissing bough, which he should have torn down the first moment he'd seen it.

'She was receiving a kiss,' Lewis said, sounding faintly amused. 'It was not the first time that has happened and not even the first time this evening.'

'You allow it?' he said, looking up to see that there were berries missing from the sprigs of mistletoe, which meant that the damn thing had been used.

'It is far better that she receives a few chaste kisses with me sitting here to watch than that she tries to pull the wool over my eyes and get them in secret,' she said with a small smile. 'This way, she has her fun at Christmas and nothing gets out of hand.'

'Where did you get such a ridiculous notion?' he demanded, giving her the same glare that had broken the nerve of many strong men.

'From my own past and my knowledge of all girls her age,' she said, unflinching.

'You allowed men to kiss you,' he said, his anger turning to fury.

'When I was young and courting.' Her expression grew distant. 'My only regret is that it did not happen more often, for once I was married there was no time for such frivolity.' For a moment, there was a deep sadness in her bright blue eyes and he had to struggle not to be touched by it. He did not want to think of her, alone and unloved, feeling that her youth had escaped her.

Then she added, 'When Jane was sixteen, she was no different. She outgrew the fascination with mistletoe when she realised that she wanted a man who would kiss her without relying on parlour games. So will Eleanor, given a Season or two.'

'Or I can forbid her to do anything so stupid,' he snapped, remembering the problem at hand.

Lewis opened her mouth as if she was about to speak, then thought the better of it and closed it again.

'You have an opinion as to how I raise my daughter?' he said.

'Yes, I think I do,' she replied, tipping her head to the side as if considering. 'She will not respond well to such a command. It is liable to make her more rebellious, rather than less.'

'Then I will lock her in her room until she sees the light,' he said.

To this, she said nothing, simply staring at him until the anger began to fade. What he was suggesting sounded unreasonable, even to him, and he began to wonder who it was he wanted to punish, Eleanor or her chaperon. He stared at Lewis, remembering her at dinner looking radiant as she did now and chatting amiably with Hargraves herself. It left him wondering about the missing berries on the ball of mistletoe and who might have used them.

'This cavalier attitude to kissing, does it pertain to you as well?' he asked. There had to be something fuelling all the proposals she had told him about yesterday.

'Certainly not.' She laughed. 'I am far too old for such nonsense.'

'Are you now?' he said, stepping into the doorway, so he was positioned under the ball of greenery.

'Of course,' she said. But now she looked uneasily from him to the mistletoe and back again.

'That is good to know,' he said, then added, 'You are dismissed, Lewis.'

She was frozen in her chair, looking at him like a rabbit staring at a fox. They both knew that, to leave the room, she would have to push past him, as he stood beneath the kissing bough. Tradition said she owed him a kiss. If there was truly nothing dangerous about the custom, then she had no reason to hesitate.

'Dismissed,' he repeated, daring her to come to him.

'Of course, Sir,' she said and he watched her stubbornness win out over her fear. She rose slowly, straightening her skirts and lowering her eyes. Then she walked towards him.

Suddenly, the room seemed a hundred miles long and time stretched as she got closer and closer. There was ample opportunity for him to move out of the way and let her pass. It would be the gentlemanly thing to do. But he could not bring himself to move. She was almost upon him now, so close that he could feel the warmth of her body as she came close.

She paused for just a moment, then tried to ease past, her breasts brushing against his coat. And in that moment, his reserve crumbled and he seized her, pulling her into his arms to claim the kiss he could not stop imagining.

He was kissing her.

She should struggle and refuse. She should pull away with a shocked rebuke and give him the set down he deserved. Instead, she melted into him, letting him crush her against his body and hold her so tightly that she could hardly breathe.

This was no innocent mistletoe peck on the lips. It was the sort of forceful, passionate possession that she had imagined when she'd dreamed of his homecoming. She was afraid to move, afraid to breathe, afraid to respond lest he come to his senses and stop what he was doing to her.

So she let him take what he wanted, opening her mouth to the thrust of his tongue, drinking in the decadence of it. His hands were on her body now, tracing her curves through the fabric of her gown. As he gripped her hips, she pressed her breasts to the front of his uniform jacket, rubbing herself gently against him and imagining his touch on her bare skin.

She would be his, if only he would ask. But that would be madness. He was not her equal. He was her employer and had hired her for her good sense and sterling character. She could not chaperon his daughters by day and be his lover by night. She would be little better than a courtesan to behave so.

But in this moment, she would be happy to let it all burn, to be left with nothing but the memory of his kisses and his love.

Then, just as suddenly as it had begun, it was over. He pulled away and set her back on her feet, and she had to resist the urge to groan in disappointment.

'Let that be a lesson to you,' he muttered. 'What you think of as a Christmas game can quickly get out of hand.' Then he walked down the hall to his study and slammed the door.

She leaned against the door frame, still weak with desire. Perhaps he was right. Tonight, the presence of mistletoe did feel dangerous in a way she'd never noticed before. Since he'd given no instruction to take it down, she left the kissing bough just as it was. But not before reaching up to pull off a berry and rolling it between her fingers as she smiled and walked up the stairs to console Eleanor.

Let that be a lesson.

Once in his study, Frederick reached for the brandy

decanter and poured himself a stiff drink, downing it in one gulp.

What had he been trying to teach anyone by that shameless display? She must think him a monster, the sort of man who took advantage of the women who worked for him, then blamed them for tempting him into despicable behaviour. He owed her an apology, not a platitude.

The trouble was, he wasn't the least bit sorry. If she came into the room now, he would likely kiss her again to see if he could coax her into responding to him. Her mouth had been sweet, her body even more so. The feel of it against him as he'd held her had raised desires that he'd been trying to ignore all week.

It was not as if he'd been celibate during the war. But the couplings he'd allowed himself had been anonymous and brief, leaving him feeling lonelier than he had when he'd sought them.

But holding Charlotte Lewis had left him wanting a future that was full of warmth and, dare he say it, love. There was no indication that she wished to offer such to him and he had no right to take it, as he had just now.

But suppose he wanted to court her. How would he even go about doing so? Anything he might suggest would be seen as a command and he was far too used to giving those anyway. How did one suggest to a member of the staff that one wanted a different sort of relationship from the professional one they shared?

She had said that she did not want to be married to a military man again. She would have the right to refuse.

And suppose she did? It would make subsequent interactions between them so awkward he might end up dismissing her, just to escape the embarrassment.

If she was happy in her position, she deserved to stay there. She had not asked for any of this. It was all down to his obsession with her. Better to get a hold of himself and remain silent than to speak and risk spoiling everything.

He waited until he was sure that he was alone on the main floor and then snuffed the candles and went to bed alone, just as he always did.

Chapter Eight

The next day was Boxing Day and Charlotte allowed herself to sleep late for the first time in months. The other servants had the day off to visit their families. Breakfast, lunch and dinner would be cold and left over from the previous day's feast.

Since her parents had died before her husband, she had nowhere to be but just where she was: with the Preston family. But there would be no guests tonight, so there was no need for a chaperon, or for someone to arrange games and scold the girls into their best behaviour. For twenty-four hours, her time was her own.

She threw back the covers and went to the pot of chocolate she'd left on the hob by the fire the night before. As she poured herself a cup, she glanced at the blue gown hanging at the front of the wardrobe and thought of the kiss she'd been given. She'd had sweet dreams last night. Fantasies of dancing at balls and being held too close, pulled into the shadows for an embrace as sweet words were whispered into her ear. Promises of a future of love and ease, of a family already made that she could be a true part of and a new family that might begin.

She shook her head and sighed. It was romantic nonsense. Though he had probably meant it as a punishment, she would view the kiss as an extra Christmas gift. In time, it would be nothing more than a pleasant memory.

Eleanor's aborted kiss was another matter. Last night, she'd sworn she would never speak to her father again. There had been tears, of course, and Charlotte had assured her that she had spoken to the Major about it and would speak again if necessary to assure that there would be no punishment for Lieutenant Hargraves, since Eleanor had been the one to step under the kissing bough to tempt him.

She went to the wardrobe and reached past the dinner gown to find one of her usual, modest day gowns, then prepared to go downstairs to visit with the girls. But she reached the bottom of the stairs to find the Major, pacing uneasily in the front hall.

'Mrs Lewis, may I speak to you in my study, please?'

Was she a Mrs today? This was different from the usual curt summons she'd been receiving. In truth, she rather liked being called Lewis. Though it was genderless, it felt to her as if he wanted to call her by her first name, but could not bring himself to do it.

But today, she would take what she could get. 'Coming, Sir,' she said and followed him down the hall and into the room to her usual seat.

He gave her a grim look. 'I want to apologise for what

happened last evening,' he said, looking as if each word pained him. 'I do not know what came over me.'

She maintained her polite smile, hoping it hid her disappointment. It was no compliment that he meant to treat the only kiss she'd had in years as an embarrassing aberration. 'That is all right,' she said automatically.

'I do not want what happened to come between us,' he said, though she did not understand how it could make them anything but closer. 'It was a mistake. My mistake, actually.'

'I understand,' she said, then turned the conversation to a topic which was a more important and less painful topic. 'And have you apologised to Eleanor?'

He stared down at the desk and muttered, 'You may have been right about that, as well.'

'I might?' she said.

'She would not speak to me at breakfast,' he said.

'Call her in here, as you do me,' she suggested. 'Speak freely to her and allow her to answer. She is worried about poor Hargraves.'

'Since I did not shoot him this morning, the matter is settled between us,' the Major said with the faintest of smiles.

'Men are simple creatures,' she replied. 'Women are more complicated. Girls even more than that.'

'I am beginning to realise the fact,' he admitted. 'And you...' He stopped again and her heart skipped a beat as she waited for his next words.

He smiled at her. 'You always seem to know what to

do with them and I would do well to listen, just as I did when I was away from home and had only letters to follow the happenings here. I enjoyed our correspondence immensely.'

'As did I, Sir,' she said.

He sighed. 'That is all, Lewis.' This time, he rose and walked her to the door and out into the hall. Then she went to the library to find a book and he went off in search of his younger daughter, to try to make amends.

It had been a quiet day and, if Frederick was honest, he much preferred it to the continual business of the last few days. Cold turkey and bread with a healthy dollop of currants and a decent claret was more than satisfactory for a meal.

To his relief, the matter of Lewis had been settled first thing. She had accepted his apology and behaved as if nothing significant had happened. It was rather annoying to see how easily she had recovered from what had been an excellent kiss, profound in its depth and, he'd hoped, capable of arousing the passions of an average woman.

But then Lewis was not an average anything. She was really quite exceptional. He had discovered that as he'd been traipsing across the Peninsula with her letters for company. Getting to know her at home had not changed his opinion.

Of course, if he'd wanted emotion, he'd got more than enough of that during his talk with Eleanor. She had erupted in a shower of tears and called him the worst father in the world. But, in the end, she had blown her nose in his handkerchief and forgiven him, and he had promised not to lurk about in hallways, guarding the mistletoe and spoiling everyone's fun.

Then he had retired to the sitting room and spent most of the day napping and reading as the girls and Lewis played cards and guessing games. The sound of their voices had been a sweet accompaniment to his shallow dreams, which had been homey and pleasant. He had hardly noticed when they'd crept off to bed, leaving him in his chair by the fire.

It was half past eleven and rather embarrassing, he supposed, to be sleeping in a common room when he had a perfectly good bed waiting for him. But dozing in front of his own fire was a luxury he'd not had in many years and surely he could not be blamed for it.

But his body argued at his careless treatment of it. His knee was stiff from too much sitting and locked from lack of use. It would hurt like the devil when he tried to stand up.

He glanced at his stick, which he'd foolishly left on the other side of the room. He would need that before tackling the stairs to get to his bed.

He sighed, drumming his fingers on his knee before gritting his teeth and hoisting himself to his feet. He'd made it only a step or two before the joint failed him, sending him lurching towards the nearest table.

But before he could collide with the furniture, Lewis was there, taking the weight of his body on to herself and preventing the fall. She could not support him for long. He was far too heavy for her. But her intervention gave him enough time to grab the back of a chair and prevent a complete collapse.

'I thought you had gone to bed,' he said, trying to distract her from his embarrassing weakness.

'It is a good thing I had not,' she said, looking up at him with her blue eyes full of worry. 'I was just checking the door before getting a candle. Are you all right, Sir?'

'Better than I was in France,' he said, attempting a laugh. 'Death is not imminent. But if I neglect to stand and stretch every hour or so, I cannot be surprised when I pay the price for it.'

'Then it is good that I was here to help,' she said, her curls bobbing. He was standing close enough to her that he could plant a kiss on that blonde head, if he wanted to. It was sorely tempting. But there must be no more of that, even though he caught a whiff of the perfume he had given her like a whispered invitation.

Perhaps she realised the direction of his thoughts, for she stepped away to get his walking stick for him. 'Here you are, Major. Are you headed to bed now?'

'That was my plan,' he said, doing his best not to think of the previous day's mistake under the mistletoe. If they were to leave the room together, there was a chance that the incident could be repeated. It left him wavering between anticipation and dread.

'I will see you to your room,' she said, giving him a firm governess's smile.

'It is still Boxing Day for another few minutes,' he reminded her. 'You have no obligation.'

'And the footmen are still gone, or I would summon one of them, no matter the day. But I am here,' she said. 'I will not leave you alone.'

Her devotion stirred something in him, reminding him of all the letters they'd shared and the confidence he'd placed in her. If he trusted her with his daughters, why was it so difficult to lean on her now?

Because he wanted her to see him as something less than her feeble employer. 'I am…' He'd meant to announce he was fine. But as he stepped away from the chair he was holding to reach for the stick, the knee buckled again. He grabbed for the chair again, wincing. 'I am grateful for your help,' he said, surrendering.

'And I am happy to give it,' she said with an encouraging smile. Then she slung an arm under his shoulder and planted herself against his side like a living crutch.

There was nothing more for him to do but release the chair and let her lead him out of the room and towards the stairs. As they walked through the doorway and beneath the kissing bough, he held his breath, hoping that she would take it as a reaction to the pain of his injury and not the very real fear that he would forget himself and kiss her again.

They passed it without incident and he relaxed and let her walk with him, tight to his side as they reached the foot of the stairs.

'This is no longer necessary,' he insisted, trying to ignore the comfort he felt at the warmth of her body against his. 'I am doing much better.' He tested the leg, sure he could manage on his own.

'Maybe so,' she agreed. 'But it is better to be safe than sorry and have a tumble on the stairs.'

'I am not an invalid,' he replied.

'Of course not,' she agreed, but she did not withdraw her help.

He bit his tongue against any further objections. If she listened to them, she would leave him alone and he would lose the feeling of her breast pressed firmly into his side and her hip against his thigh. What kind of fool would refuse such delightful aid?

They were nearing his bedroom door, the moment when he should part from her. He was quite capable of putting himself to bed without a nursemaid, even with an injured leg. But he did not feel tired. He felt alive in a way he hadn't in ages.

As he opened the door, he turned his head to the side and surrendered to desire, nuzzling the hand that was resting on his shoulder, inhaling the scent dabbed on her wrist. The girl in the shop was right. With the heat of her skin, the innocent floral he had chosen for her had turned to a heady musk that he did not want to resist. He pressed his lips to the place where her blood pulsed, allowing himself a taste of her sweet skin.

She stiffened and sighed, but did not pull away. Her body, which had been straight and strong as she'd helped him, fit perfectly against him, curve to hollow. They belonged together. For tonight, at least.

He flexed his bad leg and, though the pain was still there, the strength had returned to it. He turned into her, wrapped one arm around her waist and dipped the other to her knees to scoop her up into his arms. Then he carried her the few steps to the bed.

Chapter Nine

It happened so suddenly that Charlotte did not know how to respond. One moment, they had been in the hall, then she was on the bed, looking up at him as he turned back to shut the door.

She should protest. The least she could do was sit up instead of lounging in the pillows as he approached her. But after years of being proper and strong, she was tired of it. Tomorrow, she might have to listen to the same hollow apology she'd got this morning. But just for a little while, she wanted to feel like a woman and not a guardian of someone else's innocence.

He paused a few feet from the bed, his hands on his hips, a soldier ready to do battle. With his dashing red coat and the tiny scar above his eye he looked capable of overcoming any resistance. But the officer was also a gentleman and was waiting for some sign to proceed.

She smiled and reached to the fichu that was tucked modestly into the neckline of her gown, then drew it slowly out, waving it like a flag of surrender before letting it fall to the floor.

He gave her a roguish half-smile in return and tore at the buttons on his coat, shrugging out of it, yanking his shirt over his head to reveal a chest that was broad and solid.

Her fingers itched to touch him. As he sat on the edge of the mattress to pull off his boots she fumbled with the closures of her bodice, eager to be free of it.

But she was too slow. He was already out of his clothes and grabbed her, tearing at the buttons, pushing the cloth away, shoving her stays and shift to the side and seizing a nipple in his teeth.

She arched her back and let him take her. His kisses were rough, hard enough to mark her, she was sure. The thought of hiding those love bites beneath a prim gown tomorrow made her wet with desire. She moaned into his ear, running her fingers through his hair, pressing his head to her to encourage him, spreading her legs to straddle him in invitation.

He released her to stare up into her eyes, then covered her lips with his. His kisses were deep and possessive, leaving no doubt in her mind what he wanted from her. She returned them, unafraid. Then she felt his hands, big and calloused, rough and yet gentle as he toyed with her body before settling into a rhythmic stroking between her legs that was driving her wild.

He paused and she moaned in frustration, then he began again, only to stop as she neared her climax, lulling her back to earth with gentle nips on her throat, only to take her back to a place that was a little more desperate than before. Finally, he tipped her over the edge with a single touch.

And while she shook, helpless, he filled her with one smooth thrust, leaving her gasping at his size and power as he moved in her. Her hands found his hips, clinging to him as he moved, steadying herself to meet him as he plunged into her. She belonged to him now. No matter what happened, she had been his, just as she'd dreamt.

She let herself go again as he shuddered in release against her. Then he held her in his arms, panting as they settled back to rest together.

Somewhere downstairs a clock chimed midnight. Boxing Day was over and she was a servant again.

The sweat on their bodies cooled them and she shivered, then glanced down to find she was still partly dressed, her crisp gown rumpled about her waist, the buttons scattered beneath her, poking her bare shoulders. The pinafore top of her full petticoat was torn half off her body and beyond repair.

What had she done?

A few moments ago, it had been nothing more than an erotic game. But now she could imagine the rush down the hall to get to her room. Suppose someone saw her, face flushed and clothes torn, running from the Major's room? Would they think he was a ravisher and her an unfortunate victim? Or would they see her as a seducer, eager to improve her position by providing services far beyond her duties?

Either one would be horrible. And what if the girls found out? They wanted their father to marry, but that did not mean they saw her as a candidate for stepmother. She should be ashamed of herself and not eager to snuggle back into the covers and begin it all again.

The Major looked just as shocked as she felt. He reached out and touched the ragged muslin of her petticoat as if he did not understand how it had come to be so. 'I will pay for the clothing,' he said, then glanced away, as if ashamed.

'That is not necessary,' she said automatically. In fact, it made things worse, calling attention to their carelessness and her wanton behaviour. She shrugged back into what was left of her garments, trying to make herself presentable for the short walk down the hall.

'You can borrow my dressing gown,' he said, reaching for the robe at the foot of the bed.

'No, thank you,' she replied and rose, walking towards the door.

'Lewis,' he said, then stopped himself and whispered, 'Charlotte. This is not over.'

'On the contrary, I think it is,' she said, hurrying to open the door and rush through it, shutting it with a soft click before racing to her room before the tears could begin.

Frederick stared at the closed door, wondering if he should go after her. He had behaved like a barbarian. And this, after the apology in the morning and the promise to her and himself that there would be no more incidents between them.

There was no defending what he had done, or the way he'd gone about it. There was some small consolation in the fact that she had been a willing participant. But now the sight of her fichu abandoned on the floor where anyone might find it made him feel even worse. He snatched it up and stuffed it into a bureau drawer, where it could remain until he could find a way to sneak it back into her room.

But how would he buy her a new gown without drawing attention to the fact? Slipping her the money to replace the garments he'd ripped was equally repellent. He might as well give her one of the bracelets that worm of a jeweller had been hawking. He didn't want a mistress. What use did he have for a woman who would tell him any lie that would keep her in jewels?

He wanted a woman who would be honest with him, even when he did not want the truth. Someone who understood his wants and needs almost before he could express them. A woman who surprised him with her beauty, her modesty and her ability to cast that modesty aside when he took her to bed.

He wanted her for more than just a single night. He wanted to live and die with her, to keep her always at his side.

The thought sent a surprising thrill through him, as the idea came to fruition. He had loved Charlotte Lewis as a friend while he'd been away. But once he'd seen her, he'd wanted more than friendship. What had just happened had been the inevitable result of his growing feelings and the lack of control that sometimes came with a long-awaited homecoming.

But what did she feel for him? Just now, she had given herself to him without reservation. But she had been refusing more respectable offers for months and was adamant that she did not want a repeat of her last marriage, or to lose another husband to war. Suppose she turned him down because of his red coat?

Worse yet, suppose she only accepted him because he was her employer? Maybe she'd felt she had no choice. That refusal meant losing her position. They would have to come to some agreement, but he did not want her assenting to a marriage that she did not truly desire, just for the sake of financial safety.

A sham union would not be enough for him. He had lived too long alone to settle for a woman who did not love him. Perhaps it would be better to find a command somewhere far away, in a place where his injury did not hold him back. It would mean parting from his daughters again. But Jane would be leaving home in a matter of days. Eleanor would understand. If he left, she would still have Charlotte Lewis to care for her. She would be all right and he could return to loving them both as he had, safely and from a distance.

But that did not seem right, either. It was running from a fight and he had never done that in his life. What he needed was time to plan a campaign. And, since he could not sleep a wink with the delectable Charlotte Lewis lying just down the hall from him, he had all night to think.

Chapter Ten

Charlotte got little sleep that night, replaying the happenings of the past day in her head. How had they gone from agreeing that there would be no more kissing, to a violent tussle in the sheets and a shuddering release? And where were they to go next?

In the morning, she rose and dressed, careful to ignore the torn petticoat and buttonless gown wadded in the back of the wardrobe, an embarrassing reminder of her loss of control.

She moved the blue dinner gown to its place behind the other gowns as well. Putting on airs had done nothing but get her into trouble and she would not do it again. She was an utter failure as a chaperon if she secretly revelled in the things she was denying her charges.

And what was she to do if the Major called her into his office to give her another apology and tell her that what had happened was nothing more than an aberration of the Christmas season? What else could it be? He had said nothing about love or marriage when he'd carried her to his bed. He'd said nothing at all about anything.

If he apologised, she would accept it for what it was, a well-meaning attempt to make things right between them. But what if he offered for her, instead?

That might be almost worse than the apology. It might be just an excuse to keep her in her place, running the house as she had while he went back to the army. If he did not love her enough to stay with her, she would be left alone with his letters, just as she had been with Hiram. And eventually she might get that final letter explaining that something terrible had happened and she was a widow again. She did not want to risk her heart, only to lose it.

There was no avoiding it. She would have to go downstairs and see what he had to say. But when she arrived on the ground floor, he was not standing in the hallway, as she'd expected him to be. Nor was he in the study or the breakfast room.

The girls were there, as always. Or, at least, as they would be for one more day. Tomorrow was the wedding and, after it, Jane would no longer be her responsibility.

She gave them a falsely bright smile as she helped herself to eggs and toast. 'Where is your father?'

'Gone to the Horse Guard,' Eleanor said, rolling her eyes. 'And then to his tailors, probably to have a fresh uniform fitted.'

'I suppose it was too much to hope that he would be home with us for more than a few days,' Jane agreed. 'But at least he is staying for the wedding.'

'He is going back to the army?' Charlotte said numbly. It confirmed her worst fears.

'It certainly seems so,' Jane replied.

She sat down and chewed absently on her food as Jane began to talk about the menu for the wedding breakfast, wondering if it was too late to change the ham for salmon.

Charlotte had not known what she should do or say. But apparently, the Major had made the decision for her. There would be no further incidents between them because he would be gone again, after Christmas.

She felt a tear forming at the corner of her eye, ready to slip down her nose, and dabbed at it with the edge of her napkin.

'Oh, Mrs Lewis,' Jane said, offering her a handkerchief. 'Do not cry over me. I will always be your friend.'

Charlotte gave a shuddery sigh, glad of the excuse that the girl provided. 'I am sorry to be such a ninny. I will be fine in a moment. But I think I must write a letter this morning, if you will excuse me.'

'Of course,' Eleanor replied. 'I am sure we can manage without you for a little while.'

She left her breakfast nearly untouched and went to the morning room with its little writing desk and sharpened a quill. She stared at the blank paper for a moment, searching for the words. How did one resign from a job one loved without assigning blame or hurting feelings? There was no easy way to do it. But if she meant to do what was best for herself, she could not stay here and allow things to go back to the way they had been.

It was not healthy to moon over a man one could not have, waiting eagerly for his letters and reading and re-reading them, hoping to find a clue to his feelings. If he was leaving, so could she. It was the only way to free herself from hoping he might come back to her.

In the end, she scribbled out a few lines, stressing the need for a fresh start due to the changes in the household and the fact that her skills were hardly needed now that there would be only one girl to care for.

That was not true at all. Eleanor was as much trouble as any two other girls and should not be left alone. But perhaps Charlotte's absence would encourage the Major to remain in London to watch out for her. If so, her leaving was the best thing that could happen to this family and she would do it right after Twelfth Night.

She signed at the bottom, blotted the ink and folded and sealed the paper, writing the Major's name in fine script on the back. Then she took it to the study and set it on the desk.

She stared at it for a moment, to be sure that her mind did not change before returning to the girls who were celebrating the arrival of the bridal flowers.

Their scent was almost like perfume. But she'd had far too much of that this week. After taking one last sniff she turned away and lost herself in her other duties.

When the Major returned home, it was half past nine and the house had gone to bed early, to be ready for the big day tomorrow.

He had lingered at the tailor and then at a shop on Bond Street, obsessing over each detail of his purchases, though there had been little reason to. His mind was made up. He knew what he wanted and had no further input to give to the merchants.

Then it had been off to his club, where he accepted far too many drinks to congratulate him on his daughter's wedding and his own decisions for the future.

He should have come home earlier. He needed to talk with everyone, to explain to them the changes that were to take place, to receive the blessings of his daughters and to secure Charlotte's agreement. It was too late now, but perhaps, in the morning, before going to the church...

When he saw the letter on his desk, he recognised the hand immediately and tore at the seal and read. Then he read it again more slowly, searching for unspoken meaning in the few lines she'd written. If he could not stop her, she was leaving him and it was because of what he'd done.

The thought stunned him. He could not let her get away, now that he knew how to make things right. At least the letter said she would remain for the wedding and the rest of the Christmas season. He did not have to worry about her slinking off before he could speak to her.

There would be time tomorrow to change her mind. There had to be.

Chapter Eleven

The next morning, Charlotte arranged for a light breakfast to be brought to Jane's room, where she and Eleanor joined her to help with her toilette. She was already dressed in her wedding gown, an embroidered white muslin with a pelisse of dark green velvet that would look festive next to Jeremy's red and gold uniform.

'I do not know what I will do without you,' Jane said, staring at her in the mirror as the maid arranged flowers in her hair and took a curling iron to the fringe at her temples. She looked very near tears and was staring at her own reflection as if she did not know her self or her mind.

'I will always be there for you,' Charlotte said, trying not to think of a future without the Preston family. 'As you said to me yesterday, I will always be your friend, even if we do not see each other every day.'

'Do not be a goose, Jane,' her sister said from her seat on the side of the bed. 'You are only moving a little way away. It is not like you will never come home to visit. Mrs Lewis and I will be here, whenever you need us.'

She should tell them the truth. That she could not stand to be here any longer, to see their father so close and yet so far away. But now was not the time. She would break the news after the wedding when everyone was not so emotional.

Jane was ready now and the sisters walked down the stairs hand in hand, Charlotte a step or two behind them. The Major was waiting at the foot of the stairs and, for a moment, their eyes met. He gave her an encouraging smile that made her wonder if he had read her letter. Was he relieved to be rid of her? Or perhaps he had too much to think about today to worry about a minor problem with the staff.

She forced a smile in return and then looked away. She would be happy today, for Jane's sake.

'You look lovely,' the Major said, staring between his daughters. 'Both of you.' Then he looked at Charlotte and the look in his eyes softened. 'Mrs Lewis, may I speak to my daughters alone for a moment?'

'Of course, Sir,' she said, going outside to wait in the carriage.

A few minutes passed and she wondered what he was telling them. He had looked very happy as he'd greeted them at the foot of the stairs. He had probably prepared some brief speech with a few words of wisdom for the new bride, the sort of thing that only his daughters needed to hear. It was a reminder that she was not really part of the family, no matter how she'd felt these five years.

Then the front door opened and he ushered the girls to

the carriage, climbing in after them so they might begin their journey to St George's. The wedding was to be small, with no one but family there to witness it, and Charlotte supposed she was lucky to be included.

As the Major walked his daughter up the aisle a lump formed in her throat and she swallowed hard, fearing that it might be the beginning of tears. At least, if she were to cry today, she could blame it on the wedding and Jane's departure. It need have nothing to do with what had happened between her and Frederick.

In her heart, she savoured the name. To use it, even in silence, was an illicit pleasure, a chance to claim some small part of him before she had to let him go for ever. She took a seat at the front of the church, staring at his broad, red-coated back as he led Jane to the vicar and the ceremony began.

He stood ramrod straight beside his daughter, one hand protectively on her arm, the other resting on the pommel of his sword, as if ready to fight to the death to keep her. And then his moment came and, with a trace of wistfulness in his voice, he gave her to be married, stepping back as she turned to her love.

Then Eleanor took the bouquet Jane had been carrying and Jeremy took Jane's hand. As the vows were said, Charlotte thought of her own wedding, which had been in June in a tiny village church, and how happy she had been. Would she ever feel that way again? Perhaps it was her duty now to see to the happiness of others rather than focusing on her own.

The thought made her sigh, but she did it quietly, the barest whisper of air in the echoing stillness of the church. Then the ceremony was over and the licence was signed and they filed out of the church to make room for the next happy couple to be married.

They stopped in the portico where Jane turned back to them with a smile. 'It is time to throw the bouquet,' she said, waving the flowers at her sister. They had talked about this before, with Eleanor quite insistent that this was a tradition that her sister must keep.

'I am ready,' Eleanor said, holding up her hands to receive the toss.

Charlotte forced herself to smile, afraid to look at the Major as the bride prepared her throw. If he was upset by a simple kiss under the mistletoe, what must he think of this?

She would assure him later that the girl's fascination with marriage was harmless. It was still all a game to her. Her heart had never been broken and, hopefully, it never would be.

Then the roses were arching through the air towards them. Just before they reached her, Eleanor grabbed Charlotte by the arm and pulled her into their path.

She held out her hands in surprise and the bouquet dropped into them as if it had belonged there all along. She stared at them in dumb amazement, then looked automatically to the Major.

He was smiling back at her. 'Well, Lewis,' he said, 'what are we to do about this?'

'Sir,' she said automatically, 'I did not mean...' She looked to Eleanor, ready to hand the flowers back to her, where they belonged, but the girl stepped away before she could.

'I am far too young to be married,' she replied with a laugh.

'And you are leaving us,' he reminded her. 'Who knows what the future holds, now that you will no longer be working for me?'

Charlotte looked helplessly at the girls, who should not find out in this way that she was going. But they did not seem in the least distressed. Instead, they were smiling at her as if they knew something she did not.

The Major stepped closer to her, holding out his hand. 'If you are no longer working for me, I can ask what I want of you without fears that the differences between us will give you a reason to lie about your feelings. Charlotte Lewis, will you marry me?'

'Me?' she said, surprised. It was what she'd wanted to hear, but what was she to say?

'No other,' he replied. 'There is no other woman that I would rather spend my life with. And I will have a lot of time on my hands, now that I have sold my commission.'

'You are giving up the army,' she said. 'For me?'

'If you will have me,' he replied. 'I went out yesterday and had a wardrobe of clothes tailored and there is not a red coat or a bit of gold braid in the lot.'

'You are staying here,' she said, her face breaking into an amazed smile.

'And I had time to pick up a little something,' he replied, fishing in the pocket of his coat. He held out a ring set with emeralds and rubies. 'I saw it before Christmas and, even then, it made me think of you.'

'A ring?' she said, still unable to string her thoughts together. Not just a ring. One that would remind her of the Christmas she had found her love.

He reached for her left hand and pulled the glove off it before slipping the ring on her finger. Then he looked at her expectantly. 'You are not answering me, Charlotte Lewis. Do you have nothing to say for yourself?'

'Yes,' she said, laughing. 'Yes. I will marry you.'

'And do you love me, woman?' he boomed at her in a voice that would have made a soldier jump. 'If it is half as much as I love you, I might manage to be content.'

She laughed again and nodded, unphased by his tone. 'I love you,' she whispered. 'Since…for ever.' Then she looked to the girls, afraid of what they must think.

'Finally!' Eleanor said, clapping her hands together.

'We have always hoped,' Jane admitted.

'If we were to be allowed to pick the woman to be our stepmother, we would want no one other than you,' Eleanor agreed.

The Major pulled her close, lifting her off her feet as if she was a doll and kissing her on the lips. Then he reached up to wipe a snowflake from her hair. 'Come, everyone, let us get out of the weather. I understand there is a fine breakfast waiting for us at home. We will toast to the bride and groom and to the future.'

'To our future,' Charlotte agreed with a blush and followed her love, and her family, to the carriage and to home.

* * * * *

THE EARL'S
YULETIDE PROPOSAL

Liz Tyner

Dedicated to Bill, who helped create
one of my happiest family Christmas memories
on a Christmas Eve when temperatures hovered
around freezing and our riverbank campfire
hardly warmed the rocks surrounding it.

Chapter One

'Lord Philbrook. Lord Philbrook,' Adriana called, holding the letter high, scurrying as fast as she could in her dress, hitching it up with her left hand so she could move faster. 'Stop. Please. Wait. You must…'

She gasped, unable to run any longer. She caught her breath, shivering from the raindrops pelting her with a mix of water and ice. She held the paper high while clutching her shawl to secure the covering.

If she had to charge at him and grasp him around the ankle to make him listen, she would. She knew how that would end—with him shaking her from his boot and giving her an austere stare that questioned her sensibilities.

He paused, looking over his shoulder with the merest glance until he recognised her, then he stilled as if turned into ice. Across from the vehicle a young man in livery peered over his bundle of mistletoe and a man in a tall hat watched from a distance.

Cheeks numb, she breathed in a blast of chimney smoke

that teased her with a memory of warmth, but carried a stinging grit that she tightened her lips against.

Waving the letter again, she stepped closer.

He stared at her, eyes questioning, no longer frosted with ice.

'Lord Philbrook. You must read this.' Words forced into the air.

Then he appeared slightly gentler than the weather.

'Why are you—?' he asked.

'You must,' she said, ignoring the blast plastering a dampened curl against her face.

Hand trembling from the cold, she held the paper outstretched.

He took the missive from her, unfolded the letter and read.

'I had to stop you before you—before you—' She lowered her arm. 'Before your appointment for the Special Licence. Or I am to be sacked.'

Eyes tightening, he read the letter again. Then he studied her. 'So, I am sacked instead.' He laughed without humour and tossed the letter to the ground.

She jumped forward and lifted the paper, brushing the dirt from it. She'd already heard the contents and didn't want anyone else to peruse it. She was fairly certain one of the men watching would be too curious not to fetch it.

She turned to run back to Her Ladyship's, but Philbrook commanded her with one word. 'Stop.'

It would take a person much braver than she to ignore

such a directive. She breathed in the stabbing air, turned and waited.

'What do you know of this?' he asked.

'It's a letter from Her Ladyship,' she said, trying to keep her teeth from chattering. She glanced at her shoes, feet hurting from the cold.

'Explain.'

'I did see her write the letter.' And heard her grumble on and on about the unfairness of it all, the injustice, the disgrace…

'My grandfather's dying wish was that I wed Lady Velma. He said it was important to have strength in a union and then he mentioned his wish that I wed.'

'She is forceful.'

'Why is she calling it off? Now?' The last word was delivered with such strength it made the cold winds around them gentle by comparison.

'She heard of your…' Then she swallowed. And swallowed again.

'My?'

'Your decreased fortune.' She whispered the words. Must she spell out her cousin's shallowness?

'My decreased fortune?' he almost shouted, eyes widening.

'Your reduced circumstances,' she whispered again, giving a sideways glance to his carriage. The cumbersome vehicle had been well constructed once upon a time and could have withstood a marauding army, but it was well out of fashion.

He looked at the carriage and then his gaze alighted on her again.

'My decreased fortune.' His tone had a deadness.

'Yes. I'm so sorry, Your Lordship.' She meant it, too. Her cousin, Lady Velma, was one of the loveliest women in society. No question about that. A frail swan of a woman. A delicate wisp who could have taken Bonaparte's army from him with little more than a sigh and a tremulous gasp, and if that hadn't worked, she would have taken him prisoner. One didn't go against Velma without expecting consequences.

'How does she know about my *decreased* fortune?'

Adriana took a step away at the sound of his words, unwilling to tell him about the letter Lady Velma had received. Unsigned, of course. From a concerned, caring person.

Likely.

He studied her, waiting.

'Well, I must return,' she said. 'Her Ladyship will want to know how you took the news.'

'And what will you tell her?' A shadowy smile passed across his face, but he appeared to be laughing at himself.

'That you appeared a bit gruff. Perhaps hiding your broken heart with valour. And—' She took another step back, but the distance never increased between them. She was shivering terribly now, not because of him, but because the wind was piercing. '—that you…' her voice strengthened '…bid me farewell, wishing her the best, and made your way into the carriage, grasping the door for support…'

'You'd lie?' His eyes almost twinkled. The twinkle. Oh, she'd seen hints of it before when he'd arrived to visit Lady Vel and she'd had to make an excuse as to why Vel was running behind.

Her knees almost gave way and it wasn't from the cold. In fact, she might have felt a burst of the sun, which had to have been blazing to have blasted through all that ice in the sky.

'I'd imagine it to be the truth,' she said. 'After all, she is your beloved.'

He half snorted a laugh. 'Apparently not.'

'You will recover,' she said, pulling at her shawl to try to gather some warmth. She supposed Her Ladyship would have been a good countess if he didn't upset her often. Cajoling her husband into giving her whatever she wanted. Spending her days taking care of her appearance. Being the most beautiful woman at any event. Making him proud.

He reached out and snapped the paper from her hands, the leather from his gloves brushing her cold fingers, sending a fresh batch of trembles inside her.

He could stand there and scowl in his greatcoat until night fell if he wished. She wasn't staying. She pulled her thin garment more tightly, hoping for a glimmer of warmth, and he suddenly seemed aware of her situation. For an instant, he didn't move.

She rather felt she was being dissected, one ravelling thread at a time, and coming up a few fibres short.

He shook his head, his tone mellowing into the warm-

est sound she'd ever heard. 'You're going to catch your
death of cold if you aren't careful.'

The compassion in his voice was more in keeping with
the man she knew. He'd never spoken harshly to her before. If Velma was rude to her, and he'd heard, he'd found
a kind word to correct the situation.

'I must get back to Lady Vel,' she said, because she
knew she'd catch a verbal thrashing if she didn't return
to give a full report, including what he was wearing, how
his eyes looked, what he did as he read the letter, the intensity of his sadness, and what his coachman did, and
so on and so on.

'Come inside with me,' he said, taking her arm. 'You're
shaking from head to foot.'

She could feel the pressure of his clasp, but no warmth
from the touch, only the awareness of leather gloves.

'It's your choice,' he said.

It wasn't really her choice.

'I must get back. She's waiting on me.' And she hoped
to have enough time to at least put on a dry dress so Lady
Vel didn't complain of untidiness.

'No. You should not be standing about shivering like
this.' Clipped, commanding words, with no expectation
of disagreement.

And at that moment, she was tired of being icy and was
especially tired of freezing while he stood in a greatcoat
to his knees.

'It's December. Winter. Only two days before Christmas, Your Lordship. The sooner I get back and speak with

Her Ladyship, the quicker I will be able to find a warm spot in the kitchen and thaw out.'

But he still held her arm. 'Go inside with me,' he said. 'You're not dressed warm enough. For indoors.'

The thought of a fire tempted her, but Lady Velma's blast of fury would be intense if Adriana didn't return immediately.

'Do you wish for me to be sacked?' she whispered, but staying with a grumbling Vel might be a worse fate than searching for employment. 'I know she is my cousin, but our positions in life are so different. My mother didn't marry a peer. She wed for love. If Her Ladyship gets angry, she will be ferocious. And I need to get things ready for Boxing Day.'

He studied her. 'Boxing Day? For servants?'

She nodded. 'But I must get back to Her Ladyship. She can be most determined when she makes up her mind.'

'Well, good,' he said. 'So can I.'

His eyes changed then. Softened. And he mustn't look at her like that. Because saying no to him was difficult enough when he was upset, but when he appeared kind-hearted, she could not refuse.

He glanced at his carriage. 'I don't want my driver being out in the weather any longer than he has to be.'

She followed his gaze. The servant had a big hat, a thick scarf around his neck, a coat, gloves, and looked to have a blanket around his legs. She shivered again.

'Do you have a concern with my vehicle?' He lowered his chin and his dark eyes held challenge.

'It appears warmer than I am,' she muttered and looked up at him, feeling her teeth chatter and noticing she was having trouble forcing her mouth to say the words.

He took in a breath that seemed to start so deep in his body she wondered that any air was left around her. And she knew he'd been asking her so much more than whether she had a *concern* with his vehicle. He was likely, possibly, perhaps, thinking of returning to Velma's and trying to rekindle her affection. If so, maybe he would allow her to ride with him if she wasn't offended by the elderly state of his carriage.

If he returned her in the vehicle, she would certainly get home more quickly and perhaps Lady Vel would reconsider the courtship.

'Then step indoors with me.'

He would have to cancel his appointment, she realised. He was so much more courteous than Vel.

'Thank you,' she said, deciding she would risk the fury she would find when she returned. Her toes were cold.

'I know you have had a terrible surprise,' she said, walking with him, forcing her lips to move, 'but really, I would not expect Vel to reconsider.'

'Well, I'm not.'

'Um…' She studied his face, minding her tongue.

Then he hurried her along. Once inside, she really couldn't tell it was much warmer and now her teeth were well and truly chattering.

He took off his hat and gave it to the man inside the door, and slid her shawl from her shoulders, the tips of his gloves grazing against her skin. It must be wonderful to have gloves that had never been mended.

He removed his coat and wrapped it around her. Suddenly she was covered, head to toe, in the light scent of shaving soap and masculine wool, and in a bundle of warmth. She no longer only imagined what it was like to have such warm clothing. The wool was caressing her.

'I am…' she whispered, shutting her eyes, savouring her instant with the coat. Surprised at the weight. She loved that coat. 'In love.'

'I had no idea.' He studied her. 'But you must get warm.'

'I will hold the coat while you finish with the clerk,' she said, her teeth still a little chattery, but she pulled her shoulders higher, the cloth brushing her cheeks.

It was fortunate she had never discovered the coat while he was courting Velma, or she would have had to run downstairs to give the wool a caress while he was speaking with her cousin.

'You don't want me to reconcile with Vel?' he asked.

Vel was her cousin and best for him not to know of how easily it was to pique her. 'I should not answer that question,' she said, hiding her eyes because really her thoughts were disloyal.

'I just want to be here a moment longer with…' she whispered, hiding her face so he would not see her savouring the unspeakable joy of his winter wear. 'This is wonderful…'

With her hands inside the coat, she snuggled it closer.

'Oh, goodness. I do not even know how you take this off to sleep.'

He blinked and his words were distinct. 'My butler wrenches it from my shoulders when I arrive home.'

'A brave man.'

Silence grew between them, but she didn't find it uncomfortable. He appeared to be studying his coat.

'And even with my carriage,' he said, 'it would not matter to you? Marriage?'

'Of course not…' And then she remembered her loyalty to her cousin. 'But I understand my cousin's… She is my family. And that means a lot,' she consoled him, but she shut her eyes and hugged the coat closer.

'Her Ladyship should have wed you for the coat alone,' she whispered. She meant to say the words to herself, but the warmth was the most delicious thing she'd ever felt.

'My tailor would definitely agree.' Not a hint of humour in his words.

'I should go now.' Yet she pulled the clothing close again, raising her shoulders so that the collar covered her ears, warming her even more. 'But it's hard to leave…' She'd not been so warm since July.

He could talk about marriage all he wanted.

But she didn't want to hear another word about Lady Vel, even though he had mentioned an absence of feelings and the promise he'd made his grandfather.

Right now, that was not important to Adriana as she wasn't going to listen to him ramble on about his broken heart. She cuddled into the coat, pulling the wool tight around her ears, letting him talk about whatever he wanted. She was too busy thinking about the cloak of comfort around her to listen to anything he said. Wool was glorious. For once, she understood moths.

Then he paused and she knew she was to answer. What had he just said? Something like, 'Suitable for you? For the rest of your life?'

She heard a trace of compassion, but she wasn't really attending. Apparently, he had noticed her attention to his coat. It coaxed her to experience every thread and to enjoy the luxury of masculine warmth around her. She shivered with a whole new feeling. 'Of course,' she said. Goodness, the coat was more than suitable to warm her. It was exquisite. She did not know enough words to describe how it felt.

'If you're agreeable?'

'Yes.' She was always agreeable. Agreeable to everyone. She hid a sigh and tried to slip the coat from her shoulders to return it.

'Your full name?' he asked.

'Adriana Armstrong,' she said.

'You don't have a middle name?'

'No. Simple.'

'And your date of birth?'

She didn't see why that mattered, but she didn't care because she was going to hand over the garment and run home as quickly as possible. She told him the date, noticing he didn't even appear affected by the temperature, but it was warmer inside.

He turned to the man who'd let them in. 'Did you get that? We want everything completed at once. She's freezing.'

'Yes, Your Lordship. I will take care of getting things underway.' Bowing, he left.

She could barely walk in the coat and her fingers were tingling now. Just another heartbeat and she would leave, but he put an arm at her back and ushered her forward. And the air was warmer in the direction he was moving her. Ah, she could not refuse such an offer.

The man returned, his browed eyes seeming not to see her. 'He is ready for you, Your Lordship.'

Philbrook gave her what she supposed worked as a smile.

'Wait,' he commanded.

She snuggled into the wool. Really, she couldn't leave.

The coat was heavenly. Unfortunately, stealing it would be a capital offence. Staying longer with him was keeping her warm and she didn't care much about his broken heart, but she knew it wasn't based in love.

He'd been at the same gatherings she'd attended with Vel for years. While he'd always been kind and considerate, he'd never been one to hold long conversations with any of the ladies, though he'd danced occasionally and been entertaining before wandering on to discuss politics or projects with the others involved.

He studied her. Eyes appraising. Giving away nothing. Making her feel a little guilty for liking his coat, but it was a wonderful place to disappear into.

And she just couldn't remove the garment.

He started in the direction the man had taken.

'Surely you're not going to get the licence,' she called after him. Apparently, he didn't understand. 'If word of this gets out, she will not like it and will take it out on—'

He stopped and turned on his heel. 'I will *not* let her take this out on you. I'm getting the licence—if it is acceptable to you?'

'Yes. Of course. She will believe me when I tell her you continued on. But that money could be well spent elsewhere.'

He seemed to get taller and he looked down his most decidedly important nose. He didn't stop until he was standing in front of her, a tower of imposing strength. 'No. It will not.'

She could have easily given him about a hundred thousand ways any funds could be spent better than on a licence to wed Her Ladyship, but there was no arguing with him.

'Well, I could be wrong.' She smiled, one of the ones she used when Vel needed to be coaxed to stop throwing things about.

Apparently, he was not as gullible as her cousin could be. He didn't make a sound, but she wondered that he was not making an ironic chuckle deep inside himself.

He left and in a few moments, the inner door was opened by someone. Philbrook returned with another folded paper, which he tucked into the pocket of his frock coat.

Poor man. Lady Vel would never marry someone who could not keep her in the finest attire.

She wrenched the coat from her shoulders, took one last lingering look at it, held it to him and said softly, 'With all due respect, you should reconsider this.'

'That remains to be seen, I suppose.'

He put the coat back over her shoulders, again covering her with securing warmth.

Who was she to argue with an earl? 'If that is what you wish, Lord Philbrook.'

'It is,' he said, smiling, or at least his lips moving, and his voice sounded a rich gravelly growl.

As they exited, she reached out, holding a hand for her shawl, and he waved the man away. 'I would like never to see that again. It's threadbare.'

'Of course,' the man said, taking the garment and exiting.

'You can't.' She turned to Philbrook. 'That's my precious wrap.'

'You will have one a thousand times better.'

'No. I can't. That one is precious.'

'That is a disgrace,' he said. 'You should never be about on such a cold day in such light clothing.'

She forced herself not to throw off the coat and rush after her shawl. But she could hardly run in such a coat.

'But—' she stepped to go after the employee '—I must have it.'

'You will have a new one.' Philbrook's eyes were stone and he ushered her out.

She would have to return for the shawl and it would be a distance out of her way.

After all, he was taking her back to Lady Velma's.

He helped her into the carriage—which wasn't really warm on the inside, but it protected one from the wind and precipitation.

He settled in and the carriage took off.

Oh, he was going to regret this when he came to his senses, she decided, noting the worn carriage seat. His coat was delightful, but she needed that shawl. Perhaps she could send a footman to retrieve it as they at least had warm clothing.

'I don't think the driver was listening,' she said, expecting the carriage only to move forward enough to find a place to turn around, but she noticed the vehicle wasn't changing direction.

She turned in her seat, looking behind her. 'He's going the wrong direction,' she said, bustling forward, perching on the edge.

'No. We're not. You need a place to stay until the marriage.'

He and Lady Vel were decidedly right for each other. Neither one listened to a single word of disagreement.

'We are going the wrong direction. You are not getting married to Lady Vel. At least not tomorrow. She may change her mind as she has some funds of her own, but you will have to do some crawling.'

'I do not crawl.'

'Fine. Don't crawl. Do as you wish, but I—'

'You are the one who isn't listening. You will have a new shawl. My aunt will chaperon until the marriage.'

The aunt wasn't the kindest person, but she wasn't the vicious crone that Vel claimed must have been uncovered from a cursed burial pit. She only seemed half that bad when Adriana had attended events at his house with Vel. Perhaps she would know someone in search of a lady's maid. Even though it would not be an elevation in status, it would be much better than working for a woman who enjoyed prodding her with a fan… Or a book… Or throwing them.

He studied her. 'Is there anything you simply must have from Lady Velma's?'

'I want my shawl,' she said.

'You will have one that is better than that pitiful rag.'

She struggled to remove his coat. 'I would rather be covered by that beautiful shawl than this oversized coat.' Mostly. His coat arrested her, but she wasn't keeping it even though it caressed her.

'You'll freeze.'

'Yes. But it's my choice.'

'Your freezing is not a choice when I am with you.'

She threw the garment into his lap and it rested half on her knees and half on his. The cold hit her again.

He raised a brow. 'You don't have to wear it. And I'm beginning to question whether you are as placid as you've always appeared.'

'Whether I am or not is none of your concern.' But she was getting herself in such a mess. She didn't have her shawl. She was getting further from Lady Velma's and she must hope her recounting of his mind-altering disappointment would soothe Vel somewhat.

She studied the coat and pulled it up around her, fluffing a corner of it his way, and then shared another bit of it. Outrage was one thing. Coldness another.

He understood and pulled it around them, tenting them with warmth.

Lady Vel had made such a tremendous mistake, unusual for her. But Adriana wasn't sure she was doing much better. She would somehow have to get a hackney to take her home and that would be costly. She'd also have to fetch her shawl on the way.

From the window, she recognised the path she'd travelled with Vel and knew it wouldn't be wise to return home without a vehicle and a wrap. She'd truly freeze.

The carriage was slowing in front of his town house. One with gables and large windows and which didn't even seem aware that it was a town house, but considered itself a mansion. In truth, she couldn't argue. She'd been impressed each time she'd attended an event with Vel at the home.

Several times Philbrook had even taken it upon himself to fetch her refreshments and once he'd even danced with her, jesting about changing their slow steps into a spirited country dance mid-song. She'd refused, as she knew he expected, but the exchange had made the dance more enjoyable.

Yet now he appeared so much more serious than he had

in the past. He exited the carriage, taking his coat without speaking.

She raised her chin, took his hand and stepped out. He again wrapped the coat around her shoulders and she moved with him into the house.

Her chin, Philbrook's chin and the butler's chin were all in agreement—this might be the only butler in the world she didn't think she could cajole into helping her. She was going to have to go back into the cold on her own, but she must have a moment to think. Or to see if his aunt would understand.

Philbrook took her into a sitting room that had a case clock and a sofa that appeared sturdy enough to withstand two hurricanes at the same time, plus a snowstorm and drought—and Adriana sat. She intended to throw herself on the mercy of his aunt. Surely she was used to his ways and would be able to help her find her way home quickly.

He appeared to be lost in thought, but that was much better than hearing his fancies about marrying Lady Vel.

Then his aunt, a thin coil of hair atop her head like a coronet, strolled in, stamped her carved, over-tall cane on the floor and glared in a way that would have parted the seas if there'd been any.

'Aunt Bessie, I'd like to introduce you to my intended. Adriana Armstrong. We are going to get married tomorrow.'

'Pardon?' she said, taking a step to the side and shaking her head to try to clear her ears because she was sure she'd not heard correctly. 'We're not getting married tomorrow.'

'No more Lady Perfect?' The aunt interjected the question, waving a hand. 'Judging by her bedraggled look, I would suppose this might be Lady Imperfect.' She sniffed. 'You sure you're not trading a sow's ear for another sow's ear?' Her lips moved into a grim smile. 'Please take no offence, Miss. It's only a question. Someone has to keep the men in line.'

Adriana didn't move, trying to put the right meaning to the words she thought she'd just heard. 'Did you say married?' she asked. 'Like wedded?'

'Yes.' He stared at her as if she were the one making outlandish statements.

'We're not getting married tomorrow. It's Christmas Eve.'

'Fine. The licence will not expire for a few days. We can get married on Christmas or Boxing Day or the day after if you'd like.'

'Christmas or Boxing Day?' She repeated the words and his attention passed to his aunt.

'Miss Adriana Armstrong,' he said. 'I'm sure you remember her. A relative of my former intended. We saw each other, the air tingled and we were instantly smitten.'

'With love?'

'We didn't question it.'

His aunt gave a dismissive wave in Adriana's direction and stomped closer to Philbrook.

'I've heard about this one. And seen her before. She's a companion to Lady Vel…from the impoverished side of the family. Velma's mother parlayed her beauty into a good marriage. This one's mother wasted her beauty.'

Adriana bristled. 'My father is a good man.'

The woman looked heavenwards. 'I suppose. And you have taken after him. Poor.'

'An honour,' she corrected.

'I'm starting to like Vel better,' the burial ground woman said. 'Vel is annoying, but she is the Earl of Lawton's daughter. I hope you weren't serious about the air sparkling, but if it did it was just with ice crystals. Not anything, um, good. Perhaps I made a mistake.'

The aunt obviously didn't mind that Adriana could hear the conversation. Adriana would have expected them to excuse themselves. But neither seemed inclined. And she felt her mind must have got lost in some kind of mental fog.

'It's past time I settled into a family life. And Vel was tossing me over because she thinks I'm impoverished,' he said.

'I know.' His aunt chuckled. 'I put that about. And it took Vapid Vel long enough to get the message. Had to have it, um, spelled out for her. And told she had a wealthy secret admirer.'

So this was the person who'd written the letter Vel had received that morning, telling of the Earl's sad, sad state and hinting he was wedding Vel for her funds.

'Aunt.' His eyes darkened as much as hers. 'I should decrease your allowance if you think I am poor.'

The aunt took a step closer, glaring up at him, her posture challenging. 'And you still didn't get the message, either. I told you that Lord Weatherford's daughter was suitable. And Miss Wellston.' She tossed her arm out, palm upraised. 'And you bring home a cousin. Send the poor relation back.'

'I'm not sending *her* back. We've already received the special licence.'

That had been a special licence? How was that possible? she wondered. Everything had seemed so simple. Too simple for something as binding as a marriage licence.

The aunt put a hand to her chest and looked heavenwards, then emitted a low rumble. Next she narrowed her gaze at him. 'Even if I take her under my wing and dress her in the finest clothes and get her the best hairdresser, she'll still be a lesser cousin. You can't expect a miracle. She is not a blank canvas, but a dabbled one.'

'I'm not expecting a miracle. She'll be a good wife who doesn't demand every hour of my day. Besides, she thinks she's fond of me—'

'Your coat,' Adriana insisted, feeling her fog lifting. 'I'm fond of your coat.'

'Ha!' the older woman spoke over Adriana's words. 'She's fond of your title and all that goes with it. Nothing more.'

'His coat,' Adriana said. 'I like his coat. And his carriage is very comfortable.'

'That rolling heap of rust and bolts?' The old woman squinted. 'He needs a new carriage.'

'It has a strong roof and snug windows and doors,' Adriana answered. 'It's finer than many people have for a home.' She crossed her arms. This woman was as opinionated as Velma was.

The older woman's mouth was closed and she made a face as if she were using her tongue to get something out of her teeth, but afterwards, the corners of her lips rose.

'It was damned insensitive of Vel not to have the courage to tell me herself,' he said to his aunt. 'This one at least showed up. She will be a fine wife.'

Adriana wanted to beg their pardon, even though she wasn't the person in the room who should be doing that—and explain that they were speaking about her right in front of her. But she kept her mouth closed. And wife? *Wife?*

'May I—? May I see that licence?' she asked, remembering his question about spelling her name. About her birthdate.

He reached into his pocket and took out the rolled paper and gave it to her. She saw her name. Spelled correctly. Her birthdate. And his.

'The name is wrong,' she said.

He took the paper from her and, with a sweep of his eyes, examined it, then studied her. 'You said you didn't have a middle name.'

She stared over the aunt's head and Philbrook didn't even see her. He didn't listen to her and he didn't see her. He saw a name on a special licence and that's all she was to him. He was over-tall, too confident by far, a man used to having his way as much as Vel was used to hers. He appeared slender, but he'd stood beside her and she knew that was an impression caused by his height. The carriage had dipped when he'd stepped inside.

He pivoted, facing the fireplace, and then Adriana noticed the painting above it. A boy, ten or elevenish, shoulder-length hair, a dark coat, fawn trousers, a stare that had all the confidence of the world, left fist resting against his hip, right hand lightly clasped on a table. She was fairly certain she remembered him wearing those clothes and he'd seemed so self-assured.

It truly didn't matter if he was in financial hardship or not. His funds couldn't be less than her own. His horses were well fed and his carriage driver was dressed in thick wool.

She had lived her last few years surrounded by wealth, watching her cousin luxuriate in a wall of perfume and flick crumbs of sweets from her lips with hands unmarked by calluses, and Adriana had enjoyed the awareness of riches, but realised her own mother had known the truth: that love was more comforting than an expensive array of jewellery.

Throughout the day, the servants commiserated with each other and with her. At night she slept in a tiny room in her even tinier bed and closed her eyes in a room surrounded by gifts the servants had lovingly made for her out of little more than scraps, but which felt more beautiful than any pearl or gold she'd ever seen. She could not leave them to step into a cold world. No wool could warm it.

'A misunderstanding,' she said. 'The licence should have— You weren't listening.'

'You gave me your birthdate,' he said. 'You weren't listening.'

'I surely wasn't.' She stepped closer and he held the paper so she could read it again. Yes, that was her name.

'What say you?' he asked, flicking his gaze over her.

She couldn't say anything.

'You should wed him,' the aunt answered for her. 'He's got that amazingly ancient carriage. Or I can keep you as a companion. Yes. My other one is getting above herself. Wants to see her grown daughter, as if that was necessary.' She tapped her cane.

Adriana lowered her eyes. She had been a companion to Lady Vel, her cousin, for five years since Velma's mother had complained of her daughter's rudeness to staff and hoped that Adriana could act as a peacemaker between Vel and everyone else.

She'd been pleased to have the employment and the reason had been the wonderful people she worked with. Leaving them would be too hard. And to work for his aunt would likely be no different than Velma's without the people Adriana cared for.

She had spent hour after hour anticipating Velma's wishes and ignoring her tempers. She had made the world around her cousin as peaceful as possible, much as she'd done when they were children.

When she'd heard of Velma's marriage plans, Adriana had wondered how her life would change, but Vel had planned to leave Adriana in charge of the house.

Philbrook interrupted her thoughts.

'Will you marry me?' he asked her. 'I suppose I should have made that question more distinct.'

She nodded. Yes, he should have made that part of the conversation stand out a little more. She'd heard of men getting down on one knee to ask a question of such import and now she knew why they did it. One needed to put some sort of physical punctuation around that query.

His aunt held her cane high and motioned Adriana her way. 'Let me show you my canes. My collection is the best in the world, I'd say. You won't find a speck of dust on them and I can use a different one each day of the year, but I prefer to co-ordinate them with my dresses.'

She was in a house of daft people. She might as well play along. She could make her escape later.

Philbrook took her hand, and she couldn't look anywhere but his eyes. It was as if Christmas carollers stood around her and suddenly burst into song after gazing at him and she couldn't blame them.

'That is going to keep you busy for a bit,' he said, seemingly unaware of the choir inside her, 'so I'll leave you two to get acquainted, and please let me know if you'd prefer Christmas Eve or Christmas Day for the wedding.' He kissed the air above her hand.

She didn't answer, but gave a shake of her head. Disagreeing.

He didn't seem to notice.

She wasn't the only one who didn't pay attention.

Chapter Two

After the aunt finished showing her row of canes lining the wall of her room, a servant appeared and whisked Adriana away.

'And if you need anything…' the housekeeper said, opening the door and standing aside. 'We've readied the rooms for you. Though of course we always leave the sitting room you'll share with the Earl just as he wants it.'

She stepped inside, blinking twice. A rectangular table with square bases on its legs sat at one side, with four chairs around it, all in a wood she was unfamiliar with. A mahogany cabinet with French curved legs was behind them, with some mismatched dishes inside, and on the top, an old hat hung from one of the knobs. A large room, obviously filled from very old furniture that had seen a lifetime or two of use.

Then the housekeeper opened another doorway. 'And this.'

This was a bedroom with a blue bedcover, a simple bedside table, a door which likely led to a dressing room and more space than her other room five times over. 'The room has been empty since Philbrook's grandmother died, I believe. And if you will step this way, Lady Velma.'

Even as she opened her mouth to correct the woman, it struck Adriana as sad that such a room should be unoccupied.

'The Earl's mother left years ago,' the housekeeper continued, 'and her sister was welcomed by the Earl.'

'I'm Adriana,' she said.

'Oh, my pardon. My pardon, Milady,' the housekeeper said. 'I must have forgotten.'

'No. I'm Adriana. Velma is…'

She could not say anything else.

Then she remembered the servants often knew more about what went on in a household better than the people involved. The servants would see all the puzzle pieces and were adept at forming their own conclusions. She might as well help them fill in the events.

'Velma was betrothed to the Earl previously. That has been discontinued. I merely delivered the news of the discontinuation and it has been such a blow to the Earl that he—he has—not shared the news with everyone yet.' She lowered her chin, her eyes, and her voice. 'So terribly sad.'

The housekeeper's mouth opened and she stared.

They left the rooms, almost colliding with a maid rushing to them carrying a tray of macaroons, the scent of the almond-based biscuits wafting her way.

She paused, staring at the tray, her mouth watered.

'Do… Do have some, Milady,' the hopeful maid said,

holding the tray to Adriana. 'We made them for His Lordship's aunt, but Cook is preparing a second batch now.'

'Of course,' she said, for a moment adopting the manner of a woman who normally was called Milady. Treats were a weakness of hers and these appeared delicate, smelled of goodness, and called to her more strongly than her ethics did.

Taking one and feeling the lightness and the softness of the bite, she nibbled, then complimented the staff on the wonderful treat.

'I love Christmas biscuits,' she said. 'My favourite Christmas tradition.'

'Oh, no, Milady. These aren't Christmas biscuits. We make them at least once a week. Miss Bessie insists.'

'That must be wonderful. Like Christmas all year.'

The maid mumbled an agreement. 'I suppose it is.'

Before she finished, a screech sounded in the distance. Adriana recognised it and gathered her skirts and immediately ran to the noise, followed by maids.

As she scurried into the formal sitting room, Velma threw a wad of clothes in Adriana's direction, letting them scatter on to the floor between them, then she stomped on one of the dresses. Adriana saw her favourite garment.

'What—?' Velma shouted, eyes pinched and irises darkened into an apple-seed-sized glare. 'What do you think you are doing, sending for your things?'

'I'm so sorry, Your Ladyship,' Adriana said, arms at her side, shoulders tensed. 'I don't— I was… Um…um…'

A hand, feeling as large and strong as her back, steadied her and a baritone voice from behind answered, 'She no longer has to answer to you.'

Velma stamped a foot on Adriana's dress again. She snarled, 'I did not give her permission to leave. I gave her permission to send you packing. That was all.'

Philbrook stopped beside Adriana, clasping her hand. 'She doesn't need your permission. She is—'

'I am keeping her,' a shrill voice sounded. The aunt burst from her room, her cane moving at a fast clip.

'I'm taking her back,' Velma said. 'She is my companion and I did not give you leave to employ her.'

'We didn't employ her,' Philbrook said. 'She is—'

The aunt rapped her cane against his leg and his neck twisted when he peered at his aunt. 'Pardon?'

The aunt raised her cane as if trying to block Velma's vision of Adriana. 'She's no longer your concern,' the aunt said to Lady Vel. 'We're keeping her. I like her. Way better than you.'

Velma's mouth hinged open and seemed to lock briefly before clamping shut and widening again a little more normally. Vel turned to her, answered the aunt, but spoke to Adriana.

'She had better be home by nightfall,' Vel stated.

'It is entirely her decision,' Philbrook said. 'She's been asked—'

'Are you mad?' Velma said, ignoring Philbrook to again address Adriana. 'You cannot leave. You will miss Boxing Day and it is your favourite day of the year.'

Adriana held her breath. She hadn't known her cousin knew that.

'If you don't return,' Vel said, waving her palm from one shoulder to the next in a cutting motion, 'Boxing Day will be cancelled at my house. Cancelled. Terminated. Over. Done.' Then her voice dripped sweetness. 'Boxing Day. Gone.' And she made a fluttering noise with her lips.

'You can't do that.' Adriana touched the banister. 'You can't. The servants—'

'I can.' Velma's head bobbed sideways, then she tapped her finger to her lip. 'Mrs Ingalls, Perry, Enid, Miss Yale. Mannford. All without Boxing Day. So sad… But there will be another one next year. Perhaps…'

Vel bent at the waist, neck sticking out as far as it would go. 'Happy Christmas.'

And she turned, gave a kick to disengage Adriana's dress from her slipper and pranced out the door.

'Well.' A cackle. The aunt. 'Happy Christmas to Lady Velma as well.' She propped her cane against the wall, clasped her hands and raised them above her head. 'Crisis averted. A bad niece out. A potential good niece in. You don't have to thank me.'

His aunt took her cane and levered it if she were hitting a billiards ball, then left, singing. Adriana thought the song was about a-wassailing, but realised the aunt had changed it to *Here we go a-walloping*.

The sound of the carriage leaving echoed through the walls.

'Get that and have it taken care of,' Philbrook said, indicating the items Velma had kicked around the room.

She moved to collect her clothing, but his hand stilled her.

'I was not talking to you,' he said.

Two maids rushed out, gathering the dress and other items, and the housekeeper appeared at the corner and directed them. A horseback rider rushing through the streets shouting would have been more discreet. Servants would carry tales of this far and wide.

'I must have been—' Philbrook spoke under his breath.

'How did she know I was here?' Adriana wondered aloud.

'I sent a message to have your things sent here.'

That felt presumptuous of him.

'My apologies,' he said, turning to her 'I did not foresee this happening.'

'You didn't really know her,' she said. 'Just as you don't know me.'

'Would you ever act so?' he asked.

'I don't think so. I can't really see the purpose. Except for the drama.'

'You don't appear to be a person who likes drama.'

'No. I prefer peacefulness. At almost all costs.'

'It's better to see the truth, as I just did,' he said. 'I will see you at our marriage once you decide if Christmas Eve or Christmas Day will be better.' His hand left her back and the sound of his boots leaving clipped into the silence.

Another set of footsteps sounded.

'We'll make certain your clothing is freshened,' the housekeeper said.

Adriana didn't move.

'Are you…? Do you need anything, Milady?' the housekeeper spoke again.

'Um…yes.' Then she paused. 'Do you have a Boxing Day celebration here?'

'Of course, Milady. In this household we would not dream otherwise. The butler and I make certain that each staff member has a token of the Earl's appreciation. Everyone is assembled after breakfast and the gifts are disbursed.'

She wondered if she should have rushed after her cousin. This household was formal. Colder.

And Philbrook was marrying her to spite her cousin.

And Boxing Day at her cousin's would be cancelled.

Boxing Day. The one day of the year that she truly had Christmas.

Chapter Three

After she had finished dinner, alone in the room next to his aunt's, Adriana made a decision. She would follow her heart, just as her mother had told her to do.

She gathered her courage and slipped out the doorway, making the way to the rooms the maid had showed her, after retracing her steps a few times and getting a bit lost.

Finally, she found the familiar sitting room, and then exited it and stood in the hallway and rapped on the nearby door.

'Enter.'

He likely thought she was a servant. She didn't even have the courage to walk in when invited because it was his private rooms.

'It's Adriana,' she called out, trying to speak loud enough for her words to carry to him, but not to reach the servants downstairs.

He opened the door, standing even bigger than she remembered, or perhaps it was the shadows dancing around him making him appear commanding. The glimmer of a smile in his eyes and a spark of amusement past his lips reassured her.

'The maids rap soundly.'

Her heart thumped, forcefully reminding her it was beating. But more important was the staff that she cared for and had spent the last five years of her life with and loved.

'I can't marry you,' she said. 'You're doing this to spite my cousin.'

His eyes, unwavering, studied her. 'Two betrothals cancelled in the same day,' he said, giving a chuckle she thought was directed at himself. 'That has to be a record. And probably will remain unchallenged for quite some time.'

He held out his forearm for her to clasp. 'Let's discuss it in the sitting room.'

She reached out, touching his arm with just her fingertips and thumb. She didn't think she'd ever grasped a man's arm who wasn't wearing a frock coat and she'd not realised an arm could be so sturdy. So much larger than her own. Alive. Her insides did a somersault and she swallowed, breathing as normally as possible.

He opened the door for her and she paused before going into the room, bolstering her strength. She couldn't leave her old life and step into another that she couldn't walk away from, particularly if it was as emotionless as the room.

The room truly was bland. Nothing like her cousin's room of flounces and ribbons and delicate furniture. Not even one sprig of holly. Or one red berry. Not even a nod to the celebration of Christmas.

Sad.

She had felt concern for Velma's servants because they'd had to arrange so many festive touches. Now she felt pity for the Earl's because they'd not been able to decorate.

She stepped inside with him and he softly shut the door.

Philbrook didn't seem so foreboding when they were alone. Just overwhelming and she wasn't sure that was in a terrible way. 'Did you really intend to wed me?'

He put a crooked finger under her chin, filling her even more with an awareness. 'Of course. I've been turned down before. This very day, in fact.'

'It's not…love.'

One brow rose. 'I have not had much luck with that emotion. I thought your cousin cared for me. And I have seen other sweethearts smile and I saw my title and fortune reflected back at me. In fact, your cousin seemed the least impressed by my inheritances than anyone I know. Except you.'

'She rarely is impressed.'

'The same as her cousin?'

'I can't afford to be.'

'Wed me and you can.'

'Was the proposal for revenge?'

He took her fingertips and briefly put them to his cheek before dropping them. 'You are caring. It was good fortune to me when she sent you as a messenger. And you were shivering. It was as if I'd never seen you before and I don't think I had, really.'

'You have to see my awareness that you appear to be a golden opportunity for me, but if you look around yourself and see the binding ties, obligations and rules your wife would be expected to adhere to, then perhaps the opportunity isn't as impressive as it might be.'

'You would rather live in Velma's household?'

'She enjoys a performance, but she's generally not that expressive.'

'We may grumble under the surface in my household, but voices never rise in anger now that my grandfather is gone. He loved a good commotion. Without him, it's easier to keep the volume lower.'

'Marriage is more than a simple combination of keeping voices low. It is a combination of families.'

'With the possible addition of children.'

'Of family,' she said. 'My parents are dear to me and I do not even know any of your family except your aunt. And people marry into each other's families, particularly if the husband has a home with relatives in residence.'

'Only Aunt Bessie.'

'Your mother?'

'She's not a close relative, I would say. We only see each other at events, Christmas and perhaps if she is running low on funds. She hates this house. Has sworn never to live here again. Prefers to live with my sister and her husband.'

'Not a close relative?' She almost gasped over the words. His mother?

'My aunt has always been a part of my daily life more than my mother. My mother might be gone for months, but Aunt was always nearby.' His words were strong, even if they were gentle, yet she sensed he wore a suit of armour over his heart. 'It was an arrangement that I would hope benefited all of us.'

She could see how he had so easily accepted distance in his life. The two people he'd been closest with had been a grandfather who was stern and overbearing and an aunt who carried a cane which she shook at people.

'Did you truly ask Vel to wed?' she asked, touching a hand to his arm, wondering if she read his intensity correctly.

'I was aware that my life was missing something. And my grandfather had requested it with his dying breath. It was just not the time to disagree with him.'

He clasped both her hands and stilled the world around them.

'Love never lasts,' he said. 'It's a false emotion, like a crate decorated with an over-tied bow. When you open the box, it's just an empty box.'

'My cousin isn't truly empty,' she said. 'You just have to look a little deeper to find her goodness most of the time. Though she does make mistakes regularly.'

'Would you consider me a mistake?' His lips turned up and he quickly added, 'Please don't answer.'

'Why me?' she asked. 'Because I am Velma's cousin?'

He laughed. 'The two of you do not favour each other. You've never created such a scene as I saw today from

Velma. And I understand why she was so upset. She was scared of losing you.'

'We are family,' she said. 'We will always be family.'

'History…' one side of his lips tilted up '…has shown that family is not always the best ally.'

'At times, family is all we have.' And she had family. If she had to, she could return to her mother and father. They did not have much, but they would never turn her away.

She tried to read every emotion in his expression and see past the façade and deep into him. Yet it wasn't possible. Or was it? 'You said you weren't particularly close to your mother? I do remember seeing you with her when we were children.'

'Oh, she took me about on occasion. I was to be an earl and she was extremely proud of that. Reminded me of it often. Wanted everyone to know I was her son.' His lips turned up in a moment of whimsy. 'No one is very close to her as far as I can tell. Her sister, my aunt Bessie, is the considerate one though she can be outspoken, as you're aware of.'

'What about familial love?'

'It's a basic caring. Duties. If wed, we would each have duties and fulfil them to the best of our ability.'

They would both gain from a marriage, although perhaps she would gain substantially more. He would get a wife and she would get financial security for the rest of her life. She would never have to smile and pretend to go along with any tirades or ravings or some such, unless it was his, or his aunt's or his mother's or even more family members she'd not met yet. Instead, she would be expected to stand in the shadows and keep her opinions to herself.

The union did not sound so advantageous when put that way.

'I don't know that I can be a society bonnet.'

'You can always add a few frills and paste a smile on your face. You did it with Vel for years.'

'True. I make a special effort for her, but...' she crossed her arms '...that smile doesn't come as easily as it used to.' She was not giving a husband the same subservient smile she had given Vel to cajole her into happiness—and Philbrook had given away her wrap. Her wrap.

That was the sort of thing Velma might do. She'd not thought Philbrook that way.

She'd seen him court Velma and be most solicitous, although distant. In fact, while he'd waited for Vel, he'd seemed more gentle with Adriana and had hardly spoken to Vel when she arrived. He and Adriana had shared a smile between them at his patience when she had greeted him with the words that Velma would be along shortly. They'd both known the wait could be long.

Then she'd seen his reaction to a failed betrothal...and recover in his next breath. He said he didn't even believe in love—a false emotion.

'I thought Vel cared for being a countess and it would lead to a union of consolidated interests,' he added. 'Together we would have more power among the peers and perhaps that was what was important to my grandfather, but shouldn't be to me.'

'Consolidated interests?' Those two words whirled in her brain, forcing her to halt her musings and putting words in her mouth that she embraced. She interlaced her fingers in front of herself, palms down, swallowed, and spoke in her *Be kind to Vel* voice.

'It is with extreme regret that I beg your pardon, but I can't wed you and I will go to Vel and ask her forgiveness.'

A muscle in his jaw tightened.

'I believe,' he said, 'you must reconsider that. You don't want to live with a woman who behaves so badly.'

'She doesn't usually. Besides, it's been my home for years,' she said. 'And I want to fetch my wrap.' She could not believe she had parted with that dear garment. Her mind must have been truly frozen.

'That wrap—' he spoke the word as if it tasted of ash '—that you were wearing…'

'Yes. I miss it,' she said. 'It was a terrible mistake to let it go. I was just so cold. I just was not thinking at all.'

Now his eyes appeared to have taken on an internal ice blanket of their own and she strengthened her stance.

'I know it was not extravagant and a bit worn, but it was dear to me.' He had no right to diminish her apparel because it was not as costly as his own.

'You cannot,' he said. 'Velma acted like a child and the wrap was pathetic. You can't return to a life like that.'

'The wrap was lovely to me, my cousin is family and my home is my home.'

Chapter Four

Philbrook tried counting to five to control his temper, but he couldn't get past three. The poor woman was as intractable as her cousin. Must be an inherited trait. His aunt claimed often he'd inherited his mother's arrogance, his grandfather's pomposity and her own sweet nature— which he knew was not at all a compliment.

'Why?' He raised a brow. 'Why would you not consider an advantageous marriage?'

She took in a breath and let it out. Slowly. She studied the wall over his shoulder and he barely heard her. 'You tossed aside my clothing just as my cousin did.'

The thought that he would be considered the same as Velma speared into him. He took a step away, considering her words. He would never act as Velma had, but perhaps he had disregarded her feelings just as her cousin did. He must explain.

'No. I did not,' he said. 'The lowliest servant would not be allowed from my house in such attire. It is not controlling, it is caring.'

He firmed his lips, then stepped to the bell and rang it. Her little angry bee stare was not stinging him—overly. Then he put his hands behind his back so less of him could be stung. 'One moment, please.'

She was a bedraggled sort. Eyes the size of saucers when she wasn't trying to hide her wrath. If she'd truly been a bee, he'd have red welts over most of his skin just for insulting her pitiful wrap.

She was someone he wanted to put his arms around and protect. Such a shame she was attached to old clothing. Blast. She must have a fondness for faultiness. Vel. The wrap.

His carriage driver, Woodward, had once told him she'd even concerned herself after she'd noticed Woodward favouring a leg when the driver opened the carriage door for Philbrook to leave and checked on Woodward the next visit.

The little speck of a woman had tried to hire his carriage driver and told him that Velma's butler had agreed that the gardener could use a fine man for assistance. Woodward had insisted he wouldn't know a rose from a radish and later the grizzled old man had laughingly informed Philbrook of the encounter, but afterwards he'd always beamed when Philbrook had asked him how the garden was growing.

The memory caused him to reassess his view of her and he wondered if he should apologise. Working for Vel could not be all fun and frivolity based on what he had seen. And this woman wanted to wear a tattered cloth while returning to a floor-stomping shrew.

He might need to reconsider his attributes.

Or perhaps she was only happy when she was miserable.

A rap at the door sounded and the maid rushed in, shutting the door with a soft snap.

'Get Miss Adriana a wrap. Any cloak.' His eyes shut briefly. *'Hurry.'*

The maid's jaw dropped and she said, 'Of course.' She turned, grasped at the door, swinging it wide.

'No.' Adriana burst forward, stopping the servant. 'You do not have to get me a wrap. I need my old one.'

The maid searched his face, questioning, before she dashed from the room.

'I will be on my way,' Adriana said, stepping to the door.

'Please wait for the wrap.'

She hesitated, hand to the latch. 'I told her not to bring me one.'

'She will.' He had no question of that. 'I pay her wage.'

'It is not my wrap. I cannot take someone's wrap.'

'You cannot freeze.'

'I will hurry and keep warm by rushing.' The feminine eyes became bee-like again. And he'd never noticed before how lovely little bees could be. Those little stingers were only to protect themselves so the insects could create more sweetness.

'If you freeze,' he said, 'you'll be of no help to Lady Vel, although why you would return to a woman who stomps on your clothing concerns me.'

'Every occupation has its drawbacks.'

The door flew open again. The maid ran in with a shawl, holding it for Adriana.

'Thank you,' she said, smiling at the woman, taking it.

The maid gave a stiff nod and left.

He could see the debate in her regarding tossing it on the sofa and walking out.

'Keep it for now,' he said. 'Once we get your wrap, you can send it back with me.'

She moved to the door.

'I will have the carriage readied so I can go with you to make sure your wrap is collected.'

She hesitated and he suspected she was one heartbeat from bolting.

He indicated the window. The frigid weather.

'I can get my shawl on my own.' Her voice lingered in the air, softening it. He supposed it was her Vel voice and the thought caused his jaw to clamp.

Wide eyes studied him, with lashes long enough to sweep a lesser man under her feet.

'No,' he said. 'It's too far. It's cold. And I was going that way anyway.' To take her to Lady Velma's.

Adriana felt cosseted as he wrapped the borrowed shawl around her shoulders, filling her with a new warmth, and for just a moment they both lingered. She wondered if they were telling each other goodbye, perhaps spending a twinkling thinking about what might have been if they'd been different people.

She stepped down the stairs, passing the stone-faced butler who assisted Philbrook with his coat wordlessly, only the brush of fabric breaking the silence. Philbrook shook his head when the butler held out gloves for him.

They left the house and she could almost feel the demeanour of the butler following them. They got into the carriage, and she sat where the seat had been mended, noticing the scent of old fabrics and perhaps a hint of a cheroot.

Before they left, the driver, his countenance as solemn as the butler's, handed in a blanket. Philbrook took the covering to drape over her, surrounding her in a different household aroma.

In that moment, she completely understood why he liked the vehicle. Even though she'd not ridden in it as a child, it seemed to carry strong reminders of the past. The wheels would creak with the same sounds he'd surely heard as a lad. An envelope of memories just below the surface which didn't intrude, yet gave one a calming sense.

Or perhaps there was more to it. Perhaps it was the man sitting beside her who gave her the sense of security.

She glanced at Philbrook. He didn't appear to even see her, but then he darted a glance her way. The same one he'd sometimes given her at Lady Velma's. One of camaraderie. Distant, but somehow reassuring her that she wasn't alone. That he was giving her thoughts consideration even if they might have been behind different panes of glass.

She'd not known he was going to put the garment over her and truly it was thicker than her treasured one.

Admittedly, the shawl she wore now was luxurious, but Mrs Ingalls had knitted the other one for her. Even though the poor lady couldn't really see well enough to know if Adriana was actually wearing the shawl, Adriana would always step closer to her and hold out a side for her to feel. The clouded eyes would light up and Adriana's heart would glow.

For Boxing Day, Mrs Ingalls was getting a new shawl herself. Vel had purchased the wool, the servants had carded and spun the wool, and each servant, even the males who'd never touched a knitting needle, had been guided to knit at least a few stitches. Everyone in the house had had a part in it

Adriana had wanted Mrs Ingalls to have something each one of them had contributed to and made certain that it had happened in time for Christmas.

For Vel she was a relative and servant. For the staff, she was their leader, their confidant, their friend and the one person who looked out for their welfare. She made every person in that house have a better life—including Vel. And she loved them all.

Philbrook held one hand on his knee and used a thumb to rub the knuckle of his other one, a small scar running along the top of it.

'How did that happen?' she asked, pointing to the scar.

Momentarily his gaze widened a hair, then he studied the mark when he answered.

'I took Father's knife. He'd just passed on and the house was somehow different. I went to his dressing room, found his old knife, took it outside and decided I would cut down a tree. The knife slipped and I sliced my thumb. I was trying to hide what had happened, but I must have wiped my face, because Grandfather saw the blood and took the knife, and scolded me tremendously.'

'You must have loved your father dearly.' She wanted him to understand how he had felt love.

'Father was gone most of the time and Grandfather was a wizened old man who sat in a chair mostly and gave me lecture upon lecture.' He indicated the door. 'His. This carriage was his.'

'A reminder.'

'The carriage suits my size. And the springs. Best I've ever ridden in.'

'You don't think you have kept it the same to remind yourself of him?'

'It's larger than most. I like the ragged old seats because they're comfortable. My friends have spilled their drinks in it and I don't care. If there is a group, we take this one. Light for its size. My horses can pull it with no problem.'

'Not a memento?'

'No.'

'You don't believe you had a strong affection for him?'

'In the way one is fond of a wearied instructor. But the barbs were tiresome. After Father passed on, Grandfather believed he must be all things to me. And when Mother was with her father-in-law, a tug-of-war ensued. How was I to be schooled? Who was to have say over me? He insisted I live here and, as his heir, she really had little choice and so we resided here and she hated it. Hated it. And found reasons to be elsewhere.'

He rubbed his thumb. 'Although the three of us had the evening meal together when I was not away at school. A chance to stab at our meat, pound our vegetables and slice at our bread.'

'Sounds lovely.'

'Well, I may be polishing it up too much.' His mouth settled into a smile, yet his sight appeared to remain with his memories of the past until the carriage stopped in front of the structure where he'd purchased the licence.

He leapt from the vehicle and helped her out, taking her in to see the clerk who had taken possession of her shawl.

The clerk wrung his hands, insisting he had no idea where the shawl might be because it had been tossed into a crate of collected items going to the poor so they would have them before Christmas.

She didn't know what to do. The man in front of her had concern on his face. He leaned forward.

'We will do all we can to retrieve the item,' he said. 'I will find out where the poor are gathering and send—'

'Not necessary,' Philbrook said, 'I'll handle it.' He nodded a goodbye to the man and helped her outside, stopping just beyond the door.

'I'll see that a new one is made for you,' Philbrook said.

'I want my old one.' She bit her lip. She didn't want to

tell Mrs Ingalls that the shawl had been tossed aside like a rag.

'It was a scrap.' He stood in front of her, speaking softly. 'I will have one made for you that will wrap you three times if you wish. Or you can take the one you're wearing.'

'Oh, I could not take this one.'

'Yes. You could. The servant will make another one.'

She hid her gasp. He had taken her shawl and now he was taking a servant's. A woman would have to spend hours knitting.

The driver had opened the door to the carriage and she didn't want him freezing, or herself—but she would give Philbrook a lesson in manners once they were alone.

His long strides put him in front of her and he waved the driver aside, gave quick directions and helped her up.

She stepped into the carriage and peered at him. 'I could never, ever take someone's shawl from them.'

'It's better than the one you wore.' He sat beside her.

'And now you are insulting my lovely shawl.'

'Lovely? Lovely?' He shook his head. 'It was pitiful. Ill fitting, and that's hard to say about a shawl. Looked like something stolen off a person who had no home.'

'You—'

She fluffed about in the vehicle and made certain he saw her response in her eyes.

'I will tell Mrs Ingalls that it went to a poor person who needed it badly. She will understand and her feelings won't be hurt.'

'Who is this Mrs Ingalls?'

'A member of the staff. She's— It was indeed an honour that she created it for me.'

'A maid? It's her job.'

She pressed her lips together firmly and inhaled slowly, thanking her good fortune that her cousin did not marry the barbarian. She turned. 'If I had a fan, I would tap your fingers with it.'

'Pardon?' he said. 'If you'd like to reprimand me, just hit me full force with a slap and I will not bat an eye. In childhood, my friends and I used to call it having a slap-out and I could handle it better than any of them. But don't punch me with a fist. The damage would be massive—to your hand.'

Her jaw dropped and she squeaked a breath. 'You are, quite frankly, very self-assured. Much like Velma.'

'The woman who jumped on your clothing and acted like a spoiled child?'

'One and the same,' she said. 'But at least she allows the servants to have a wonderful Boxing Day.' She hesitated and her voice wavered away. 'Or at least she did.'

'Boxing Day?' He perused her. 'It's a bit of a nuisance but understandable. The servants take care of it themselves.'

'*I* take care of it at Lady Velma's.

'You are, in a sense, her servant.'

'Yes, I am. So, Boxing Day is *my* Christmas. Everyone has a grand day and it has taken effort because it is very hard for some of the staff to keep secrets. In fact, I think the sharing of secrets, and the spilling of them, contributes to the joy of the day.'

She thought of the previous month. 'It really isn't only the day, but the time beforehand when we are furiously thinking of what we might plan and how we might surprise each other. And Boxing Day is the reward. The moment when we all chuckle together and share tales.' She touched his arm for emphasis. 'It is endearing.'

He appeared to be pondering the thought. 'But you could create that day wherever you are.'

'Perhaps. Perhaps not.'

'You would be in charge of the housekeeping staff at my house.'

'But they are a different staff. Not the ones I love. And it is their home, and for me to arrive and start upending things would be unnerving to them.'

'They are adults. They can handle it.'

'How uncaring.'

'You would not be unkind to them. And instead of having your own household, you prefer to stay with your cousin.'

'Better the...er...not-saint you know than the one you don't.'

His head tilted low to the side. 'I've never been called a not-saint before. At least to my face.' His eyes half closed. 'Many other things, perhaps, but not a not-saint.'

He put the scarred thumb to his chin. 'Is that a step above or below a not-sharp-tongued woman?'

Then she saw the little smile in his eyes and she did slap his knee with the shawl.

'That may bruise,' he said, rubbing the knee, and his smile increased. 'And the driver could have to help me into my house.'

'You are insufferable,' she said. 'Insufferable. If you worked at Lady Velma's, you would be let go.'

'I don't. And I was.'

'You were let go because Vel is—'

He raised a brow.

'Not a saint either. The two of you would have been… not perfect together.'

'But the licence is in your name.'

'Well. You could have spent those funds more wisely.'

'I disagree.'

The carriage rolled to a stop and he got out and helped her alight.

Then she took his arm and turned to the driver. 'I apologise, kind sir, but please wait for the Earl. He will be back shortly after he meets Mrs Ingalls.' She pulled at the shawl, and held it to the servant. 'And please return this to the maid with my heartfelt thanks.'

'Pardon?' Philbrook said, feet planted. 'I should not be in Lady Velma's house now. I am agreeable to the end of the betrothal.'

'You had best be agreeable to the end,' she said. 'It's in your own interest. There are plenty of mindless beauties to take her place.'

'Thank you. But I believe I will decline your invitation. I have found my beauty.'

She didn't know which invite he was declining, but she had had enough of pettiness over her attire. First, he gave away her shawl and then Lady Vel stomped on her dress. She was going to show him that she did have friends and good ones.

'It was not an invitation, Lord Philbrook.' She stared up at him. She clutched both hands on to his tree trunk of an arm, looked at his eyes, and held on. He took in a breath and slowly expelled it. 'I suppose, not-saint that I am, I should go with you.'

He took a step.

'Not the main entrance,' she insisted. 'Will your boots be able to step over the threshold of the servants' entrance?'

'I suppose I can limp across it.'

'If I need to drag you, I will do the best I can. I can get a footman to help.'

'I will manage. Thank you.'

She flounced to the outside stairs descending to the plain door mostly hidden by shrubs.

He followed along and she couldn't read his thoughts, but it didn't matter. He was going to meet dear Mrs Ingalls.

Opening the door, the familiar scent of Christmas baking spices wafted over her and took some of the irritation from her.

The door behind her clicked closed as he shut it. And in

that moment, she realised she had dragged an earl into the realm of the servants and…perhaps it would be best for him to exit from the front steps. Or just exit. Immediately.

Chapter Five

'Why, Miss Adriana,' a maid said, popping around the corner, 'I am pleased to see you. Lady Vel is in a prop—'

Then the maid's eyes halted on the Earl and she froze.

'We're just going to see Mrs Ingalls for a moment,' Adriana said. 'Is she polishing?'

'No. Cook needed peeling done.' The maid bobbed her head and darted away.

Adriana moved to the kitchen and opened the door. A trim lady, who wouldn't reach much higher than his elbow even with her mobcap on, looked up.

'Is that you, Adriana My Heart?' Mrs Ingalls asked when the door opened, her dim eyes lighting with the same warmth of the biggest fireplace. 'Talk had it that you were leaving us, but I knew better. My girl wouldn't leave me.'

'No. I couldn't,' Adriana said. 'But I'm sad to say I don't have the shawl you made for me any more. It went to someone who needed it badly.'

'Oh.' The brightness in her eyes dimmed. 'I've not

enough yarn…' She squinted. 'Is that a man with you?' she asked.

'Yes.'

'My goodness me,' the woman said. 'Have you hired another footman?'

'I'm just on loan,' he answered. 'To make sure Miss Adriana made it home safely.'

'You have to watch her,' the older woman said. 'She is always trying to fit another member of staff into the house, but if the older ones don't like the new person, she just helps the new staff member find other employment, our Miss Adri—'

'Now, hush, Mrs Ingalls. Let's not—'

'And no one in the entire world can keep Lady Vel in as good spirits. Why, our life is a paradise compared to before. Well, compared to anything really. Miss Adriana is our best gift ever.' The older woman beamed. 'I'd never slept as easy as I do after she arrived and put things to order. My old eyes don't work as good as they once did, but she watches over me as if she thinks me her own grandmother.'

Adriana stepped over to give the older woman a gentle hug.

'She really didn't want to give the shawl away,' he said. 'She is a gem and an asset to any household. As you seem to be. She was torn to see it go.'

'No matter about the wrap,' the woman said, blushing. 'I'll be happy to knit her another, though I might need a bit of help from Miss Tuttle getting the threads picked out and getting the stitches started, and winter will be long gone before it's finished.'

She patted Adriana's hand. 'You're a dear one. I would not be able to make it without you.'

'You won't have to,' Adriana said. 'Everyone here is my family. I didn't grasp how much until today. This is my home. And no one can ever take care of me as well as you and the others do.'

'Don't lie to yourself, dear heart, you're the one who makes this home a joy.'

The older woman turned to Philbrook.

'We had a problem footman here when Adriana arrived, she suspicioned him out and, the next thing you know, he was gone,' she said.

'She doesn't have to send me on my way,' Philbrook said. 'I'll find my way out.'

He knew he was walking away from something he'd never find again, but oftentimes life went its own direction and a person had to adapt or be unhappy.

'Nonsense,' Mrs Ingalls said. 'Adriana don't need to be looking after me all the time. Show the young man to the door,' she instructed Adriana.

He gave a respectful nod of his head to the older woman, then, realising she might not be able to see it, he said, 'I must thank you.' And he truly did.

Walking over, he took her fingertips, feeling the lines of time. 'It has indeed been an honour to meet you.'

He moved to the door.

'Goodness, Adriana, this one has a silver tongue and

a golden voice. I don't think I've ever heard such a handsome voice.'

He stopped. 'This one?' he asked.

'Oh, yes.' She waved away his words and her own. 'Adriana has so many suitors that we have to shoo them away. Once a baron's son even sent her a note.'

'Mrs Ingalls,' Adriana said, gasping. 'The Baron's son was just thanking me for being so kind to his sister who was awkward at events.'

The older woman shut her eyes and shook her head. 'And she's such a dear one she thought that was all it was. But, of course, we couldn't talk her into sending him a nice note in return.'

'Well, he must have been wise if he saw her sweetness.'

'I have told her she shouldn't let her devotion to us keep her from living her life, but I don't say it enough.'

'I understand,' he answered.

'Your compliments have travelled straight to my head,' Adriana told them. 'I shall soon be expecting the floor to be brushed in front of me before I put each foot down.'

'Where is a broom?' he asked.

'Nonsense,' she said, laughing.

'Perhaps. Perhaps not,' he said, voice low, indicating she precede him to the doorway.

Mrs Ingalls waved them out and they moved into the hallway.

At the exit, he rested his shoulder against the door frame. Leaving would place her out of his life for ever. He knew that. Few chances would occur for a happenstance meeting and she would not instigate them. 'If you wed me, there would always be room for Mrs Ingalls.'

'You are still asking?'

He held out a hand, palm up. 'Of course.' He studied her face. 'And I suspect you're still refusing.'

'I suspect you would be right.'

'But Mrs Ingalls approves of me.'

'She is fond of your voice.'

'Lady Vel will eventually wed and you need to consider what could happen then. I could provide a good home for Mrs Ingalls.'

'That is caring.' She took his hand and rested against him, curling into his strength. 'But she would be displaced,' she spoke with her head at his shoulder. 'It would be hard for her to navigate a new place.'

'I think you are the one worried about navigating a new place.'

'You might take in Mrs Ingalls.' She didn't respond to his comment. 'But there's Maud, and she's courting a footman here, and Mrs Ingalls loves her like a daughter. And there's Enid, and her fingers are getting stiff and Maud helps her as well.'

'I can take the whole household.' He would do it for her. He would do anything for her. Then he bent closer, lifted her chin and placed a kiss on her lips, her softness and femininity reaching all parts of him, and for a moment they just looked at each other.

Then he kissed her again before forcing himself to stop.

'I can find room for all the servants.'

'You only have so much space. It would be a tremendous upheaval for everyone. Everyone.' She touched his chest. 'Your aunt would react to a household of new servants. And the expense would be enormous.'

'You would stay here, with a woman who stomps on your clothing...for servants?'

'No. I would stay here—for my friends.' She took a step away and he saw the farewell in her eyes. Their first kisses would be their last. He could not leave her without presenting his cause.

'You would have your own household,' he said.

'I have one here.'

'You have Velma's.'

'She is my family and I am needed here. Everyone seems to depend on me. I truly feel like I solve the problems and make things go more smoothly.'

'You would always be able to do that at any home.'

'That isn't a reason to leave,' she said. 'I have the love and care that I have built up over the past five years.'

The moment was at hand to go.

A male servant stepped into the hallway and Adriana moved away from Philbrook, but before the servant walked on, his eyes assessed the situation, greeting her warmly, and giving Philbrook a glare he'd never received from a servant in his life.

He couldn't leave because he knew the moment he was out the door, that servant would return to make certain Adriana was still smiling and would be hoping to catch her attention.

'We need to talk privately,' he said after they were alone again.

'There is nothing you can't say to me that the whole world can't hear.'

'Yes. There is.'

She didn't speak, but debate flickered behind her eyes, until she appeared to lose the argument and advised him to wait.

Then she went to the room where the older woman remained and a heartbeat later she returned. 'We can use Mrs Ingalls's room.'

She'd asked permission of a servant.

In the little room, he first noticed the oversized chair crammed into a spot by the foot of the bed. Adriana moved to the shelf not filled with necessities but vases with holly sprigs and she rearranged the holly, although he could see no true change in it. A little glass bowl had some dried green in it and he wasn't sure what it was, but he supposed that was where the woodsy perfume originated from. A large, framed, flowery print hung on the wall with words elaborately written in red: *Shall I Compare Thee to a Summer's Day?*

The walls had so many samplers and drawings and even little twigs connected with leather strips that he felt oversized, but he also felt something that he didn't understand. He could feel the spirit of the people Adriana loved.

She reached out and ran her fingers over a little box by

the bedside, then she lifted it and twisted the knob. Music filled the silence.

'Mrs Ingalls was having trouble sleeping.' Adriana put the box back on the table, her voice a new music. 'Losing her sight and the frailties included was upsetting her. The servants and I collected our funds so that she might have the best music box we could get. At night, before she sleeps, she plays it. And if any one of the maids has a problem or a concern, she might slip down to the room, sit in the big chair and talk with Mrs Ingalls while she rests, then Mrs Ingalls plays the music when she feels all has been said, and the world is so much better.'

Adriana stood by the spindly chair, touching the wood as gently as if she touched a babe.

'I would have a sketch made of this room and every thread would be relocated.' He took her hands.

'You can't sketch our hearts,' Adriana said. 'If you moved a palace into a desert, it is a palace, but it is surrounded by dry land. Arid land. Where nothing grows.'

'You could make a desert a palace,' he said. 'With your presence.'

'No. I couldn't.'

But then, proving her words wrong, she kissed him. Shimmering blasts of her spirit melded itself into him.

She moved away too soon, reminding him again what a desert felt like.

'You could make the land verdant,' he said. 'Summer showers create beauty.'

'Vision is clouded by water and it might appear to be

raining, but what if it turns out to be tears? And I will always be known as the one who took Velma's cast-off husband.'

He never wanted her to believe, or anyone else to believe, that she was second to Velma or anyone else. 'I understand.' And he truly did.

But he'd also realised something else in his life. It wasn't love he'd not believed in—it was an Adriana. He'd not known a woman like her existed. She was the only one who could provide a different life for him. Who could walk with him, joined in purpose and meaning, and could give him an existence beyond any he'd otherwise feel.

'Can I hear the music box one more time?' he asked. He could walk out of her life for ever—truly, it would be easy to find someone who would stare at him with daydreams in her eyes and be blinded by the pretty things he could get for her, the soft words and the gifts recommended by the servants. But it would be pointless to him. Because Adriana was the one woman in the world who could give his life meaning.

She'd always been in the periphery of his life, showing kindness around him, yet his eyes hadn't truly opened to the treasure she was until he saw her appearing so bedraggled and alone, but she took the time to pick up a bit of refuse he'd thrown to the ground. That was Adriana… doing what needed to be done quietly and risking even more discomfort to herself. Her friend had created a shawl for her and, no matter how tattered it might appear, she proudly wore it in friendship.

She moved, twisting the music box's knob with a series of clicks and releasing it. He listened, taking in the moment. Then, when the tune ended, he stood, moved to the box and ran his fingers over the maker's mark on it.

'You could be in charge of a mansion.'

A mansion in a desert. He saw the words without her speaking them. Not even if he were a duke or a king. She would not be purchased.

'That's very kind of you to offer,' she said, softly. 'I will consider it.'

Consider.

A kind way of saying goodbye.

'I must go,' he said. 'I have a very important errand to attend.'

He had to find a shawl.

He'd stopped on the way home to talk again with the clerk and in the morning the servants searched the most probable areas. The butler was co-ordinating their hunt and had made arrangements for everyone to meet at a central location where he would make certain they could have tea and warmth.

They were to bring the owner back because anyone might claim to own a shawl for the high sum he'd offered to purchase it and he would need to inspect it. The servant would get a nice vail.

Philbrook's last hope for another chance to impress Adriana.

He'd not been able to keep from pacing. Finally, at midday, a butler knocked and stepped inside, leading a man with a hat missing part of a brim, and a footman presenting a tattered shawl out as if he held a pillow with a crown perched on it.

He'd touched the garment reverently and produced payment, and more.

Before the first man had time to exit, a second man and garment had followed and he'd discovered he didn't know exactly what the scrap had looked like, but he'd paid the man.

Then a third man arrived.

He was left with three faulty garments in his hands—he couldn't decide which was which. Adriana would have to be the judge.

Imagining stars of gratefulness in her eyes, he relished the happiness in her heart and his chance to see her again.

Moving to his carriage, his delight appeared contagious when the driver gave a jaunty nod after finding out where they were going.

After he arrived, strides long, he didn't go to the main door at her house, but the servants' entrance. Once inside, he found the area where Mrs Ingalls had been sitting and knocked. The older woman wasn't there, but a curious maid told him she would fetch Adriana.

He waited in the empty room, feeling a little sheepish for the three tattered shawls in his hands, but he really didn't know which one was the correct one. Even the wisest of men might decide on three separate gifts.

Adriana walked in the door, hesitant.

Every moment had been worth it, ten times over. He was in her presence again and truly felt he viewed her for the first time. He wondered if every moment for the rest of his life would be that way when he saw her and he knew it would. Adriana stirred something in him that had been dormant his whole life. Something he'd not known existed.

'I found Mrs Ingalls's shawl,' he said.

She moved forward and, with fingers outstretched but not touching the closest one, she said, 'This isn't—I've never seen any of those garments in my life.'

The air seemed to leave his body and he searched her eyes while he lowered the goods. Apparently, the shawl he felt so tattered was quite the fashion.

'Truly. I never have,' she said.

One faded shawl looked the same to him as any other faded shawl, but the disappointment hit him so deep in his chest he could barely breathe.

A blast of words directed at himself, but that he never said in front of women, whirled through his mind. He bit his cheek to keep from speaking them.

'Where did you get them? Did you think you could give me another woman's shawl? And these poor women…' She touched the fabric, accidentally touching his hand, jarring him with warmth to the bottom of his boots. 'The poor women will freeze,' she stated.

'I paid triple what they were worth.' He said the only thing that came to his mind. In truth, he'd likely paid more than three times their value. They were mere rags.

'That was kind of you,' she said, expression unchanging but then her eyes immediately brightened. 'Do you think...? Do you think they can be returned? I hate to think of the women being without their wrap so close to Christmas—and they might not have wool at hand to spin into yarn.'

'I can direct the clothes to be returned,' he said.

He wanted to say he wouldn't return to her. But he couldn't speak the words. They would be too true.

She saw the goodbye in his eyes.

She wanted the women to get their shawls back. She wanted them to stay warm.

She didn't want her life to change. The servants were her true family next to her parents. They had been together through Velma's tantrums. Through illness and celebration. Many had told her she was the daughter they'd never had, the sister they'd longed for, the reason their days had brightness in them.

Even Vel needed her.

'I must stay where I am.'

'I will see that they are returned.' His jaw firmed.

'I'm sure they will have a much better Christmas with the funds from the shawls—if you don't take the funds back.'

He separated each shawl, held it out, studied it and wrapped it over his arm, before giving her a glance she could not read.

'You will not ask for your money to be returned?' She

didn't have any funds left to give him to replace the money he might take. She had spent it all on gifts for the servants.

'Of course not. It was my error.'

Her heart practically tied itself in a knot. He had done the right thing. He had made an effort.

'If you wait just a moment…' she thought of the abundant baking taking place in the house, and she knew many poor did not have ovens '… I can have some Christmas treats gathered for the families' children.'

He patted the shawls over his arm, giving her a bow. 'I will wait in my vehicle and you can have one of the servants bring the treats out. My driver will make certain the others receive them.'

He left, leaving chilled air behind. Her throat didn't want to work and neither did her feet, but she scurried around, finding the largest basket she could and assembling treats.

Then she collected two large buns still warm from the oven to give to the drivers. She ran out with the basket, the wind slicing into her.

He had a point. The servants treated her like a treasured guest. A friend. And they sheltered her. She depended on them so much. They cossetted her as much, or more, than she helped them.

Perhaps as she was so scrupulous about telling the truth to others, she was telling herself the biggest lie of all. It was not just her taking care of them. They were taking care of her.

She stopped before reaching the carriage, staring

through the window at a profile that appeared a continent away from her and perhaps he was.

The driver hopped down from the perch and she looked at the man, unable to say anything at first, feeling the loss and seeing the reflection of awareness in the driver's eyes. He was telling her she was making a big mistake.

'The two wrapped on top are for you and the other man beside you,' she said, lingering just a breath, not turning to the carriage to see if Philbrook was watching, knowing she had already said goodbye.

Without preamble, the driver jumped away when something caught his eye.

'Lord Philbrook,' the driver called out, scurrying to kick a wheel. 'Just aware. The bolts are sticking out. We can't risk leaving now. Just give us some time and we can fix it for you. And we should probably test it. Wouldn't want to send you to your maker so close to Christmas.'

He nodded to Adriana. 'Sorry, Miss. Don't want to lose a wheel or cause a horse to be lamed. It would be kind of you to let the Earl wait inside while we tend things. It'll only take a few— And it's so cold.' He shivered, an exaggerated move.

Philbrook stepped out, able to melt ice with his stare.

'It's fine,' Philbrook said, studying the wheel. His eyes raked the servant. 'I appreciate your concern, but the wheel will get us home.' He reached for the door.

Adriana touched his arm. 'You cannot risk injury. Or your life. Or cause the driver to have to work even more in cold weather. He could be frozen.'

His eyes had a hint of stone and steel, but then he blinked the coldness away and his voice was wry. 'I wouldn't want to risk the drivers' safety.'

'Please come back inside,' she said. 'You can wait in the kitchen. Mrs Ingalls will be there for company.'

She led him inside and, sure enough, Mrs Ingalls was in the room.

They spoke and Adriana could not stay. It would only make saying goodbye to him again hurt more. She was in her home. With her family. And she needed to stay there and not risk moving into a social world that would not accept her. To make a quick decision that would haunt her for the rest of her life. Being the recipient of yet another of Vel's cast-offs and everyone noting that she was the poor cousin he'd married in what surely was a moment of pity.

Adriana forced herself to leave. He would be gone soon and she would muddle on.

He was too much for her. Too much man. Too powerful. Too far above her in standing.

On the next floor, she stopped, watching his carriage from the window. The two drivers were just talking. Not fixing anything.

Vel walked up to her, looking out the window. 'What is that rickety rattletrap doing here?'

'Something went wrong with it. Philbrook is with Mrs Ingalls now, waiting while it's fixed.'

Velma turned away, shuddering. 'Can't believe I let him squire me around in that thing. But, oh, well, there'll be someone else wanting to be a countess as soon as they hear he's available again. He's just so blasted cold. Never wanted to kiss me.'

Then she left, leaving Adriana to keep watching the carriage.

Adriana kept staring out the window. The carriage driver took out a cloth and it appeared he was polishing a wheel. Then he talked to the other driver. One took a pinch of snuff. They really didn't seem overly concerned about the vehicle.

The vocal driver walked to the house and she watched until he was too close to view, then she turned away from the window, listening until she heard the carriage leave. Philbrook was gone and she still had the important things in her life. Her family.

She went to her room, reached under her pillow and pulled out the elaborate shawl she'd finished with thick yarn. The one they'd made for Mrs Ingalls. Adriana had wanted Mrs Ingalls to have the warmest shawl ever and the servants had called it a knitted hug.

She couldn't help herself. She put away the shawl and returned to the window. She peered out. The carriage was gone. All the Christmas spirit seemed to have left, squeezed out. Wrung out and tossed out into the cold, and trailing along after that vehicle which certainly wouldn't stop to have a few sprigs of holly be collected, mistletoe or a yule log.

It just irked her.

And it irked her that Vel had said she would cancel

Boxing Day. In truth, Adriana would have found a way to continue it, but she couldn't leave the people she cared so much for. Especially to always be the second choice.

She had everything. Everything. And it was not causing a burst of happiness inside her as it usually did. Something had taken her peace. A few words and a proposal had caused her to doubt herself. And she shouldn't really. All was right with the world. Things were just as they should be. Although the house was quiet for Christmas time.

And she had been just the substitute for another and she would not live like that. It was one thing to work for Vel. It was another to be second place in a marriage.

She straightened her shoulders and decided she would go help Mrs Ingalls. Working hands strengthened the heart and head, as Mrs Ingalls would say.

When her foot touched the last rung on the step, she heard laughter. The servants must be celebrating early after all.

Then she walked into the room and heard a masculine voice say, 'I ate one a day until my mother found out and then she put a stop to it. Mother told me green persimmons never made anyone grow taller. But I got the last laugh when I finally outgrew the lad who'd had a jest on me.'

The servants were all standing around Philbrook and they were laughing. Laughing. They hesitated when she walked in, except for Mrs Ingalls.

'Didn't your carriage just leave?' she asked him.

'I suppose it did.'

'The driver wanted to make certain it was safe,' Mrs Ingalls said.

'And risk himself?'

'Oh, goodness,' Mrs Ingalls said. 'The driver is safe. It was just a bit of horse fluff caught in the spoke.'

The older woman studied Philbrook through dimmed eyes. 'I think he's sweet on me.'

'I am,' Philbrook said.

She knew they were jesting. Knew he was playing along with the dreamy gaze he gave Mrs Ingalls. But she was envious of that adoring, breathless expression.

'I would propose to you,' he said to Mrs Ingalls, 'but I have been turned down twice recently. I do not think I could take a third refusal.'

'You wouldn't have to,' Mrs Ingalls said.

The maids all blushed.

She felt as if her family turned against her.

Mrs Ingalls put her hand on the table and pushed herself up. 'I think we all have chores to do, don't we?'

The maids giggled and the footmen left with everyone else, and Mrs Ingalls crept around the table by Philbrook and pulled a sprig of mistletoe out of her pocket. 'I'll leave this with you.' She placed it in front of him, smiling. 'You need it more than I do.'

Then Mrs Ingalls made her way out the door, placing her palm on the wall to feel her way along.

'You have sweet-talked them,' Adriana said.

'Did I?'

Oh, he knew very well he had. The silkiness of his voice told her he agreed completely with her assessment.

'How did you get your driver to leave without you?'

'He did that on his own.'

'Truly?' The man had noticed her staring at Philbrook. Or the driver was trying to earn favour with his employer.

'I must be going,' he said. Then he narrowed his eyes and appeared in exaggerated thought.

'Is there something on the horizon?' he asked.

'Only Christmas and Boxing Day, as you well know.'

'Christmas?' he asked. 'I guess I must have overlooked it last year. Probably missed dinner that day, or the staff forgot to prepare our usual Christmas treat, a spun sugar confection over a pyramid of fried dough balls that doesn't consist of anything filling.'

'Sounds delicious.'

'Why don't you have Christmas dinner at my house?' he asked. 'You might have some ideas to make it more festive.'

'I always have Christmas with my parents. Vel is with her father's family so I use that as a chance to visit with my parents and my siblings.'

'May I join you?' he asked.

'It's Christmas.' She emphasised the word. 'A day for family.' She couldn't say anything else.

'I know.'

'Your family…'

'Aunt will understand.'

'Your mother?'

'Will complain no more than usual.'

'I don't know.'

'Your choice,' he said. 'It's all your choice.'

He waited and she noticed he still held the mistletoe cluster, giving the stem a little roll within his hand.

Then he put his free hand under hers and tapped it just enough that she lifted it. He put the mistletoe on her palm, his lips turned up and his eyes focused so intently on her that she blushed.

'You're welcome to hang on to that for use when I'm around,' he said. 'But really, you don't need it.'

'Neither do you,' she said, a dare rising in her body.

She ran the greenery up his sleeve and rested it on his shoulder.

'Which would you rather have?' she asked. 'A kiss or an invite to my parents'?'

'There's no reason not to have both.'

She could feel his gaze deep inside her, connecting her to him in a way she'd never known before.

'I will pick you up tomorrow,' he said, taking the greenery and holding it over her head. But he only brushed her cheek with his lips and moved his mouth so close to her ear she could feel his words. 'Your two lips work better than any Christmas tradition ever will to make me wish for a kiss from you.'

He finished by holding her close and his lips found hers, finally showing her what mistletoe truly meant.

He instructed his servants to have a good time. They were to be all smiles and frivolous. They'd stared back at him as if he'd instructed them to hop on one foot while doing their chores and in a way that was what he felt he'd done.

His butler had been affronted and he'd seen the man literally biting his lip. 'Merry, sir?' the servant had asked. 'I am. Every day.'

'We always give good wishes to the tradesmen who arrive at the house during the two weeks before a festive season.' The housekeeper put a hand to her chest. Upset. 'And we are careful to pass along a token of your appreciation as has been done since before your grandfather's time. We take pride in knowing this household runs as a well-constructed clock. When we are prepared for a bell before it rings, we give ourselves a silent salute.'

'Understandable and appreciated,' he said. 'Miss Adriana will likely visit on Christmas Day and I want her to see the reflection of the true happiness of my staff. She spends Boxing Day with her friends, but I would like her to see that the staff here has everything needed to have the best Boxing Day ever. No expense is to be spared. I want Cook's spun sugar sculpture supported by mounds of sweet balls of dough prepared, not only for the family, but for the staff. And I want Boxing Day to be an extravagant, pleasant event for everyone. Better than ever before.'

'Us?' the housekeeper had said, her voice ending in a squeak.

'Yes. I have been remiss in the past,' he said. 'And I want you to make this Christmas and Boxing Day superlative for you.'

They had stared at him. 'What needs to be changed?' the housekeeper finally asked.

'Everything possible, I suppose,' he said. 'More. Better. Bigger.' But time had been short, so he had rushed out to join the stablemen to find more holly, mistletoe and other greenery that might give the servants' hall a more festive air. He would show Adriana that his staff had the Christmas spirit.

And when he was returning home with a coach that smelled of a woodland and hardly had any place left for him to sit, he had more awareness of a Christmas spirit than he'd ever felt. Of what it truly meant. Of rebirth. Of the future.

And he knew the misguided path he had been on in the past had had one purpose. To bring Adriana into his life.

Chapter Six

Christmas dawned almost warm, sunny and bright. Adriana rushed to visit Mrs Ingalls and share a bite of breakfast with her and the other servants bustling in and out.

Vel was still abed after a late-night event her mother had planned suddenly so she could recover from the cancelled marriage plans. News of the broken betrothal had been broadcast far and wide as Velma's mother thought it best for any marriageable man to know her daughter was unfettered. The betrothal had, she announced to all and sundry, been merely a jest Velma had been playing on her and everyone else. She and Philbrook had had a laugh and remained friends.

Then the sound of creaking carriage wheels stopping caused everyone to quieten.

'I bet that is Lord Philbrook,' Mrs Ingalls said. 'Do you think he's returning to court Lady Velma?' she asked, all expression leaving her face, except innocence. 'Or is that the reason you didn't ask the carriage driver to prepare the vehicle for you to borrow and Cook lent you a wrap?'

'He's not returning for my cousin,' Adriana said, unable to keep the smile from her face as she rushed out the door.

His frail-appearing coach waited and she knew that she was tumbling forward into something that could be difficult to stop.

She went to the servants' door and saw him striding up the walkway, and her body responded with the feeling of potently spiked punch making its way throughout.

He whisked her to his carriage, and she gave direction to her parents' house. Inside, a wool blanket rested and he carefully unfolded it and wrapped her inside.

'Are you sure your fondness for the carriage isn't because it's a memento of your grandfather?' Surely he recognised his affection for his grandfather.

'It fits my size and is the most reliable vehicle I have ever seen, crafted by the best carriage maker in the world who was given all the time and funds he needed, according to my grandfather.'

'Your grandfather...'

'Was stern. Once he came in my room and saw my clothing scattered about before the maid arrived. But my chest swelled with pride when he said I was a man now and he appointed me a trusted valet.' He rubbed the scar on his hand again. 'Only this valet's duty was to see that I was trained to take care of my clothing and straighten my room. And he was to inspect it.'

'You were to take care of your room?'

'The valet would catch me gone and turn a shirt wrong side out, stuff my stockings into my pillow case, or wrap threads around my waistcoat. He's still my valet, but now he truly does take care of my clothing.'

'Perhaps you're fond of him?'

'After he sewed my shirt sleeves closed, I left a smelly fish under his bed,' he mused. 'Two days in a row. We both enjoyed that.'

'Like having a brother?' she asked.

'More like a favourite uncle,' he said.

'Well, I have brothers,' she said. 'Four of them and I suspect you're about to meet them. Prepare yourself.'

'I am,' he said, not looking concerned at all.

She bit the inside of her lip. Her family's home wasn't the fine estate of her cousin, Velma, but rooms above a shop where her parents worked.

She was anxious to see her family. When the carriage pulled up to the shop, he appeared to be looking for a house and didn't seem to know what she meant when she indicated the rooms overhead.

The sight of her brother arriving at the same time distracted her and she stepped out of the vehicle.

'Auntie. Auntie. Auntie.' Suddenly she was surrounded by nieces and nephews and sisters and brothers and more hugs than she could count.

So much revelry burst around her she couldn't introduce him and she was swept into the shop as her family surged forward.

Her mother greeted her, handkerchief in hand, and gave her a hug before stepping back and dotting the handkerchief to her eye.

'We've missed all our family so.'

'Yes,' her father said, voice gruff with emotion.

'I would like to introduce you to—' She reached back, her nieces clutching her skirt, but he wasn't as close as she'd expected. She turned, realising he was standing, watching, no expression on his face, his thoughts deep inside himself.

'A friend of mine,' she said, fingers seeming lost in the air. She couldn't tell them he was an earl. Her mother would be overwhelmed to have a peer in the household. She had never even had her brother-in-law to tea. Only her sister.

'He must be a good friend if you risk introducing him to us,' her brother said, picking up his son and swinging him to rest on his hip.

'Now, be on your best behaviour,' her mother said. 'We have a guest.'

'I'm Edmond,' he said, 'as Miss Armstrong appears to have forgotten to introduce me.'

'Those your cattle?' her father said, indicating the carriage on the street below after she concluded introductions.

He nodded.

'Well, you must have grand employment,' her father said. 'If your employer lends you such a fine equipage.' Then her father knit his brows. 'Oh, are you a hackney? Don't believe I've seen that rig around here much, though.'

'I am partial to it, the cattle and the carriage,' he said, not answering the question.

Then the uproar continued and her mother sat them

across from each other. And he seemed to be taking it all in, conversing enough to be sociable, laughing in the right places, yet, somehow, remaining apart from it.

And she was more aware of him than she was her family. She noted each flicker of expression, each movement of his head, sip he took, tilt of his lips. It seemed her happiness rested on her awareness of him.

Once in the carriage to leave, she told herself that his impression of her family didn't matter. She told herself the words again. It didn't matter.

The wheels creaked away, not moving with any speed.

'What did you think?' she asked, forgetting her statement to herself that she didn't care about his opinion.

'I liked them all, except that one little boy who bit my boot.' He shifted and peered at the scuff on his boot. 'Not my fault he didn't like the taste of leather.'

'He wanted your attention.'

'His yowl worked very well.' He laughed. 'And got everyone's notice.'

'Something like that always happens when the whole family is together.'

He clasped her hand. 'Thank you for inviting me. Now though, I would like for you to go with me to my family's house. Will you?'

'But…'

'I asked my mother not to leave until tonight. I told her that I hoped to bring someone I would like her to visit with.'

'I've seen her from afar. Just as I have with most of your family.'

'But you've never spoken with her, have you?'

'No.'

'You place a great emphasis on togetherness. On this season. On how well the servants are treated. I'd like you to see Christmas at my home.'

He clasped her hand and held it between them. 'If you don't want to do so, then I understand, but it would mean a great deal to me and I hope it would mean something to you.'

He spoke in such a way that she could hear the hope in his voice. Refusal was impossible to her. In fact, it seemed no one had ever asked her before to do something which sounded so important to them.

Even before she reached the entrance, she could see Christmas greenery overflowing the window sills.

When they walked inside, the butler wasn't there to take cloaks and Philbrook took his off and placed it crosswise over the chair, then helped her with her wrap and put it on top of his coat.

With the greenery in the windows and the two garments on the chair, the room felt in chaos and she felt a bit disarrayed herself.

Philbrook led her into the servants' area, then to a door which he opened. The staff had gathered inside the room and suddenly everyone's backbone straightened, except one older woman wearing a large apron. She was sitting, head forward, eyes closed, dozing.

A sideboard was filled with pies—currant, plum and mince that Adriana recognised. Sugar cakes thick with almonds. Biscuits with nutmeg sprinkled atop. A spun sugar golden web covered a tall triangle of cooked balls of fried dough.

Each collar was starched, each hair was in place and, except for the one asleep, shoulders were tensed.

The room appeared to have sprouted a forest. Enough greenery surrounded them that much of it was placed on the floor, One corner was stuffed with boxes and cloth bundles and paper parcels.

'Lord Philbrook,' the butler said and everyone jumped for space to stand and a maid tapped the sleeping woman's shoulder. She jumped awake, collected herself, gazed around and rose.

'Welcome to our Christmas celebration,' the butler intoned. Tree bark had more personality than the butler's face, but she noticed that he appeared to be communicating with Philbrook via eye movement and she caught the barest nod Philbrook gave him.

'We are just having the most festive of occasions.' The butler waved a hand around. 'Please join us if you'd like.'

The housekeeper, dark smudges under her eyes, pointed to the spun sugar confection. 'Oh, yes, and Cook has provided special treats for us.'

'So many gifts,' the butler said. 'What a joyous Boxing Day we'll have tomorrow.'

Palms patted together in soft applause and every face smiled.

'Thank you,' he said. 'Please enjoy your treats.' He pulled the door closed behind him, then stood outside the door, holding the latch. He examined her face.

'They couldn't all fit at the table.' She paused.

He should have had the butler do a test earlier. That was not his servant's mistake. It was his.

'When did you tell them to do this?' she asked.

'We started work yesterday. I gathered the greenery with the carriage drivers because we had so little time.'

'You gathered the greenery?'

'Yes. I would imagine they hardly got any sleep because by the time we returned with it, they all joined in arranging it as I'd asked them to do as a gift to me.'

'How early did they start this morning?'

'I'm not certain, but everything was perfectly in place when I awoke. I suppose you could ask them.'

He opened the door, hand remaining on the knob. Some of the servants stood, filling their plates. They realised she was standing there and a burst of smiles replaced all the tiredness.

'What time did you start working this morning?' he asked.

'Why, our normal time, I suppose,' the butler inserted and she could tell instantly that no one would disagree with him.

'My pardon that you are not having a superior Christmas,' he said. 'Hopefully Boxing Day will be better to-morrow.'

'But we are enjoying today so,' the housekeeper said, eyes darting from side to side, a stare instructing all the maids to agree. A chorus of voices concurred. 'And thank you for giving us the rest of the day to ourselves.'

'I appreciate your efforts,' Philbrook said, shutting the door after he spoke.

'Your servants don't even know how to relax,' she said.

'Yes, they do. It is just in a different style than you are used to. I have a stellar staff.'

'But you don't love them as much as I love the ones I live with.'

He raised a brow. 'It's not necessary for me to love them. It's necessary that their wages are given them and they are respected. They are staff.'

'That is heartless. And they probably care deeply for you.'

'If they were given the choice between receiving love or a wage, I think all my staff is sensible enough to choose the wage.'

She stared at him for a brief moment, then put her arm firmly around his and attached herself to his side, more secure than any pair of gloves he'd ever donned.

She tugged at his arm. Nothing moved but her feet, but then he let her pull him back into the servants' dining hall.

Again, the movement stopped.

'Everyone,' she said. 'Please tell Lord Philbrook what you think of him. One by one. I'd like to hear it.'

~ The employees' countenance outshone the sun.

'The best employer.' The butler took the lead.

'Efficient.' The housekeeper.

'The best employer.' A maid next to her.

'Precise.' The answers went around the table with each one speaking after the person standing next.

'The best employer.'

'Even better that what he said.'

'Upstanding.'

Philbrook raised a hand, stopping them. 'I pay their wages.'

'Yes, but there must be some affection between you.' She studied the faces.

'Oh, no, Miss,' the housekeeper said. 'He is an exemplary employer.'

She asked the butler, 'Does he not share a jest with you from time to time?'

'Of course not,' the butler said, huffing. 'He is an exemplary employer.'

The words thudded into the room.

'You'll get no argument from me,' Philbrook stated.

Servants stared at her. She could never live in a household so perfect. So austere. A home in which Christmas greenery appeared out of place,

'Very well,' she said, 'I hope everyone has a joyous Christmas and that your Boxing Day is relaxing.' She thanked them all for their well wishes and walked out with Philbrook, aware of how fortunate she was to have an assemblage of servants that she lived with and loved.

Suddenly it became more important to her than ever to understand Philbrook's thoughts and not just important for him. Important for herself.

He stopped when they were at the stairway and she had no option but to halt if she continued to hold on to his arm.

'Life is not about love,' he said. 'It's about duty. Love is like the spun sugar confection in the servants' area. It's a good treat, but it doesn't last long.'

'I like treats.'

'You may believe that.' He shook his head. 'But your actions prove they are not your first priority.'

She didn't respond.

'People are your first priority.'

'Love. I stand by it. And if what you say is true, it doesn't matter. Love and people go hand in hand.'

'Respect is important. Integrity,' he said.

'You can have them both.'

'Love causes men to be foolish. To leave their families. It's the height of self-regard with no thought to anyone else.'

'That's not love. It's selfishness.'

She peered at the greenery. 'I still believe in love,' she said, 'and Christmas.' It was true, she just didn't know if she believed you could decorate the world with holly and make it Christmas. Or you could put a wedding band on and have a marriage.

With her servants, the spirit of Christmas reached them all. With her family, the gaiety stretched to everyone. And her parents genuinely loved each other. Affection filled their lives. It had been around her from childhood.

Perhaps his family had more of the Christmas spirit than he realised.

'You mentioned me meeting your mother,' she said. 'Is she still here?'

'Yes.'

From the distance in his face, she knew where he'd received his schooling on love.

Chapter Seven

When they walked upstairs into a small sitting room where his aunt sat, there was another woman who could be her mirror image—if it were drenched in cosmetics—perched in an opposite chair. Another difference between them was that the other woman's dress appeared more suitable for a fancy event and his aunt's, while fashionable, had nothing special to commend it. A huge platter of biscuits sat between them, some looking of fluffed egg whites, some of crisped flour, and some of nuts dipped in boiled sugar.

'Mother, this is—'

Immediately his mother interrupted. 'Lady Velma's cousin Adriana,' she said by way of greeting. 'I remember you from years past. And today my sister has been telling me about Velma's little dance on your dress. The two of you have always been close like that, I suppose.'

'We normally get on,' Adriana said and saw the disagreement in the faces around her. 'We do, even if we ruffle each other's feathers on occasion.'

His aunt Bessie lifted a biscuit, broke it two pieces and stared at her sister. 'She's better than Velma. You don't know how close we came to a disaster. I had to help.' She popped one half of the biscuit into her mouth.

The aunt rose, took the platter and offered the biscuits to Adriana. She shook her head, then his aunt walked to the door while carrying the platter, tapping the door facing with the side of her cane. She spoke over her shoulder. 'You could be right at home here, Adriana. My sister could make you feel as if you had never left Velma.'

'Well, I'm not enjoying this Christmas,' his mother said, directing her words at him, which held a bit of censure in them. 'The servants have been running through the halls almost like lost children, so befuddled and rearranging greenery after already having it in place. You know I can't stand the smell of woodsy things. I hate things being out of order just because it is December the twenty-fifth. We have eleven other months with a twenty-fifth. I'm sure Christmas could be better celebrated in the spring. Your grandfather and I were in complete agreement on that. For once.'

'Perhaps he was wrong.'

'Oh, it's totally unfair to expect servants to put out twigs, then expect them to clean up afterwards. If today is any indication of the normally superlative staff, I cannot imagine Boxing Day with the servants not working,' his mother said. 'I'll be happy to return home to my daughter's house. She understands that greenery is best left in the woods.'

She stood, gave a moment for everyone to appreciate her stature and perfection, then spoke to her son. 'Your aunt seems to believe the two of you are courting. I suppose it's true or Adriana wouldn't be here.'

'That is entirely up to Adriana,' he said.

'I am not at all surprised,' she said. 'Your grandfather is getting everything he wanted.'

'My grandfather wished for me to court Velma.'

She shut her eyes, let out a breath through her nose before raising her lids and said, 'No. He didn't. Why would you think that?'

'Because on his deathbed… With his last breath. He said he wanted me to wed… I nodded. I could not refuse him a dying wish, but it pained me to follow through with it.'

'That's a little cold to say that in front of Adriana, isn't it?'

'I understand a grandson doing his duty,' Adriana said, 'and wanting to carry on as his grandfather instructed.'

'Happy you do,' his mother said. 'I knew not to trust the old tyrant and I wanted to see how he would trick you. I was not surprised. Trying to control his grandson with his last breath. And Philbrook was so upset because his grandfather's illness came as a complete surprise.'

'It was a horrific day for me. I didn't realise he was dying until those very last moments and then he asked me to wed Velma.'

'Are you daft?' his mother said. 'He didn't say that.'

'He did.'

She put her palms to her temple. 'Didn't you hear him say cousin? *Velma's cousin?*' She gave a nod to Adriana. 'Pardon, the old goat never could remember your name and you were not around as much as she was.'

'He didn't even know me.'

'Yes, he did. Remember when you weren't very old and got mud on Velma's dress?' She chuckled. 'He saw it. He told my husband who told me. The old goat detested Velma from then on.'

Adriana put her fingertips over her lips. 'I shouldn't have done that. Mother was furious.'

'But you didn't tell on Velma. She pushed you into the mud and no one but my father-in-law saw it. Then you got up, covered in mud, told Velma you loved her and gave her a big hug, and he said she squalled like a little baby. He thought it so fitting.'

'I shouldn't have done it. I knew I was doing wrong. Mother was so embarrassed. Clothing was so dear and Velma could give away her dress, but we couldn't afford a new one for me. The stains didn't come out and I still had to wear it.'

'I wonder if you've not changed that much,' his mother said, glancing at her son. *'Pardon me, Velma, while I wed your betrothed. Love you dearly, Cousin.'*

'It's not like that,' Adriana insisted. 'It's not.'

'It's absolutely not,' Philbrook said.

His mother nodded, didn't answer and, with a roll of her eyes, disagreed as she left the room.

Adriana dealt with the thoughts bombarding her. To believe she was always getting her cousin's cast-offs was bad enough, but believing she was somehow using machinations to put her cousin behind her was even worse.

'I can see why you're not fond of love,' she said.

'But can you now see why I want to marry you?' he said. 'Why it would mean so much to have you near me? A woman strong from childhood. Who creates a warm home around her and wants to take care of the people she cares for. Who stands up for herself even when she does it in a calm way.'

Adriana didn't know if she could agree. Her thoughts tangled around what she had just discovered. She wondered if she was still getting revenge and calling it love. 'I should go home now. It's been an eventful day.'

He led her to his vehicle.

At the carriage, she stopped and greeted the driver whom Philbrook had waved away so he could open the door himself. The staff member gave her a respectful nod and climbed back into his seat, the carriage creaking its acceptance of the weight.

She needed to talk with the driver alone and she would find a way.

'I'd like to give Mrs Ingalls a Christmas greeting,' he said, when they arrived at her house. 'It would be remiss of me not to speak with her.'

Adriana and Philbrook walked into the servants' hall and Mrs Ingalls was sitting with her knitting needles. Her face glowed when she saw him.

'Did you get use of the mistletoe?' she asked him.

'Sadly, not as much as I'd hoped,' he said. 'I suppose it wasn't full strength.'

'Bah,' she said. 'You could put a dried twig over your head and I'd claim it was mistletoe.' Then she lowered her chin and glanced at Adriana. 'Any one would be wise to do the same.'

Adriana watched as Philbrook then took a holly twig from a small bough sitting on the table, and put it over Mrs Ingalls's head, and kissed her cheek. She chuckled and fanned her face.

'I suppose I must be going.' He twirled the twig and put it back where he'd found it, then left, without giving Adriana more than the most proper and briefest of farewells.

The room felt more silent than any room she'd ever been in.

Mrs Ingalls locked eyes with her. 'You are making such an error,' Mrs Ingalls said.

'He was betrothed to my cousin. I did the right thing. Otherwise, I will be seen for ever as the one getting Velma's cast-off love.'

Mrs Ingalls pushed her hair back in place and adjusted her cap. 'I don't know. It doesn't feel to me like you're doing the right thing.'

'The right thing doesn't always make you feel happy at first. That's what the wrong thing does. The right thing makes you feel better later. The wrong thing starts out with the joy and leads to sadness or more of the wrong thing lying to you that the right thing doesn't matter.'

'Please stop over-explaining,' Mrs Ingalls said, waving her words away. 'That's what happens when you do the wrong thing.'

Chapter Eight

B oxing Day dawned with none of the fanfare she usually felt in her heart.

She knew Velma would sleep late and early morning was Adriana's time to use the carriage if she needed to go on any quick errands.

Her only errand was to find Philbrook's driver. She wanted to speak with him alone so she made arrangements to go to visit the man.

When she found him, he was even more grizzled than he'd been the day before.

'You did not want to leave Philbrook when offered employment,' she said. 'Why?'

'His wages is good. To me the only good garden is a hay field.'

She bit her upper lip. 'And why did you give him that folderol about the carriage wheel potentially being loose?'

'Well, if he was sweet for you, I thought you would make a better mistress than that...er... Lady Velma and you were kind enough to offer me employment. He could do worse. He has.' He rubbed his knuckles against his whiskers. 'He thought he was going to marry that other one, but he wasn't happy about it.'

'He tried to give the household servants Christmas off, but they ended up having to work twice as hard.'

'True,' he said. 'They were all so flummoxed. They feel he hardly has any Christmas at all and they wanted to make his Christmas special for him. And if he wanted them to pretend it was for themselves...' He shrugged. 'Whatever he wishes for, we wish for.'

'He seems so firm with them.'

'It's them that are firm with him. They want to be the absolute finest for Philbrook.' He tilted his head. 'That's the best man you'll ever find. If you have half a chance with him, take the opportunity and run with it, right to him. If I'm wrong, I'll spend the rest of my days growing them overgrown weeds called carrots.'

She considered the driver's words carefully. 'But he doesn't believe in love.'

The man's voice strengthened. 'He's a good man and it don't matter. He believes in doin' what's right and fair. He didn't get that from his mother or grandfather. He inherited those traits from his father and grandmother, and maybe a little part from his aunt. And maybe it's all just from his own thoughts.'

He chewed his inner cheek for a moment before continuing. 'And one other thing you got to think of: if he don't believe in love, maybe it's 'cause he never felt it. And you can be the first one he feels it with and with any children you might have. I'd take that wager. If you're wrong, you still get a good man. If you're right, then you get something only a few in the world ever have.'

She returned home, ruminating over the words the man had said. Her mother had always claimed love was the reason she was so happy in her marriage, but maybe it was their basic integrity. Her father was a good man and treated them all so gently that they all wanted to please him. Her mother was much the same.

When she stepped out of Velma's carriage, she turned and looked back at it, and realised it meant absolutely nothing to her. She couldn't have described it if she'd been asked.

But she could describe that old vehicle Philbrook drove. In fact, it gave her a feeling of warmth no other carriage had and perhaps it was because of the man who'd sat beside her.

A maid ran to her at the servants' entrance. 'Her Ladyship is calling for you. Hurry.'

Adriana rushed forward, then stopped and walked up the stairs at a normal pace.

After a quick knock, she walked into Vel's room.

'Were you at Philbrook's house this morning?'

'Yes.'

'Well, you can't take my carriage to his house any more and I don't want him being here. He is not welcome.'

'He is welcome in my world,' Adriana said.

Velma's eyes hardened. 'You are sacked. I mean it. I will have your things sent after you. But you must stay until tomorrow.'

She'd known when she said the words what Velma's response would be and she had known it would be the only way she could walk out of the situation she found herself in.

'I will leave now.'

'You can't until tomorrow,' Vel said. 'Today is Boxing Day. You must stay in case I need a handkerchief or a comb.'

'You will manage.'

Vel glared and crossed her arms. 'I will cancel Boxing Day. In truth. And I am going to tell that to Mrs Ingalls and everyone else. It is cancelled. Over. Done. No Boxing Day here this year because of you. And it is everyone here's favourite day of the year.' She peered at her closed hand and checked her fingernails. 'Or it was until this year.'

And then the little girl inside Adriana resurfaced. 'I love you. And I am leaving now. This is going to be my best Boxing Day ever.'

At Mrs Ingalls's room, she knocked and walked inside. 'I am leaving,' she told the other woman. She rubbed the side of her thumb. 'I will be with my parents. Please tell everyone to pick up the handkerchiefs with their initials and other gifts I have in my room.'

'You can't go now.'

'I can't stay,' Adriana said. 'I cannot. She is unbearable. And she sacked me.'

Mrs Ingalls said, 'Shakespeare mentioned that smooth are the waters where the brook is deep and I think that fits Philbrook. I believe you would rather have the still waters in your life and the substance of a man like the Earl at your side. Don't run from him. Run to him.'

She had to go. Even if she'd not been sacked, she had to leave because if she remained, she could not see Philbrook any more. Then she hesitated. 'But I can't leave everyone. And his house is too far for me to walk.'

Mrs Ingalls haltingly stepped to her and reached out. 'Don't fret about that now.' They clasped hands. 'You go on to your parents, dear one,' Mrs Ingalls said. 'We will send your things after you. You are more important to us than Christmas. We will be fine and it is vital to us that you are happy. That knowledge will be our celebration.'

In Mrs Ingalls's dim eyes, awareness shown through that Adriana's decision was the right one.

She ran outdoors and the sky wasn't spitting moisture, just gloom and the dreariness that only a cold Christmas season could add to a person. But she could almost feel the sunshine hiding beyond the clouds.

It didn't even matter that she was unlikely to get a hackney. All the drivers were as they should be. Home with their families.

The day remained overcast, but the clouds thinned some and the silence around her gave her a feeling of hope.

She was taking one step at a time to get closer to her future. She didn't know what it would be, but she was walking out of her cousin's shadow and into her own life.

* * *

Philbrook was late waking because he'd slept so fitfully. Immediately upon summoning his valet, the man had appeared with a note. Then, as Philbrook started eating breakfast, the valet said he'd fetch the carriage driver to speak with Philbrook because the driver had insisted he needed an audience with him when he woke.

Soon, the carriage driver knocked on Philbrook's door and came inside the room, hat in hand, eyes shining with happiness. 'I had a visit from a dear lady this morning.'

'Does your wife know?' Philbrook asked.

'Not yet,' the carriage driver said, 'but the woman wanted to ask me about, um, er, a certain unwed man who may be a bit sweet on her. Wanted to know what kind of employer he was.'

'What did you tell her?' Philbrook asked.

'Well, I said he wasn't half bad. That she could do worse.' He stepped back to the door. 'And you could, too, as you well know.' Then he left, whistling 'Deck the Halls'.

Before the door was even shut, Philbrook's mother appeared in the hall and she grimaced at the tune. 'I must be leaving because my sister is warbling on and on about how lovely it is here and she knows I don't like this house. I don't know why she wishes to stay.'

'Did Grandfather really say that about Adriana?' he asked.

'I'm not sure. I think so.' She shrugged. 'But there is one thing I know. He would not have wanted you to wed Lady

Mudbath.' She touched her bottom lip. 'But it doesn't really matter. It was the other one who always made you smile.'

'I didn't smile at her.'

'You may not have thought you did, but that's a better story to tell your children.' She shook her head. 'Son, you need to think of these things.'

She gave him a pat on the shoulder. 'Now take care of that crotchety old woman who lives in this house with you. The world needs more mean old women like the two of us and we need you. And you should think about adding an additional person to this household. One who has enough spirit to like that crotchetiest old woman who lives here. Don't let the opportunity pass you by.' She sighed. 'You'll likely never find another woman my sister can tolerate as well as Adriana.'

She left and he understood what everyone was trying to tell him. Everyone recognised it and he did, too. But it wasn't enough to recognise it. He needed to be willing to work for it and he would.

Adriana wanted him to love and he would find a way to unlock love with her.

He wanted a permanent love, not the nonsensical ones his friends told him about that caused them to turn their back on all they had committed to.

Instead, he wanted a feeling so deep and so intrinsic to him that it didn't feel like love but a part of himself.

None of the servants or his aunt let their feelings bubble to the surface, but it didn't matter. They were the people he needed in his life and who needed him.

But if Adriana needed someone in her life who demonstrated his love and that was what made her happy, then he would become that person. She was too dear to him, and to everyone else who mattered, to risk losing.

If Adriana wed him, then he intended to find a way to make sure his feelings burst into the world and shone so brightly that no one would ever doubt them. Because he wanted her at his side, day and night, and in his life—and carriage and family and everything else around him.

He smoothed the paper he had been clasping in his hand and smiled.

Chapter Nine

Her parents greeted her with welcome surprise and after a bombardment of questions that she really didn't have answers to, her nephew stumbled and bumped his lip and everyone's attention turned to him, and she was back in her family, almost as if she'd never left.

She'd hardly got seated when a wagon stopped in front of her parents' house, the vehicle stuffed with servants who all waved to her as she stepped out.

'Boxing Day was cancelled at Lady Velma's,' Miss Yale called out, laughing. 'So, we decided to have it here with you.'

Then she noticed a second wagon, with Mrs Ingalls sitting beside the driver, and the conveyance itself was filled with crates, sacks and what appeared to be hastily gathered clothing.

The wagon containing Mrs Ingalls stopped in front of Adriana and one of the footmen jumped to help the older woman exit.

'We also gave notice,' Mrs Ingalls called out. 'And then we were all sacked.'

'Well, it was hard to tell who was sacked and who wasn't,' Miss Yale said, 'so we decided it was best for all of us to leave.'

Adriana didn't know what to say. She couldn't think of anything.

'We couldn't stay without you,' Mrs Ingalls said. 'We just couldn't.'

'We can make pallets in the shop at night for all who won't fit in the house,' her father said. 'If these people care that much for you, then we cannot let them be homeless.'

'Well, I was hoping…' Mrs Ingalls had a wistful contemplative look '…that you might pass the problem on to someone else who can help us, as it is his fault.'

'Man about so high,' her father said, raising a hand, 'having a carriage that would likely fit my whole family?'

'That's him,' Mrs Ingalls said, holding out a sprig of mistletoe. 'And I brought this with me in case we found him here. Your daughter needs it much more than I do.'

'We have discussed it,' the butler said to Adriana. 'We decided you might need a nudge to go visit that certain man.'

'I'm freezing,' Mrs Ingalls said, pulling the wrap Adriana had given her closer. 'It's Boxing Day,' the older woman added, 'and we are all without work. Of course, we would do it all again…'

Her father waved them to the doorway. 'They are welcome to come in, but, Adriana, if they need that man to help them, I don't see what the problem is.'

'But…'

'You can't let them starve, or be forced back to Vel,' he said. 'Particularly not on their one day off in the year.'

'He'll take you to Philbrook's house,' Mrs Ingalls said, pointing to the driver. 'We decided it would be our gift to you.'

Philbrook didn't know what Christmas was, but he knew what it wasn't. A life without Adriana. He clasped the paper again and smiled.

'Vehicle at the door, sir,' his butler said, peering inside the sitting room. 'It's the woman who places so much importance on Boxing Day and staff. I can get the door, of course, but you could earn some hearty acclaim by telling her you gave me the rest of the month off.'

'Thank you,' Philbrook said, standing, still in shirt-sleeves. 'But I believe I will just earn some good spirit by telling her we shared a jest and by greeting her at the door. Now, hand me a cravat.'

The butler laughed and fetched the neckcloth.

He threw on a waistcoat and the butler helped give the cravat a quick tie. Philbrook buttoned the waistcoat as he navigated the stairs.

Her eyes widened when he opened the door.

'You were expecting me to be here, I'm sure,' Philbrook said 'After all, it is the servants' day off.' He peered at her. 'I thought you'd be celebrating with the staff.'

She gave a slow shake of her head. 'They are with me—in a sense. They've left her. En masse. And moved to my father's house. And he is not wealthy. They must have jobs and I am here in anticipation that you might be able to help me find employment for them.'

'I had hoped you would say you were missing me and wanted to spend the day with me instead of the servants.'

'I've decided you are partly right,' she said. 'True caring is the measure of a person. I can't feed all the people I love—on love. Their stomachs would be empty.'

'How many staff members left?'

'All of them. Everyone. From the butler to the cook to the scullery maids to the footmen. And they wanted me to ask you for help.'

'I will find employment for the ones that do not fit into my household.'

'You probably will not need to,' she said. 'My cousin's parents will beg them to return. It's me the servants were trying to find a home for. And I knew it. They wanted me to come to you. All of them did. And they risked their livelihood in order that I might speak with you.'

He put a hand on her shoulder, the warmness of her reaching deep into his heart. 'You don't have to try to teach me about love. I understand now. I feel it every time I think of you. There is a belief that you should care for others as you do yourself and that is true for the way I feel about you,' he said. 'The staff who are around me feel a part of me and so does my aunt. And when I look into your eyes and see the compassion you have, I know you are quality beyond measure.

'I need you,' he continued. 'The staff needs you. We all need you. You created happiness in your residence. You have already made a difference in my home. Everyone has been mellowing, chatting about the efforts I wanted them to make for you.'

He reached into his waistcoat pocket, took out the note and gave it to her.

If you do not win Adriana you will be making the largest mistake of your life, though we are not sure you are quality enough for her. Our Boxing Day gift to you should arrive today: the sight of Adriana. If you don't convince her to wed you, we pity you.
Adriana's friends

'How can I win you?' he said. 'That is what it seems I must do.' He touched her cheek, warmness rushing into him.

'You have won me already,' she said. 'When you understood about my love of the servants and wanted yours to experience a day off as well.'

'Some people may say they fell in love at first sight,' he said, 'but I believe that I started to love at first kindness. And that is a feeling which stays with a person for ever.'

The day after Boxing Day, the wedding took place with the servants of both houses looking on. His aunt said she had no reason to attend, it was just paperwork to further the lineage. Though she felt she was responsible for the union, she didn't want to have to stand around and watch all that blasted happiness.

Velma sent a note, telling her the servants must be returned at once as she did not have time to find replacements, and Adriana had best not keep them because, if she did, Velma would have no option but to move in with Adriana. The servants agreed to return, but only on the condition they could visit Adriana regularly.

His mother had decided to stay one day longer and she felt she was responsible for the union because her son would not have realised his true feelings if she hadn't told him his grandfather's wishes.

And Mrs Ingalls mentioned she was certainly pleased she had given Adriana the original shawl because it led to the proposal.

His staff basked in the knowledge that they had helped show the devotion they had for him and convinced him it was time for him to wed.

Both households celebrated their pivotal actions which led to such a happy event.

All the servants planned to return home except Mrs Ingalls. She'd said she was not leaving Adriana and a convenient room was prepared for her with all her possessions arranged just as she liked them.

Philbrook insisted he must give Adriana a present and she saw a multi-coloured shawl with extra thick yarn and wide spaced stitches wrapped over his arm.

'That's not mine either.'

'I know. It's a gift from my servants. When they understood that I had accidentally given away a shawl you liked, and that we were to wed, they spent last night making sure you had a gift from them that I could give you today.'

Their hands touched when he gave it to her and she ran her fingers though the fibres.

'Now we have three festivities to share,' he said. 'Christmas and Boxing Day and the celebration of our anniversary the day after Boxing Day.' He paused. 'No. Four. The rest of the year we can rejoice in our love.'

With that, he led her beneath the mistletoe and kissed her, his heart expanding more than he would have ever believed possible. Now he understood that the best kind of love was the feelings he had waited his whole life to experience and felt for his beloved Yuletide wife.

* * * * *

LORD GRANGE'S
SNOWY REUNION

Elizabeth Beacon

To all the Historical Romance writers past, present and future—you lighten dark patches and give us a good place to go when the outside world feels sad and gloomy. Love you all and long may you continue!

Chapter One

1819

'You can't ride to Chantry Old Hall with only a dog for company, Juno,' Lady Colby protested, '*and* the gardener says it will snow.'

Juno looked at the hazy blue sky and decided he was wrong. Just as well, as she *had* to be home in time for the worryingly early birth of her uncle's first child.

'I can join Sir Harry and Viola the rest of the way, but they will go without me if I don't hurry,' she replied, pulling on gloves as she sped down the path with Pard, her Dalmatian dog, at her heels and her godmother scurrying behind.

'It's easy to get lost in the hills, so they might go before you can get there,' Lady Colby argued.

'The innkeeper gave me good directions when I hired his best horse and Sir Harry will drive the carriage himself to get his wife there for the birth if he has to, so it's my quickest way home,' Juno said and pulled on the velvet jockey cap she wore for riding.

'He was wild to a fault until your aunt's sister and all those children tamed him, so I'm not surprised, but you're *not wed*, Juno—you can't attend a birthing.'

'I can pace outside the bedchamber with my uncle. Marianne and the Yelvertons stood by me when I needed them, so I must do the same for them. She will need all our support if the baby is too small to survive.'

When Juno's life felt shattered, just like her heart, Marianne had taken her in. She had been so kind and patient, helping Juno to pick up the pieces. At seventeen, her grandmother had planned to force Juno to marry a venal old man if he paid off the Dowager's debts, so she was left with no choice but to run away. When her uncle Alaric returned home from diplomatic duty in France, he was so furious to discover what his mother had done that he paid her debts one last time and publicly disclaimed responsibility for any more.

Juno now lived with her uncle and Marianne, but hadn't told them why she had refused another London Season. There was no point since she had loved and lost and it had hurt so much that she never wanted to experience such pain again.

'You *might* get there in time if the weather holds, but it would be so much better if you hired a carriage,' Lady Colby said.

'Not fast enough,' Juno argued and thank goodness

they were in the stable yard of the inn so she could say a hasty farewell and ride away.

Uncle Alaric and Marianne were her family, but even they didn't know she had fallen in love before she ran from London. She had taken one dazed look at a handsome, dashing and hopeful Lieutenant Nathaniel Grange and lost her foolish young heart. Then he had marched back to war and taken her heart with him and the only way for her to escape a forced marriage was to run to Herefordshire where her former governess was living.

Uncle Alaric had been determined that Juno would have a better life, so he had employed Marianne as Juno's companion. He and Marianne had fallen in love, so some good had come of Juno's youthful troubles. And at least she was a strong and independent woman now and very happy to stay that way.

An hour later, Juno blinked snowflakes from her eyelashes in order to see the road ahead and Lady Colby and her gardener were proved right. It wasn't far to Sir Harry Marbeck's beloved home in the hills, but she wasn't going to get there and needed shelter from the storm. She fought panic before she saw high walls and a gate that was wide open. The lodge was shuttered, so she urged the horse into the avenue and prayed for sanctuary at the end of it.

Yes, there was a grand old house there, but it was shuttered and no smoke was issuing from its chimneys. For an awful moment she thought she was imagining it—she had heard of people losing their reason as they froze to death. She wasn't that cold yet and it looked real enough as the horse forged on to the stables. The first door she tried opened, but no reply came to her shouted greeting as she led the horse inside and Pard dashed ahead to make sure it was empty.

The place smelt of old dust rather than horses, but two stalls were strewn with clean straw for someone's return, so she led the horse into one while Pard rolled in the other and wind keened around the stout old building. They had a roof over their heads; she could snuggle in the straw of the empty stall with Pard and wait out the storm. Yet what if they were caught napping by whoever had left these stalls ready? And the deserted mansion was making her imagination run wild, so she had to be sure it was really empty before they settled down.

She shivered with nerves as much as from the cold when the back door opened easily and she stepped inside the mansion, feeling like the heroine of a Gothic novel. Best not think of the horrors waiting for them as they explored places they were not supposed to be as she crept past the dark, cold kitchens. Pard's toenails sounded loud on the flagstones as Juno pushed open the door between servants' quarters and grand state rooms, hesitating in the shuttered gloom.

'Who the devil are you?' a gruff bass voice growled at her from the shadows and she gasped in shock.

The sound of that voice had haunted her dreams for so long she felt the ground lurch under her feet as her heartbeat jarred, then galloped on in shock. *He* was here? But was he just one of those delusions she had been worried about? No, that deep, rich voice was so uniquely Nathaniel Grange's he really must be standing in the shadows waiting for her to reply and he didn't sound very pleased about her intrusion.

The echoes of his gruff demand died away in the dusty gloom and she was still silenced. A younger, freer Juno wanted to rush into his arms and feel them close around her again at long last. She wanted to feel fully alive again for the first time in so long, but then she remembered how long it had taken her to live well without him and stayed where she was.

'I thought you were abroad,' she said numbly and it was his turn for a shocked silence. Pard sensed the tension and growled belatedly, but she had no words to reassure him.

'Not now,' Nathaniel said as if that explained everything. 'And if you think he's a guard dog, best think again,' he added so coolly that she must have imagined he was as shocked as she was. Pard wagged his tail as if he thought the stranger wasn't a threat.

'Traitor,' she murmured as he sat and offered the wretch a paw. 'You have neglected this house quite shamefully,' she said as Nathaniel came closer and her heartbeat sped up again at the reality of him, here and seemingly all alone.

He had grown a great beard and his physique seemed even larger and more formidable than the youthful one she remembered so fondly. He was so unlike his old self she wished she had happened on almost anyone else. She had loved that boy so much and this man wasn't even pretending to be pleased to see her.

'You can leave if it offends you,' he said curtly and she felt tears threaten because he wasn't her Nathaniel at all. The past was dead and it wasn't safe to mourn it with him watching.

'I wish I had stayed in the stables now,' she said bleakly.

'They might be cleaner. I wish I had got my manservant to light a fire in the grooms' quarters before he took my horse to be re-shod.'

So you would have stayed there and not come bothering me, she thought up the words for him.

How she wished she had taken Lady Colby's advice and hired a carriage now. 'Give me a tinderbox and I'll light one myself,' she said with a sniff to let him know he was being a terrible host, but that was all.

'Even I am not that much of a yahoo, my lady,' he said.

'I'm not married,' she said brusquely past the mournful thought that although he had once sworn he loved her he must have lied.

'You didn't marry the fat old lord, then?'

'Of course I didn't! I ran away.'

'Nobody told me.'

'Why would they?'

'True,' he said. If she added up the hours they had once spent together, they should be strangers.

Yet five years ago she thought he was her one true love—the hero that shy Juno Defford never quite dared believe she would ever find until he found her hiding in the shadows one night in Mayfair. Now he was shrugging her off as if they had always been strangers, but she had learned to hide her feelings, too, so he wouldn't know how much it hurt.

'You have been away too long,' she said with a sharp look at the dust and cobwebs she could now see in the semi-darkness.

'I thought it was being cared for by my late uncle's land agent, but clearly I was wrong.' A pause and even he must have decided that brusque explanation wasn't one at all. 'My uncle and I argued last time I was here. He wanted me to sell out after my bill of divorce was passed in the House, but I thought it was better to remain in the army while the dust settled.

'I was an arrogant young puppy and thought I was untouchable,' he said as if talking to himself now. 'I was wrong and that stupid war with America they are now calling the War of 1812, although it went on longer, was more or less over by the time we got there. We were shipped back just in time for Waterloo so no time for home leave before the battle and then he died and I was…' He hesitated.

'Injured,' she finished the sentence for him. 'I saw your name on the list of wounded.'

And longed to dash to Brussels, but you had made me promise to wait for you to come for me, so I stayed at home and bit my nails, and you didn't come.

'Yes, then came the news of my uncle's sudden death and poor Dorinda's a few weeks later,' he said flatly.

She could weep for the bright and hopeful boy of nineteen she remembered—unbowed by his divorce from 'poor Dorinda' and three hard years at war in Spain and France. If only she had ignored his orders to stay away from him until the scandal of his failed marriage faded, how different their lives might be now. Except if it was only real love on her side it was best he had stayed away.

'Your former wife hated the military life and the countryside, but you were a soldier and your uncle's heir, so why did she marry you?' she asked boldly because she didn't have anything to lose and she had always wondered.

'Because we were both seventeen and too green to know the difference between love and passion. We were friends as children, so it probably felt real to her at the time.'

'I am sorry for your loss,' she said, wondering if he still loved Dorinda, despite her infidelity.

Juno would have followed him to war barefoot and unwed if he had let her, but had he mourned his unfaithful former wife so dearly he forgot her? He had stolen Juno's heart when he found her hiding from the lord she didn't want to marry and Lieutenant Grange was too kind to walk away from a girl fighting tears, so he stayed to joke her out of them. Then he kissed her to make it better and changed her world.

Had he been too kind to call a halt—was that how he had ended up married to his *friend*? She hated the notion history could have repeated itself, if he hadn't thought better of marrying Juno. She saw the closed expression on his once-open face and, once again, mourned the bright youth she remembered.

'Why were you out alone in a blizzard?' he asked and his turn to change the subject. 'And this fine boy is no protection so don't tell me you were not alone.'

'He usually is.'

'His instincts aren't working today, then,' Nathaniel murmured so softly she must have misheard.

'Do you have somewhere warmer where we can argue?' she said as cold seemed to reach into her very bones and she knew it wasn't caused by the weather.

'The agent's house,' he said with another frown— maybe he didn't want her there either.

'It's very cold in here,' she said with as much dignity as she could find as her snow-wet clothes clung to her— no wonder she was shivering.

'Agreed,' he said and strode off into the gloom and she supposed he meant her to follow him. 'But where *were* you bound on such a day?' he asked without turning round.

'None of your business,' she said and scurried in his wake.

Chapter Two

Nate knew he was being an appalling host and to Juno, of all people. He was so shocked to find her here and so aware of her as a woman that his wits had gone begging. He was struggling with a mess of feelings which he had tried so hard to shut down since he had left her behind five years ago.

It was as cold as charity in here and so was he. Or at least he thought so until her voice shattered the silence and love, longing and sheer need almost smashed through the barriers he had built to stay sane. He couldn't blight her brightness and beauty with the dregs of the hopeful young fool she remembered.

Idiot, a remnant of the eager boy argued, *beg if you have to, but don't dare let her go again.*

But the boy was wrong. His arms might ache to hold her, but it was weak to want her to stare back at him with wonder and innocent, youthful passion in her bluest of blue eyes again when he didn't deserve it.

He had wanted the shyest debutante in town so badly

five years ago that he had kissed her passionately and she responded like a flower in the desert to rain, so he knew he was a villain even then. He had still lived on the fire and sweet promise of her kisses until the horrors of Waterloo had slapped him brutally awake.

He had been nineteen and a selfish young peacock when he first met shy Juno hiding in the shadows at a *ton* ball, but he still knew more about life than he hoped she ever would. He had felt like a fully grown man, desperate to introduce her to the joys of the marriage bed as soon as he could put clear water between them and his first hasty marriage and divorce. Then he would try to convince her uncle that he, Nathaniel Grange, deserved to marry his niece and ward, but he had been wrong.

A year on Waterloo had taught him better. He led his men into hell time and time again, feeling like a butcher as they fell around him and he urged the remnants on, until he was wounded himself and was almost relieved to be dragged into a square with the wounded and dead. Even when he came back to consciousness in Brussels to find his faithful batman, Jackson, was fending off the army surgeons' saws and knives, the misery didn't end.

He got word his uncle was dead and a few weeks later found out Dorinda had died trying to birth a love child. He felt so sorry for that terrible ending to her wild, young life. Yet he could not weep or go home to Juno, who had taught him what real love felt like, because she deserved to marry a better man.

He had ruined Dorinda's life when they married too

young and how could he have risked doing the same to Juno? He recovered from his wounds after Waterloo and sold out, but nightmares woke him screaming as he fought it again in his sleep and still everyone died. That was why he had stayed away and, while he was much better now, he wished he had stayed away a little longer.

Walking and riding through war-scarred Europe while working for board and lodgings had made life bearable until he beat most of his demons, but there wasn't much left of the gilded youth Juno had met five years ago. So, he must hope for a rapid thaw and watch her leave as soon as a way was clear. Then he would learn to live without her again and the less she had to do with him in the meantime, the better.

'The land agent's house is on the other side of the house,' he explained as every nerve he had tingled with awareness of her. 'Someone must have told him I am back, so he fled so fast he left some of his ill-gotten gains behind.'

'Slow down, Lord Grange.'

'Sorry,' he said. He hadn't used his title as a wanderer so it still felt like his uncle's, not his. 'I was so busy cursing the man I forgot my manners,' he lied. 'Best hold my coat so you don't stray,' he said and opened the door on the furious storm.

'Yes, sir,' she said as they stepped outside.

'Safe?' he gasped as he paused to get his bearings.

'Safe,' she confirmed with a sharp tug on his coat. 'Don't lead me into a ditch.'

No hysterics, just a reminder to keep his mind on where they were going. He felt bereft when they reached the agent's house and she let go.

'Where's your cloak?' he demanded testily, pushing the door open and trying to brush snow from her shoulders as she went past him.

'There wasn't time,' she snapped and reopened the door to let her dog in.

'Why?' he demanded, leading the way to the best kitchen Hodges had filled with luxuries from the main house. With what the rogue had stolen from the estate and years of servants' wages in his pockets, he was set for life. 'You could have frozen to death out there today.' She was stubbornly silent. 'Towels and blankets,' Nate said distractedly as he tried not to stare at the lithe feminine form outlined by her wet habit.

'Pard *is* very cold.'

'And you are not?' he said, gently pushing her into a chair by the fire because she would stand and shiver if he didn't.

'Don't manhandle me,' she said crossly. He wanted to kiss her bad mood away but, instead, he clenched his hands behind his back.

'You will only stand on your dignity if I don't and your dog is bred for the road, so stop fussing over him and worry about yourself instead.'

He marched out of the room, trying not to think at all as he ran upstairs to snatch his robe from the chair by the bed where he had slept last night. He remembered how she used to watch him with wonder in her blue, blue eyes and ached for her to do it again as he found those towels and blankets and wished he had staff to care for her every need. He felt he had failed her yet again.

Juno watched Nathaniel escaping her company with unflattering haste and tears stung, but she forced them back. Five years should have taught her not to care, but even the warmth from the range couldn't touch a coldness deep inside because somehow she still did and he plainly did not.

'You *can't* care,' she whispered.

She must not look for the charming young rogue who had sat out balls with her and made her feel so much that she didn't want to think about it right now. Pard got up from the mat by the fire to lay his head in her lap. 'It's all right, beautiful boy,' she murmured, 'or will be when we leave.'

'You must get out of those wet clothes,' Nathaniel said from the doorway and she knew he had heard.

'I have nothing to wear.'

'You set off in a snowstorm without any luggage?'

'Yes, but it wasn't snowing.'

'Someone must have told you it would, so why did you ignore them?'

'I am in a hurry.'

'Strong men die in these hills in winter so that's not a good enough reason.'

'I am alive and I'm not a man.'

'Obviously,' he muttered.

'Or accountable to you.'

'I'm sorry you think me overbearing, but it's for your own good.'

'Words that usually precede a lecture I don't want to hear.'

'I have no right to lecture anyone, but it was foolish to set out so unprepared.'

'My life, my risk.'

'What about his?' he said and Pard looked bewildered and whined.

'You just told me he was bred for the road.'

'This is life or death, not a game!'

'I know,' she said, 'but it's not Pard's fault, so stop shouting.'

'I'm sorry,' he said stiffly, but came over to fondle her dog and Pard licked his hand as if he thought Nathaniel needed comforting more than he did.

This close up, she saw a few white hairs in Nathaniel's beard and he was only four and twenty, so maybe Pard was right. She almost wished she had stayed in the stables and gone on remembering her passionate young lover instead of this austere great bear who obviously wanted her gone as soon as possible.

'Pass me a towel, please. My hair is dripping everywhere.'

'I wish I could provide a bath, but it would take too long to heat enough water,' he said and his concern nearly undid her.

'I have nothing to change into,' she reminded him, trying not to blush at the thought of being naked in the same house as him.

'You should have thought of that when you set off.'

'So you have said.'

'It bears repeating,' he said grimly.

'I told you, I am in a hurry.'

'Not good enough.'

Reminded why she was in such haste, she glanced out of the window at the relentless storm, feeling dejected and helpless. 'You aren't responsible for me,' she said blankly.

'Thank heavens.'

'Oh, go away,' she said, torn between wanting to stay here so he could infuriate her some more and the longing to be with her family.

'Take off your wet habit while I try to find you something to wear, then.'

'I can't sit here naked!'

'Wear this,' he said, throwing a vast man's robe on to a chair. 'I will go and see if my sister left anything wearable behind when she wed, although it would be outdated since she would make two of you nowadays, but anything is better than wearing a wet habit all day.'

'I'm not a lady of fashion,' she said, secretly relieved he didn't expect her to wear anything his late wife left behind since she would rather freeze.

'Then strip off those wet things and dry yourself while I'm gone.'

'Yes, my lord, three bags full, my lord.'

'And bolt the door after me,' he added curtly. 'Hedges

might not be as far away as I'd like him to be and the locks haven't been changed yet,' he added.

She felt a fool for not thinking harder about such comfort here and neglect elsewhere. The land agent must have dismissed the servants, closed the house and pocketed all their wages. In Hedges's shoes she would run hard and fast, but he must be a fool to abuse such a comfortable position.

'Very well,' she said, following Nathaniel to the door. 'Be careful,' she said when she saw the storm was fierce as ever.

'That's rich coming from you.'

'Be reckless, then,' she said and slammed the door.

'Bolts,' his deep voice rumbled through the wood and she shot them into place so fast he should know how she felt, then she watched him dash away until his powerful figure was masked by snow and anyone would think he cared.

'Stupid idea,' she muttered softly and went back to the fire.

Chapter Three

Juno closed the shutters before stripping off her habit and everything else she had on. She put on Nathaniel's vast robe and it felt intimate against her bare skin, as if his touch was going places that no other man would ever see or touch.

'I must look ridiculous,' she murmured and rolled up the sleeves so her hands were free to reopen the shutters.

She sank back into the chair to stare moodily into the glowing fire. How silly to feel wrapped up in gruff care as she tried to sort the scent of clean man from something elusive and woody. If he hadn't spoken first, she might never have recognised him, but his voice had always been unique, as if an echo of it was lodged deep inside her to make sure she could never forget him.

It felt decadent to sit naked but for his robe with her long hair loose on her shoulders to dry. She must remember she was caught in a snowstorm with a man who had done his best to forget she existed. When she had first met Nathaniel she had endured her grandmother's contempt for so long that she hid in dark corners to avoid her icy disapproval as well as the man the Dowager Lady Stratford wanted Juno to marry. Why must she brood on the night they met? And thank goodness her grandmother lived abroad now and she would probably never see her again.

She glanced out of the window and knew it was too late to keep her uncle company as he paced and raged, worrying about his beloved wife and child. The snow had set in and she must pray all was well despite Uncle Alaric's despairing letter. She could picture him furious and frustrated not to be with Marianne and desperate for news as his thoughts turned gloomy. Was that why he sent out those hasty messages?

Juno sighed and envied Marianne's brother living close to Prospect House. He and his wife, Fliss, Juno's former governess, would have got there before it began to snow in earnest. Juno felt as remote from them as if she was on the moon and she might just as well be for all the chance there was of her getting home today.

Nate ran into the main house and shook snow off like a wet dog—just as well nobody was here to sigh at the work he had just made them. He smiled at the thought of Juno's dog shaking off snow much the same way and the house didn't seem as desolate now they were here. Servants would disapprove their lack of a chaperon and whisper Lord Grange couldn't keep his eyes off this unexpected guest. He couldn't bring himself to sincerely

regret the emptiness of his poor house now she was here
to share it.

He smiled at a fanciful image of Juno's dog dressed in a
wig and spectacles and looking down his nose at unworthy
Lord Grange as the only chaperon available. Nate ran up
the stairs he had climbed so reluctantly an hour ago and
strode past the rooms he and Dorinda once shared to his
sister's old room. He sobered at the suspicion Hedges had
been one of Dorinda's lovers, recalling how bare her old
room was. He hadn't suspected why until he searched the
agent's house for blankets just now and found Dorinda's
discarded things in the attic.

Now he lifted the lid of a Spanish chest and smelt lav-
ender and spices although his sister had wed a decade ago.
Everything here had run smoothly when his uncle was
alive, so something must have turned Hedges to fraud.
Dorinda could have flirted and maybe more with the man
to relieve her boredom in the country. She always thought
each lover could be *the one,* until she found out he wasn't.
Nate realised he wasn't that one and only just weeks after
they married…

But what if Hedges blamed him for Dorinda's loss of
interest? Nate felt a fool for struggling on with a dead
marriage as long as he had. He should have admitted his
uncle and sister were right to say it was a huge mistake
to elope when they were both so young—better to end it
cleanly before more damage was done. In the end Dorinda
had begged him to. She had left a trail of disappointed
lovers behind her for Nate to pick one rich and cynical

enough not to be hurt if he was sued for criminal conversation with another man's wife, so Lord Grange could get a bill of divorce through the House on his nephew and ward's behalf.

He shook off the past and worried about Juno instead, as he searched for warm clothes to fit her. He was surprised his sister, Ella, had left so many behind when she wed. Maybe she thought she would spend more time here than she had. Meanwhile Juno was naked but for his dressing robe and he must not linger on such a heady idea. He scooped up warm gowns and a winter riding habit, knowing she would leave before her habit was dry if it stopped snowing.

The idea of her perishing of cold if it started again made him shudder and swear to do anything he could to stop her. If he stayed away from the agent's house, she would feel more secure and might not try to outwit Mother Nature again today. He would hand over his sister's clothes and sleep in the stables to let her know she had nothing to fear from him if she stayed.

He would wrap himself in guilt and horse blankets, sleeping in the stables where he and Jackson had inspected the chimneys and decided it was safe to light a fire. That way she couldn't leave without him knowing and the road from the village must be blocked or Jackson would be back by now.

Thanks to Hedges squirreling away luxuries at the agent's house there was enough food and firewood to prevent them freezing or starving. He had planned to live there while the chimneys were swept and this lovely old place had the grand clean it needed. He cursed the damage Hedges had done to it as he found a valise to pile undergarments, gowns and a warm shawl into. Where was Ella's old cloak? He found it then braved his dressing room, looking for the heavy military one he had sent home when he sold out.

Glad of it now, he hurried to the garden door, worryingly eager to see Juno again. After running through the snow again, he knocked on the door of the agent's house and waited a minute before hammering on it anxiously. He was about to shout and maybe batter it down when the bolts were drawn back and Juno opened it at last.

'I was asleep,' she admitted, blinked her sleepy blue eyes and yawned.

He felt his heart lurch and had to stamp about pretending to remove all the snow he could from his boots. She looked as if she had just got out of bed and he was desperate for it to have been his. He was a man, so of course he wanted her, but a painful sort of tenderness at the sight of her heavy eyed and undefended made his heart seem to turn over in his chest so he dared not look again until his defences were stronger. She could have *died* today. Imagining her freezing to death in some windswept corner if she hadn't found his forlorn old place made him stifle a moan of protest.

He wanted to grab her and hold her, feel her heart beat and reassure himself she was unharmed. He knew where that might lead and refused to rob her of future choices.

She was very different to the shy girl he remembered. He guiltily missed the shy adoration she had once watched him with as sleep receded and she dared him to laugh at the vastness of his robe on her when that was the last thing he felt like doing.

'Along with your fierce hound?' he said, fussing the dog that seemed far more pleased to see him than she was.

'He knew it was you,' she said and scurried back to her chair by the fire as fast as his trailing robe allowed. He would never be able to wear it again without feeling she was wrapped in it with him and that wasn't the right way to think when she was blushing as if she had read his mind.

'Are you warm yet?' he said, trying not to notice she was tucking her bare feet into his robe as if the sight of them might arouse the beast in him.

'Yes, thank you,' she said politely.

'Shall I light a fire in one of the bedchambers for you to change by, or would you prefer me to see if your horse is missing you while you do it here?'

'I only hired him this morning, but I suppose he could be missing his friends.'

'You were in such a hurry you hired a job horse?'

'He's not one of those and it was urgent,' she said and frowned as if reminded she still needed to be somewhere else.

'He's not worth risking your life for,' he protested.

'Who isn't—the horse?'

'No, the man you ignored a raging blizzard to get to.'

'What, Sir Harry?' she said and blinked as if still fighting sleep, so had she been dreaming of the damned rogue
behind Nate's back?

'Harry Marbeck?' he asked, past jealousy and bitter
hurt. 'He's married.'

'To my aunt's sister Viola,' she snapped and glared
as if he was despicable and he probably was, 'whom he
loves dearly.'

'*Harry's* in love? He swore he never would be, nor
marry.'

'Then he has learned some sense.'

'Well, I never,' he said. So much had changed since
he left maybe impossible things were possible after all.
Maybe if he was a very good baron for a very long time
he could deserve to tell Juno that he had always loved her
and always would, even if he would never deserve her.
Wild Harry Marbeck hadn't deserved his Viola either, but
she had married him anyway. Yet Harry had always been
a good man at heart and Juno was better off without an
idiot like Nate Grange.

'How far is it to Chantry Old Hall?' she asked.

'A couple of miles as the crow flies, three by road.'

'It might as well be fifty,' she said with a mournful sigh.

'Why?'

'I must get home and Sir Harry and his wife will hasten
to Herefordshire now so I wanted to beg a ride.'

'I thought your uncle's principal seat was in Wiltshire,'
he said. Relief she was desperate to be with her family,

not a lover, made him sound clumsy and uncaring and she clearly thought so, too.

'He hates Stratford Park so he and Marianne have bought a near ruin not far from her brother's manor.'

'Hasn't Stratford got enough houses already?'

'Marianne likes creating order from chaos and he likes to help her. He was very bored living in grand houses and playing the dutiful Viscount.'

'I suppose you are going to tell me they are in love as well,' Nate said wearily.

'Of course.'

'Anyone else?'

'Marianne and Viola's brother, Darius Yelverton, who married my former governess, but you don't know them so never mind their love story.'

'Darius Yelverton? There can't be two with a name like that and he was a captain in the light infantry with a sister who married one of his sergeants. The poor fellow was killed at the Battle of Badajoz.'

'Yes, that was Marianne; she is married to my uncle now.'

He heard the defiance in Juno's voice so his shock was showing. Hard to imagine dignified and aloof Lord Stratford marrying the widow of an artillery sergeant, but Nate envied their passionate marriage. It must be passionate for Stratford to have wed her for love, so nobody was safe. Except Nate, who didn't feel worth loving and what if he bored Juno as easily he had Dorinda? Juno deserved to wed a good man with an innocent heart, not a weary fool trailing scandal and tragedy behind him. He might bore *her* when the ink was hardly dry on their marriage lines as well and that was a disaster he couldn't contemplate.

'Yelverton and your governess are in love as well?' he said.

'Very much so.'

'Whatever *is* the world coming to?'

'A better place.'

'I can see how your uncle's marriage connects you to Yelverton and Marbeck, then, but not why you are in such a hurry to reach Stratford's wreck in the country.'

'Former wreck,' she argued absently.

'Stratford can afford the best care for his wife in child-bed, so why were you taking an appalling risk to get there in weather like this?'

'You wouldn't understand.'

'I might.'

'You are not close to your family.'

'I was when my sister and I grew up here,' he argued. 'Our uncle and aunt made sure we had a happy childhood.'

'Your uncle died soon after his wife, though, didn't he?'

'A year and a half later.'

Nate had doubted his uncle's will to live after his beloved wife's death, but he still did not sell out and come home. He thought he was saving his uncle more gossip about his own unhappy marriage, but perhaps it was really because he was too much of a coward to face it himself.

'A heavy blow for you and your sister,' Juno said gently.

'Aye,' Nate said bleakly. He was such a cold fish it was

no wonder she was silent. It hurt to feel, so he had locked his emotions down so tightly he felt as if he had grown a hard shell around them and was still too much of a coward to break it. When he left her behind five years ago, he had intended to come back and marry her, but after his last battle it had seemed kinder to stay away.

Chapter Four

Juno didn't know whether to pity Nathaniel or be furious he was pretending not to care. She pitied the fierce feelings that drove him from a home he clearly loved. Why did he think it was a weakness to feel much at all nowadays?

'We were discussing your relations,' he said stiffly.

'You were. I was trying not to.'

'I'm not a gossip,' he snapped.

'They still won't want your pity.'

'You think me such a weeping willow?'

'No.'

'Then tell me why you are so desperate to get to your uncle's former wreck in the country and maybe I can help you.'

'How?' she said, glancing at the relentless snow outside.

'Using some common sense would be a good place to start.'

'Love trumps it and I love them even if you think me a fool for doing it.'

'Not for loving. For not looking after yourself.'

'Then I'll tell you if you promise not to scold me any more.'

'I promise to try,' he said with a rueful shrug.

'Please do. My uncle and aunt were overjoyed when she realised she was increasing earlier this year as they had resigned themselves to it never happening.' Juno stopped to remember their stunned joy when they finally realised why Marianne had been so out of sorts. 'The baby is due at the end of January, so I was visiting my godmother before Christmas instead of after when I got a message from my uncle to say Marianne's pains have begun. The babe may be too small to survive and if she dies it will break his heart, so I must get home in a hurry.'

'Love matches look a bad risk to me.'

'I have seen them in action and they seem a risk worth taking,' she said, trying not to mourn the one they could have had if only he had cared enough for her.

'So-called love fooled me into marrying a woman who could never love one man,' he said cynically.

Her heart bled for the boy who wed a girl who couldn't be faithful if she tried, but if he couldn't see that wasn't love it was as well he didn't come back to marry her. Knowing he was waiting for her to get bored and stray as well would have been worse agony than living without him.

'As one risk didn't pay off, you will never take another?' she said and he avoided her eyes.

'No, I won't.'

'Then I pity you. Love is the finest emotion one person can feel for another.'

'I don't want anyone's pity,' he said as if she was rasping his pride raw.

She raised her eyebrows to say she doubted he was immune to all human emotions and maybe that sparked his temper, or perhaps he was trying to prove a point as he swooped in and kissed her. Fire shot through her and his mouth was so yearning and tender on hers she couldn't pretend to be outraged.

'Hmm,' she murmured instead, 'more.'

'You don't know what you're asking,' he said shakily, but lowered his head to meet her eager lips with such ardour it felt familiar and new and even more wondrous than it was before.

He still held back, his mouth teasing and not as intense as she wanted. She sensed fierce needs fighting to get out, but he would not lose control of them. There was a tremor in his hard muscle to say it cost him an effort to raise his head and meet her gaze. His eyes were dark and stormy, and maybe there were too many dreams in hers, but she couldn't look away.

He kissed her again, as if he couldn't help it, but didn't sneak his tongue into her mouth to dance with hers as he had in shadowy corners of *ton* ballrooms five years ago, with all those people so near as he taught her about delicious pleasure in his arms. The emphatic burn of need deep inside her was familiar, but she had wanted more for so long that his control made her angry.

'I *do* know,' she argued fiercely. 'I know I want *you* and you showed me how.'

'You were so young, I shouldn't have,' he murmured before kissing her again as if he couldn't fight such powerful needs alone.

'And you were such an old, old man,' she teased when she could. 'Touch me,' she murmured with a breathy sigh.

She wanted his big hands gentle on her naked skin, wickedly arousing in secret places only ever eager for him. Sensual promise burned in his dark eyes as he tugged the knot in the robe's belt free and wild excitement leapt inside her as the soft stuff parted, She gloated at the hard flush of colour burning his cheeks as he eyed her naked body and she felt breathless and so hotly needy. The way his pupils flared, then contracted as she gazed up at him without shame, felt delicious.

She was proud of the womanly body he eyed with such hunger and settled her shoulders into the cushions to flaunt her aroused breasts. She wanted sheer need to drown his scruples so he couldn't help but love her fully and freely at long last. Thrilling heat coursed through her at the very thought of him deep inside her and she wriggled against the cushions to demand he do something about it right now.

'I can't,' he murmured, despite watching her half-prone body so hungrily she knew he was lying. He most definitely could, but he didn't want to. 'I would have to shave this off first,' he said, running a rueful hand over his beard as his eager eyes roved her body and her nipples went pebble hard and never mind his confounded beard. 'I would scratch and burn you, here,' he murmured, trailing a wondering finger around the tightened areola of one nipple. He gently flicked the startlingly responsive tip of the other and made her gasp as heat shot through her so fiercely she moaned for more, but he had already moved on.

'And here,' he added huskily as he trailed his caressing finger down her flat stomach and stopped just short of the dark curls hiding her sex. Fierce longing threatened to blaze out of control as the breath stalled in her lungs. She rasped in more as his fingertip settled on yearning skin for a pulse-thundering moment.

'Especially here,' he said huskily, his gaze so intense as he nearly touched her most intimate secrets and the wild ache at her feminine core scorched so hotly she writhed against the cushions in desperation and without an iota of shame. She wanted him to join with her, to forget beards and beds and everything else but finally becoming lovers.

'You want to kiss me all over?' she murmured softly. It sounded like bliss to her, so why didn't he just get on with it?

'All of you,' he confirmed huskily, 'everywhere.'

'Then why don't you?'

'If only I hadn't grown a beard, I could show you so much pleasure without despoiling you, but I did so I can't.'

She closed her eyes to shut him out as bemused wonder faded to utter loneliness. *Despoiling you?* How dare he say so? She had felt such magic, such sweet need for him as her lover at long last and he could say that?

'And we don't want you *despoiling* me, do we?' she snapped because fury was better than hurting so much she didn't want to think about it.

'No,' he said so coolly she wanted to kick him.

'Go away, then. Keep my horse company; wander your poor old house brooding, but I must change now and you are confoundedly in the way.'

She jumped to her feet as if impatient to don his sister's clothes while she still ached for him, but refused to beg or cry over more shattered dreams. Frustrated desire might be burning and twisting inside her, but she would *not* be ashamed or humoured with half-measures. She had learned to live alone when he left her last time. So she tied the belt of his robe to hide the womanly curves he had gazed on with lying hunger and stared out of the window at more snow and an early dusk.

'Give me time to pack my valise again and I'll leave you alone for the rest of the day,' he said so expressionlessly she wanted to yell and scream and force him to admit he was devastated and lonely, too.

Make him stay—show him how good being your lover would be, bad Juno urged.

But Lord Grange was impatient to be gone and she had endured enough hardship for one day.

'I'm sure the horse will be glad of your company,' she said and bent to comfort a bewildered Pard.

'My fault,' Nathaniel said guiltily.

She closed her eyes to fight the tears. He was taking

blame now and it felt worse than not *despoiling* her. 'That's almost as bad as saying it's for my own good.'

'It is, but I'm still sorry.'

'Are you, my lord?' He was silent. 'Just go, Nathaniel,' she said wearily. 'Worry about your poor old house because I can take care of myself.' He still didn't move, but she had to make him go somehow. 'I will leave food in the hall and a pot to cook it in,' she added, wondering why she cared if he starved. 'No doubt you learned how to during your wanderings abroad.'

'No doubt,' she heard him murmur as the door shut quietly behind him.

Moments later she heard him pile firewood on the back porch so she didn't have to fetch it in. Blinking back tears, she changed into his sister's old clothes as more logs thumped on the floor outside and he wouldn't look so there was no point in closing the shutters when he already seen her all and walked away.

You bungling idiot, Grange!

Nate trudged through the snow with a cooking pot in one hand and a valise in the other. His body ached with frustration and his heart felt so sore he wanted to rub his chest to soothe the ache, but knew it wouldn't help. He felt bereft and so lonely he wanted to go back and beg for her warmth and all the wonders she had just offered him. Even if she ached as well and cried the tears she had refused to shed in front of him, at least she would wake up free of him tomorrow.

He closed his eyes, torturing himself with a picture of her stiff with pride as she watched him go and the pain in his heart said *you fool*. Yet if Juno ever told him *she* had made a mistake and didn't love him it would break him, so he was a coward and decided not to risk it. He stood still in a new squall of snow and let the cold creep over him so he could stop thinking about Juno warm and naked and wanting the unworthy lover she had stumbled across in a snowstorm and so utterly desirable and…

Oh, damnation take it, Grange, just stop torturing yourself!

War should work; the last grim battle when he was so dazed by smoke and gunfire he was deaf and half-blind by the end of it and there was his best reason to stand here in the snow. It chilled him down nicely until he got to the stables and saw the fine horse Juno had hired and had to curse her reckless bravery. The thought of her thrown off in an icy wilderness made him want to stamp back to hold her close and love her with every last inch of his shaking body until he was convinced she was safe and properly warm from head to toe.

Juno was so bold, brave and magnificent, and fantasies of making love to her had haunted him for so long he should be able to fight them off better than this by now. Yet his fantasy Juno was still a girl; the real one was every inch a woman and why the devil did he kiss her?

Nate climbed the rough stairs to the grooms' dormitory, trying to think of anything but Juno, deliciously warm and heavy-eyed as she lay naked in that chair and wanted *him*.

It took every scrap of willpower he had to push away and not take until they were sated and bound together for life.

He could be making love with her right now if not for Dorinda's ghost whispering, *Be very sure Juno won't tire of you soon after the wedding as well.*

At the time he didn't know why he couldn't be as disloyal to Dorinda as she was to him, but maybe it was the idea of Juno, a woman so loyal, strong and brave, that stopped him. He had never deserved her and now she was breathtaking—all elegant limbs and slender curves and dark hair long enough to touch her neat derrière when she sat in that confounded chair and he wanted her so much how could he *not* kiss her?

Everything else had faded from his mind when he saw heat and need and something more in her gaze that he didn't want to think about now. He felt as if he had killed his own men as well as the enemy in battle. He had seen things he never wanted her to know a man *could* see. He had failed to love his wife enough to stop her straying. So, yes, he was tempted by Juno naked and wanting him, but maybe the only worthwhile thing he had ever done was to leave her free to find a better man. Even if she hated him now, at least he hadn't ruined her chances of marrying that better man one day.

It was nearly dark inside the stables and he remembered the tinderbox in that pot of Juno's as he fumbled for a lamp in the tack room and luckily the glass had kept the mice from eating the candle. He finally managed to get it lit and safely closed, but nothing could keep his thoughts from Juno long and he hated the thought of her riding away in the morning if a thaw set in. She was such a fascinating and contrary woman he felt the stark ache of frustration bite again.

So don't keep thinking of her naked, then, you fool.

He needed more distractions and climbed the rough stairs to the loft where the stable boys and unwed grooms had slept. It should match the comfort his horses would enjoy if he still had any. He frowned at the thought of all the fine ones Hedges must have sold, but if he sat brooding about the villain he could freeze to death.

He drew up imaginary plans to house the stable boys and grooms in far more comfort as he searched for the kindling and logs the lads had chopped for a fire none of them was here to enjoy once Hedges had purged The Grange of all servants except the ones who served him. Nate hated the man for pretending to be acting on His Lordship's orders when he closed the house as if the people meant to care for it didn't matter.

His forlorn homecoming had forced Nate to realise how much he loved this place, but he had to make up fantasy bloodlines to fill the empty stables next to distract him from aching for Juno. She was more important than a house or this land and if only he was a better man she would feel like his true home.

He added a new forge and indoor school to train riding horses to his plans, then ran out of ideas and stared into the fire he had managed to light in the cold hearth.

He might as well give in to memories of Juno when he almost thought he deserved her, because nothing was big enough to stop him thinking about her tonight.

Chapter Five

Young Juno was the magic he didn't deserve when he found her in the shadows that first night. She distracted him from his woes, enchanting him with unexpected humour and her deep-down courage and integrity. He had been amazed nobody else noticed how lovely she was under the shyness, but she was never shy with him. That first night he had kissed her because he was free at last and why not? She was utterly delicious and watching him adoringly.

You young cockscomb, he accused the younger self who enjoyed her adoration and thought he deserved it.

Then he went away, left her facing such horror alone that he wanted to howl a protest at the thought of her running from a forced marriage at a heartbreakingly young age. The acute danger she had faced because of her own grandmother's coldness and greed made him feel so sick the thought of making a meal from the food Juno packed into the pot turned his stomach. The marriage that wicked woman intended for Juno was no more than legalised brutality.

He thought of Juno saying *I ran away* and of course she did, but what a useless fool he had been to leave her with no choice but give in or do just that. He had thought he was being so noble, sailing away from the temptation to make her his and brave her furious uncle's wrath afterwards. Putting an ocean between them so that his second marriage would not seem the reason why his first had failed felt like a fine sacrifice to that arrogant boy. If he could go back in time, he would break the smug idiot's nose and order him to wake up and realise he was just a heedless young fool.

He should have sold out as his uncle had wanted him to. He was always less than Juno deserved, but she had wanted him so he could have worked hard to become better. And now it was too late, wasn't it? They should probably marry because they had been marooned here alone. The idea of marrying Juno felt wondrous and he wouldn't even need to say he loved her, but he had killed the chance she would accept him for mere propriety's sake when he stood back from fully loving her.

He stared at the fire and waited for dawn, knowing his nightmares would come back if he slept with *I ran away* pounding in his ears. He pictured all the horrors a lonely girl running across England faced as he shivered in a room unheated so long it would take weeks to be truly warm, thinking he deserved every cold second of the long night ahead.

* * *

Juno had spent the night in the chair by the fire because lying where Nathaniel had slept last night was impossible. She must have dozed since Pard's loud sighs woke her when the fire burned low and he was cold. Uncle Alaric said she spoiled him and he was right. Reminded of the true reason she was sitting brooding while Nathaniel was probably doing the same elsewhere, she prayed Uncle Alaric and Marianne were both safe and not grieving their longed-for baby. She felt guilty because although she was desperate to see them, she wanted to stay here with Nathaniel as well. There was more between them than he was willing to admit and she wanted to know what it was before she left.

Suddenly she heard manly stamping about outside the front door to let her know he was back from wherever he had spent the night. She should leave him to shiver, but yawned and stretched cramped muscles instead and went to let him in.

'Good heavens, Nathaniel! What a difference,' she gasped as she took in the sight of him clean shaven and even more handsome than the young man she once knew.

'I need a barber,' he said, sheepishly smoothing his dark locks. 'Luckily there were sharp scissors and a razor in the kit I left here, although it's so long since I used one I had nearly forgotten how.'

'You still need new clothes and a valet,' she told him with a critical look to pretend he didn't make her heart race even faster without the whiskery disguise.

'I need maids, carpenters, grooms, a butler and a house-keeper more,' he said ruefully.

'And they would have to get here,' she said as they went back to the kitchen.

'True, drifts will be blocking the roads, so staffing this place must wait.'

'Do you think I could walk to Chantry Old Hall?' she said hopefully.

'No, it's too far and the snow is too deep.'

'There must be some way to get home now it's not snowing.'

'You wouldn't get a hundred yards on foot today.'

'How do you know?'

'Because I know how deep the snow is and up here, we sometimes get cut off for weeks in winter.'

'I am stuck, then?'

'Yes.'

'For how long?' she asked and he shrugged.

'Until the weather changes or we dig our way out. It's early for such a heavy snowfall so it *might* turn to rain.'

'Or stay on the ground until Christmas.'

'Yes,' he said and didn't look as worried as he should be.

'What sort of Christmas would it be with your house closed and me desperate to leave?'

'But we would have each other, Miss Defford,' he said with a soulful look and a hand on his heart like a stage Romeo. She knew he was trying to cheer her up and didn't want to be touched by his playacting.

'Idiot,' she said with a reluctant smile. 'Be serious, Lord Grange.'

'Very well, then—Jackson, my former batman and travelling companion, will persuade the villagers to dig through the snow so he can get here quickly since he thinks me helpless without him.'

Juno nearly asked why when Nathaniel was so self-sufficient. 'What shall I do when they get here?' she asked instead.

'I thought you would be delighted to see them.'

'They will be shocked I was trapped here with just you.'

'When they see my makeshift quarters in the stables and yours in here, notice your dog is large and might be fierce if provoked, they will marvel at our joint strength of character and propose me for sainthood.'

Pard wasn't very fierce yesterday, but Juno hadn't resisted Nathaniel's kisses. Now she didn't know what to make of the man hiding under that great beard. How would she feel if they had kissed until his control snapped so they woke up this morning as lovers? Wonderful, she decided defiantly—she would have been fully, urgently loved by the only man she ever wanted to make love with, but she didn't feel like that now.

'Make love to me before they get here, Nathaniel,' she blurted out impulsively. Where was her pride, for goodness' sake?

'How can I?' he said huskily.

'Since you shaved off that ridiculous beard the excuse

it will scratch me won't wash and men and women have been doing it since time began.'

'Don't joke about it, Juno,' he said so huskily he must feel something, even if it was only embarrassment.

'I was never more serious in my life,' she argued and wasn't prepared to lie that she felt nothing when he touched her, even if he was.

'I could get you with child,' he told the wall on the other side of the room as if every word must be paid for. 'I couldn't hold back once I was inside you,' he added, gazing at the kitchen clock this time and it had stopped.

'And you wouldn't want that; would you?' she said bitterly.

'Not for you, not like that.'

'Oh, well, there is nothing else to be said, my lord.'

'I would have to marry you first,' he shocked her by saying anyway.

Her breath stalled and her heart raced, but he still refused to look at her, so she knew it was only his conscience talking. 'Perish the thought,' she said flatly.

'Don't,' he said, putting a hand on her shoulder as if he wanted her to look at him. His touch scorched her skin through his sister's old clothes, but she couldn't watch him pretend it was what he wanted. 'Don't dismiss us, Juno,' he added, so hoarsely he must feel something. *Yes, that embarrassment you were just wondering about.* 'Marry me.'

'Why?' she countered so warily he took his hand away and she missed it so much she shivered.

'We suit one another,' he said as if it was a good enough

reason and a frozen silence argued otherwise. 'We wanted each other when we were not much more than boy and girl and it hasn't gone away. I'm not worthy of you, but we could have a good life together—be two halves of a better whole than I shall ever be without you.'

But don't expect me to say I love you, she added in her head, mourning the boy of nineteen who'd said it so easily she had believed him.

He wouldn't have left her so lonely and for so long if he meant it, though, would he? She refused to wed him now for the sake of their reputations if the gossips found out Lord Grange was alone with Miss Defford for a day and night. 'I ran away from being a *suitable* wife five years ago,' she said bleakly.

'Don't compare me with that randy old goat.'

'Why not? He wanted me for much the same reason.'

'No, he wanted a shamefully young wife to get an heir on. Don't lump me with him, Juno—I can't endure it if you truly think there's nothing to choose between us.'

'Very well, then, I won't,' she said with a sigh. Not even to protect herself from more hurt could she compare young, vigorous Nathaniel Grange with the elderly lecher who had made her life a misery five years ago. 'I always wanted you as fervently as you wanted me,' she admitted.

Probably more so, her inner pessimist added.

'He wanted me, willing or no, and unwilling excited him so I ran and kept running after my purse was stolen and I had no money for the next stage. I walked twenty miles to the town where my former governess was staying and hid whenever I heard anyone coming rather than risk him catching up with me.'

'Tell me!' Nathaniel barked as if she had left a crucial part out of a report to a superior officer.

'I just did.' She couldn't tell him she had been terrified throughout that endless-seeming journey and so wretched and confused about him as she ran she wasn't careful enough with her purse so every penny she had was stolen too easily. She could not let a slavering old man do things she longed to with Nathaniel, but *he* went away.

Love wasn't supposed to be that hard for girls just out of the schoolroom, yet it felt starkly real for her as she sheltered from a storm in a remote barn all night and dreamt how wonderful life would be if Nathaniel was there with her. She pitied her young self, so lost and alone, wishing she could tell her she would make a good life without him. Yet now Nathaniel was here, independence didn't seem quite so wonderful.

'What a damn fool! I knew Stratford was in Paris, yet I didn't sell out to protect you from the cur,' Nathaniel said as if he hated himself for it now. 'My uncle and sister begged me to when Boney abdicated, but I wanted to escape the scandal when Dorinda begged me to divorce her so we could both be free. I thought you were safer with an ocean between us—hah! Safer?' he barked as he paced. 'You would have been safer in a bear pit than with that disgraceful lecher and your stone-hearted grandmother.'

'I survived—indeed, I found out I could look after myself so there was no need for a knight to ride to my rescue.'

She saw him wince as if she had stuck a knife in him and at least he felt *something*, even if it was only guilt.

'I couldn't marry you so soon after my divorce, the tabbies would have eaten you alive,' he said bleakly.

'You could have if you loved me,' she said coolly.

That was the real hitch in her grand love affair—he had been so desperate to marry his *friend* Dorinda he had eloped with her, but he had put an ocean between himself and Juno rather than do the same with her. He could have married her, but he didn't want to. He could have done so, then taken her with him if he did, so how dare he offer to now they had been forced together by the snow?

'How well do you think that would have worked?' he said. 'Whispers would have done the rounds I only rid myself of Dorinda to marry you and you were too young and vulnerable to be pilloried like that. Indeed, your uncle would have put me in the stocks himself and told the mob to throw stones if he hadn't killed me first.'

'Either you weren't brave enough to face him then, or you only wanted a few stolen kisses from a green girl—I vote for the latter.'

'No, I thought you would have met a better man than me by now and married him instead,' he said stiffly.

'Why would I put myself back on the Marriage Mart after I had escaped it? Why be ignored or mocked until I hid in dark corners with bored libertines and let them fool me about love all over again?'

'Ah, don't, Juno—you would have learned how to cope in time. You are a fine and fiery woman, and some lucky and untainted young man would have snapped you up if only you had let him meet you.'

'How do you know?'

'Because you are magnificent. The promise and strength under your shyness was the reason those silly little cats persecuted you when you were too young to realise what they were up to. They knew you would outshine every single one of them one day without even trying.'

So magnificent you don't want to make love with me even when I all but beg you to? I don't think so, my lord, she thought starkly.

'Thank you,' she said out loud.

Chapter Six

∞

Nathaniel sighed as if she was being contrary and Juno wanted to scream at him for being obtuse. 'You still haven't told me exactly what happened after I left,' he said.

As if it mattered now. 'I escaped the room my grandmother locked me up in when I refused to wed a lord who promised to hand over my dowry if she made me marry him. I picked the lock and crept out of the house one dark night, paid for a seat on the Dover stage because I knew they would expect me to flee to my uncle, then I went the other way to ask my former governess for help until my uncle came home and I was safe again.'

'You must have been so frightened,' he said shakily, as if imagining the fear and danger of that frantic journey. *You have no idea,* she thought with the desperation of it sharp in her memory and missing him every step of the way had made it worse.

'Not as frightened as I was of marrying a man I detested.'

'Brave girl,' he said.

'No, I was terrified. I expected him to catch up and force me up the aisle with my grandmother's consent until my uncle rode to the rescue and I was safe at last.'

'While I crossed the Atlantic pretending we had never met,' he said as if he was furious with his younger self for leaving her so alone and maybe she still was, too. 'Because I wanted to keep my hands off an innocent girl that I should never have dallied with in the first place.'

'You went because of me?' she asked and horror outran hurt at the idea he thought it was just dalliance.

'What if I had stayed and bored you as soon as the gloss and passion of being married to me wore off and you were stuck with me for life, Juno?'

Never, I would never have been anything but enthralled by you, Nathaniel, the old, besotted Juno protested silently.

But there was such a gulf between love and passion it felt pointless to say it out loud. Only love was big enough to bridge the void and she refused to let it be one-sided.

'And, yes. I went because of you,' he admitted. 'I had to give you space to be certain I was what you wanted and how could I ruin your life as I did Dorinda's with my blind passion and impulsiveness if I was not?'

She would have argued no, it was really love if he had given her a chance back then. 'I was so afraid for you,' she admitted shakily instead.

'Don't you know the devil looks after his own?'

'You're not his and I know you were wounded at Waterloo so stop being flippant.'

'I recovered though, didn't I?'

'Did you, Nathaniel? I wonder.'

'Enough to know I wasn't good enough. I couldn't watch *you* turn away from me with bored eyes, Juno. I would have wanted to kill any man *you* loved instead of me.'

She tried not to be flattered by the difference he made between her and his former wife, then saw the insult in his words. 'You thought *I* would flit from man to man like your precious Dorinda? I *loved* you, Nathaniel. How dare you make my decisions for me. I can make my own mistakes, thank you very much. You look like the worst one of all right now and don't you dare touch me, I couldn't bear it.' She paused and took a deep breath, but he didn't try to and didn't speak either. 'I'm not a pale shadow of your wife. How dare you think I would follow her example?'

'Of course you're not like her, but when Dorinda married me she swore she loved me and I must not leave her behind when I went off to fight. She got hysterical every time someone even mentioned my commission, but she was bored within a week so I must have been a poor husband. I dragged her off to Spain and let her suffer the privations of life on the march and she hated every rough billet and missed meal and the smells and dirt and everyday dangers.'

'Yet she begged you to take her with you.'

'She had no idea what life was like on campaign and it made her miserable.'

'So miserable she slept with your commanding officer? And you didn't know what it would be like either—at

barely seventeen you were a boy and no doubt you thought
it would be a grand adventure.'

'I was still her husband and who told you she did that?'

'I forget, but her lovers were hardly a secret.'

'She wanted me to divorce her, but I was too stubborn
to admit we had made a terrible mistake when we eloped
so she could go to war with me.'

'It was her mistake as well.'

'Both our mistakes, then, but a very good reason to
make sure you were certain about your feelings for me.'

She wanted to rage at him for lumping her with Dorinda,
but felt so sad he had taken the blame for the failure of his
marriage when Dorinda sounded like a spoilt brat who
only wanted what she should not have.

'The lack was in her, not you, Nathaniel,' she said gently. 'It was beyond me why she wasn't content with such
a fine and handsome young man even before I met you
and afterwards I hated her.'

'Why?'

'Because you hid in the shadows with me to avoid the
gossips and, though you pretended to be merry and teased
me out of my misery, your eyes were so sad I ached for
you and hated her for making you feel less than you should
be.'

'It was mainly my pride that was hurting.'

'Poor boy,' she said softly and, looking back at how
young he had been, she did pity him and even found a
little of it to spare for poor, dead Dorinda.

'Say idiot boy rather and you'll be closer to the truth.'

'Because you married her?'

'Because she had grown so lovely, I was flattered when she said she loved me. We were so hungry for adult adventures we mistook youthful urges for far more.'

'And she *was* very beautiful,' Juno admitted reluctantly.

'Nowhere near as beautiful as you are,' he said and looked as if he meant it.

She wanted to believe him, but couldn't manage it. 'Everyone said how lovely your wife was and she must have been to lure the boy you were into a hasty marriage. I know I am not a beauty, so keep your empty flattery, my lord.'

'It's not flattery, but I'm not a boy now and can resist temptation if I try hard enough now.'

'You didn't yesterday.'

'You have no idea,' he said and closed his eyes as if trying to shut her out.

'You kissed me and walked away, so it wasn't much of a temptation, was it? You were dallying with me again, weren't you?'

'No, I didn't walk away because I don't want you; I did it because I do.'

'True intimacy requires emotion and you don't want to feel any for me.' He was stubbornly silent and she sighed and shook her head. 'I absolve you from any duty you may feel to the girl I was five years ago and the woman I am now, Lord Grange. I will not marry you for the sake of my good name or yours.'

'I don't have one so do it because you want to,' he urged her.

'And know you are waiting for me to be as big a light-skirt as your late wife? No, thank you; I won't walk in her shadow.'

'You're nothing like her.'

'I know, but you don't.' Tears threatened when he stayed silent and confirmed her worst fears, despite his hot and hungry kisses yesterday. 'Go away, Nathaniel. Do what you always do and leave me to fight my demons alone,' she said coldly.

He looked offended, bowed stiffly and did just that, the great, stupid ox. She heard the door slam behind him and let out a shaky breath. She wanted to sit and weep for the young girl who had fallen so deeply in love with the wrong man five years ago, but it would be a waste of time and tears. Instead, she found a handkerchief, blew her nose and refused to cry any more tears for Lord Grange.

There were plenty of kind and sensible men in the world and it was high time she found one and married him. She might even be glad she had met Nathaniel again in an-other decade or so now she knew what a mistake it was to go on dreaming of him loving her back.

She opened the window a bare inch to grab some snow from the sill to cool her sore eyes, so the wretched stuff was useful for something. Pard must have followed Na-thaniel outside and he needed a walk, but she missed him. Nathaniel obviously liked her pet's company, but she wanted to stay cross with him so how dare he be human?

Finally, she was as neat as she could be without a maid, so she drank a cup of the finest China tea and felt almost ready to face the world.

If only the chimneys in the main house had been swept fires could be lit and it would start to come alive, but there was old soot and jackdaw nests to make it too much of a risk so she couldn't be busy in there. She found the boots he must have brought over for her and she wasn't inclined to be grateful as she followed Nathaniel's tracks through the deserted kitchen gardens to see if the horse was still happy.

It wasn't actually snowing at the moment and if only Nathaniel had come home after his uncle died this place could have been neatly tended and smoke would be rising from the bothy and hothouse chimneys. A gaggle of indoor and outdoor servants would be sweeping the paths clear of snow and she hoped they would laugh and throw snowballs because she wanted Nathaniel to be a good and kind employer. It felt wistful for her to have this image of being at His Lordship's side as they joined in the fun. Silly idea, she informed her inner dreamer and shut the door on the walled garden where nothing was stirring except the odd hungry bird, then marched to the stables, careful not to walk in his footsteps this time.

Her skirts were wet, but the horse seemed happy, and Nathaniel had groomed and mucked him out. So, she closed the stable door behind her and wondered what to do next. Building a snowman seemed childish and having a snowball fight with dignified Lord Grange impossible, and he was right about the depth of snow. She could wander through what was left of the pleasure gardens or follow his footsteps and force her company on him, since raiding his late uncle's library for a book didn't appeal and there was nothing else to do. The agent's house was warm and comfortable, of course, but Hedges's malice seemed to linger in every stolen luxury he had squirreled away there so she didn't want to go back yet.

It made sense for her to know where Nathaniel was. They were alone here so she would track him down and go away before he noticed her. His footsteps led around the back of the big house and, as his legs were longer than hers, she had plenty of exercise jumping between them. The wind had piled snow across the lane leading down to the village and she was glad of the path Nathaniel had already cleared, then she rounded a bend in it to see him digging snow as if he was desperate to get away from her. She should take the slap and go back to the agent's house, yet he looked so lonely striking at a drift with an old wooden spade although Pard was digging happily at his side.

Chapter Seven

'You will wear yourselves out,' she said softly.

Pard wagged his tail, but Nathaniel stopped digging and didn't turn to look. Why hadn't she gone away as she had promised herself she would when she tracked him down? Hope, she decided bleakly as it faded and every time he rejected her it hurt more.

'That's the idea,' he told the wall of snow in front of him before facing her with defended dark eyes.

His newly shaven face was so unfairly handsome in the full light of day her heart thumped at his sheer masculine beauty and her breath went shallow again. Did he feel as exposed to her gaze without his beard as she had when she rejected her brazen offer of her body yesterday? She doubted it and turned away.

She had better look for that book after all because she needed to escape from a snowy world where nothing was as she wanted it to be for an hour or two. Her long-cherished fantasy of them being reunited and free to love was only ever a fantasy and he didn't share it.

'I'm sorry I was so forward yesterday and just now. I embarrassed you,' she said stiffly and only because it was cowardly to retreat without saying her piece. She must face facts even if they were painful and painful they were when he looked shocked at her mentioning her unlady-like behaviour.

'I'm the one who should apologise,' he said austerely.

'Better forget it happened, then,' she made herself say despite the blush burning her cheeks. 'We can go our separate ways and pretend to be strangers if we ever have to meet again, my lord,' she added coolly.

'Ah, don't, Juno—I could never forget you.'

'However hard you try?'

'I had to last time; I was married and divorced before I was even of age.'

'I would have risked anything, done anything to be with you five years ago.'

'Then why won't you marry me now?'

'Because you have a guilty conscience and don't love me.'

'We can't wipe out who we were five years ago or even now, so of course I feel guilty about wanting you as fiercely as I did.'

Past tense, Juno, remember that.

And guilt felt such a flimsy reason for marriage.

'Forget the past; worry about getting us out of here in time for me to be of use to my family,' she said.

'I was a rogue and you were innocent when I kissed

you in the shadows back then, Juno, so how can we pretend it never happened?'

'I kissed you, too, so stop being so damned noble that you set my teeth on edge.'

'And they are such nice teeth as well,' he said with the sudden smile that reminded her why she fell headlong in love with him five years ago.

Even his mane of overlong dark hair suited him ridiculously and maybe his mouth was sterner than it used to be and no longer had a quirk of laughter waiting to break free, but he was even more devastatingly handsome. Yet the years since had drained the hope out of him, and she mourned it with a sidelong glance. He would be irresistible if he ever got it back, but he had grown into his boyish looks even if he lacked the old edge of humour to make him less austere.

He had always been able to make her go weak at the knees and it seemed unfair that he still did. She scooped up a handful of snow and threw it at him because he was so infuriating, and she was proud of her aim until his snowball hit her throwing arm and of course she had to retaliate. Battle raged and Pard barked delightedly, dashing between them, then digging at the drifts so eagerly most of the snow he dug out flew back at her and she shook it off as best she could.

Nathaniel laughed so hard she redoubled her efforts to cover him in as much snow as she was and suddenly there he was—the laughing, reckless young man she had fallen for so hard five years ago. Joy at the sight and sound of the man he was meant to be threatened to make her dream impossible things again. So, she fought their snowball battle even harder to stop herself saying any more foolish things.

'Pax,' he said at last as she paused for breath and she eyed him warily. 'Pard is worn out,' he added innocently, yet his dark eyes gave him away and of course he wasn't as innocent as he was pretending to be. She looked from his face to her dog panting happily at his new friend's side.

'Hmm,' she said dubiously and was quite right since Nathaniel's next snowball hit her in the face.

'Oh, no, I'm so sorry,' Nathaniel said and strode over to brush snow from her hair and even her eyelashes. 'I didn't mean to do that,' he said huskily, his touch so gentle it warmed her despite the cold snow she shook off her face. She felt her stern hairstyle fall down and must have looked flushed and dishevelled as she blinked up at him.

'I hope you weren't a sharpshooter,' she said shakily.

'No chance of that,' he said ruefully and outlined her brows with his index finger before running a shivery line down her nose and over her mouth, then lifting her chin to persuade her to meet his suddenly serious gaze. 'I feel something deep and real for you, Juno, I always did,' he admitted gruffly, but he didn't look very happy about it so she refused to be flattered. 'But I don't deserve you now any more than I did back then.'

'Did I ask you to, Nathaniel?' she argued softly.

'I would have to be a better man to do so now, though, wouldn't I?'

'You could be good enough as you are if you really wanted to be.'

'Ah, don't, Juno,' he whispered painfully, yet he soothed another shivery line along her jaw, as if his fingers had a mind of their own. 'Please don't tell me you have been waiting for me to come home.'

'I fell deeply in love with the wounded boy you were at nineteen, Nathaniel, so why wouldn't I? And please don't say there wasn't a scratch on you because we both know that's a lie.' She cursed the hurt his late wife had put in his dark eyes, the sad quirk war made in his sensitive mouth when he wasn't trying to hide it with humour.

'Aye, it hurt,' he admitted roughly. 'Dorinda used to say she loved me as much as she could love one man, but it was impossible to settle for just one.'

'She didn't try very hard,' Juno said, feeling cynical again.

'I realised that when I met you, but it was already too late, if only I had had enough sense to know it.'

She wished she hadn't made him serious and sad. He deserved to be the carefree young man he should be, the one who had laughed and thrown snow and enjoyed Pard's company. That man was worth fighting for. 'Why do you make excuses for her?' she asked him.

'Because it was my mistake, too,' he said wearily.

'Was I one?'

'No, you were the wonder I didn't deserve.'

'Yet as I fell in love with you when you were so newly divorced from your late wife, half the guilt is mine.'

'No, you were an innocent—a lovely, lonely girl I should have left in peace as soon as I realised your dark corner wasn't empty.'

'I think you were too kind to do that.'

'Kind to myself, then, and not you.'

'Ah, but I was so lonely, Nathaniel, so bewildered by the world I was pitchforked into so suddenly I couldn't catch my breath. *You* didn't judge me tongue-tied and unworthy of effort like other men and I was always at ease with you. Everyone else thought me such a mouse there was a rumour doing the rounds I couldn't talk properly and was only pretending to be shy, but I wasn't a mouse with you.'

'What silly young puppies they were and why would you want to know them?' he said and she had to smile because he was younger than most of the gentleman who had ignored and avoided her during her first and only Season.

'When they spoke to me my mouth would go dry and I couldn't think of a single thing to say, yet I could talk to you.'

'Perhaps because you couldn't see me properly in the gloom.'

'No, because you made me feel better and the rest didn't matter.'

'You weren't shy when I kissed you.'

'I grew up in one glorious moment when you kissed me. I was my true self and it was such a lovely surprise not to be the one everyone seemed to think me, so no wonder I kissed you back.'

He chuckled at her remembered astonishment, but sobered too soon. 'I still kissed you in dark corners, then ran off to war. My true self is the worst of rogues and you were wasted on me.'

'No—only think how I would have felt if my first kiss was forced on me by an avid old man, Nathaniel. It would have put me off kissing for life and knowing how it should be gave me courage to run when saying no didn't stop him insisting he was going to marry me whether I wanted to or not. I couldn't let him do the things we did and more, so please stop pretending you bent my life out of shape. You showed me how a kiss should be. I didn't want him spoiling it, so I ran and I'm glad.'

'I could kill him.'

'You would have to stand in line after Uncle Alaric, Darius Yelverton and Sir Harry Marbeck.'

'Why haven't they done so yet?'

'Because I asked them not to.'

'Why?'

'Partly because they have wives and families who would have to flee to the Continent to spend time with them if they were caught duelling and what sort of life would that be for the people I love?'

'*I* don't have a wife or much family.'

Ah, but I love you anyway, her inner Juno insisted, but she told her to be quiet.

'You are nothing to do with me, Lord Grange.'

'Exactly, so nobody will know why I challenged the…' She reached up to stop him saying whatever he was going to call the fat old rogue and Nathaniel confused her by gently nibbling at her fingers with mischief in his dark eyes. Her heart felt as if it was going to turn over with frustrated love for the stupid great oaf.

'I don't want you to have to leave the country before you have hardly got your feet over the threshold because you recklessly fought a man who isn't fit to wipe your boots on,' she said huskily. 'Promise you won't shoot him or do any of the other things I know you are thinking of doing to him, Nathaniel?'

'He should pay for what he tried to do to you, Juno, even if it was with the help of your stony-hearted grandmother and I can't fight her,' he said with such fury in his eyes she felt as if a cold hand had closed around her heart.

She smoothed out the frown from his dark brows with a tender smile she hoped he was too busy being furious to notice. Distracted by seeing his face in the full light of day this close up for the first time, she realised his eyes were a deep moss green, not the dark brown she had always thought.

How strange they had only met in semi-darkness until now, so she hadn't known such an important thing about him. What a luxury to see him with the brightness of reflected snow and the sun trying to peep through a veil of cloud. It did finally break through and shone lovingly on his raven-dark locks to turn them blue-black. She tried to stamp an image of him so alive and unique on her inner eye so she could gloat over it when they had to part again.

'Haven't you heard that the best revenge is to live well?' she said shakily.

'You don't though, do you?'

'I am loved and useful,' she argued. 'I help Uncle Alaric and Marianne to rescue young outcasts as they once did me. I have a purpose in life and a family who love me, so of course I'm happy.'

'Not as happy as you should be. You should not have to do it all alone, Juno.'

'My choice,' she said with a shrug and turned away from his gaze because it had been his choice to leave her solitary when he didn't come home and marry her.

'My blame,' he argued softly.

'Don't think I haven't noticed you didn't promise what I asked,' she said rather than go over the same ground again.

'As long as he stays out of my way, I will stay out of his.'

Chapter Eight

'Not good enough, Nathaniel,' Juno said and held his gaze with a challenge to tell him she wasn't going to let him evade making her that promise.

'He hurt you,' he protested with a fierce frown.

'Not really. I hated being a debutante and evading his unwanted attentions was the push I needed to flee the *ton* and break from my grandmother's control.'

'I hope you aren't trying to say he did you a favour.'

'He did in a way, but he also wed a widow twice my age later that summer and they have a son, so I don't want them to suffer for his sins.'

'Yet the innocent often suffer for the guilty,' he argued.

'For the last time, I am not a wide-eyed innocent. I was very happy to love you when you weren't nearly as cynical as you are now. Promise not to go after him, my lord. I won't get out of your way until you do and my feet are confoundedly cold.'

'Not until you take it back. You *were* an innocent until I came along and…' He tried to say whatever he was going to about his not-quite seduction of the girl she was to his boy, but she clamped her hand over his mouth to stop him again and it could be habit forming.

'Don't you dare say you nearly *despoiled* me,' she said fiercely before she took it away and tried not to let him know the feel of his mouth under her fingers made her forget how cold it was for a heady moment.

'That stung, did it?' he said with a wry smile.

'Only like a serpent,' she said and turned her head away to refuse to let him laugh her out of that promise. 'Promise me,' she challenged a nearby pile of snow and the cold air.

'I have already promised not to seek him out, but if he says one wrong word about you in my hearing, I won't be able to keep my hands off him.'

'You give with one hand and take away with the other.'

'Apparently I'm good at it, but I'm also human, Juno. I won't promise not to react if he tries to blow on your reputation when his should stink like rotten fish.'

'My uncle dealt with him when he got back from France.'

'I suppose he would.'

'He did, so why don't you trust him to silence the repellent old toad?'

'I suppose I should.'

'Make me that promise, then.'

'Nag,' he teased, so she raised her eyebrows and tried to look superior. 'Ah, very well, then; I promise not to kill him.'

'Or force a quarrel on him so you can wing him in a duel?'

'That as well, if he stays away from me and mine.'

'I'm not yours, though, am I?'

'No.'

'So?'

'Away from you as well, then.'

'And?'

'I won't seek him out if he does so, that's all I can promise.'

'I suppose it will have to do.'

'I almost feel saintly,' he said and how could he think he was cynical and not worth loving when he made her heart flutter and warmth rush through her when they were standing on packed snow and her toes were nearly frozen?

'I wouldn't go that far,' she cautioned.

'No, and it's even colder now the sun has gone in again and you have snow down your neck thanks to my clumsiness.'

'And Pard's paws must be so cold now he has stopped throwing snow at me.'

'Despite being a man and supposedly beyond needing a meal in the middle of the day I could eat for my country,' he said, although she knew he would have gone on digging for hours if she hadn't interfered. What that said about his need to get to the village as fast as possible and hers for him not to she was unwilling to think about too closely.

Once he abandoned his digging and followed her back to the agent's house for a hearty luncheon of potatoes baked in the range, good strong cheese and pickles followed by sweet apples and yet more smoky China tea, Juno hoped for so much from the rest of the day. Instead of sitting with her and wiling away the day as she wished he would, Nathaniel spent it splitting logs and shovelling snow from the paths to the stables and main house.

By the time he finished it was nearly dark, so she hoped for a long winter evening in his company instead, but he took the meal she had cooked while he was busy away to eat in the bleak loft over the stables. She sat in the best kitchen of the agent's house, missing him while she nibbled at her meal without much appetite. He *had* only wanted to marry her to prevent a scandal, then, and she would choose scandal over a loveless union with the man she still couldn't help loving every time.

Pretending to read a book she found in the late Lord Grange's library to pass the time, until she realised it was upside down, she sighed and shook her head at her own stupidity, then let Pard out one last time and banked up the fire before going upstairs to bed. She would try to sleep in the one Nathaniel used on his first night here and what a miserable homecoming that must have been.

If she'd accepted his dutiful proposal earlier today, His Lordship might be with her in this lonely bed right now. She had no doubt he would give her great physical pleasure and she longed to bear his children nearly as much as she ached for him, but not as a duty to her good reputation and his title and lands. But, oh, if only he had waited to meet her instead of marrying Dorinda!

Would a shining youth like dashing Lieutenant Grange have sat out any dances with Juno when they did meet if he wasn't so recently divorced? If he hadn't once eloped with a flirt and brought their marriage to end, he would have been too busy bedazzling more sociable young ladies on the dance floor in his dress uniform. He would not have had any time to spare for shy Juno Defford who hid in gloomy corners. With all those eager young ladies competing for his attention he would never have noticed her at all.

Dissatisfied with her gloomy conclusion, Juno thumped the pillow and wished she had stayed downstairs with Pard. At least there she could listen to him sleeping and watch the quiet glow of the fire. She sighed and closed her eyes again to lie in the dark and try not to think of what might have been, but when she finally drifted off to sleep, she dreamt of Nathaniel as eager and urgent for her as she was for him and what a fine fantasy that was.

It seemed like only minutes later when Pard barked downstairs, so Nathaniel must be out there since Pard sounded excited and not alarmed. She pulled her borrowed gown back on, thankful she had slept in her underclothes, but feeling dishevelled and sleepy as she ran downstairs to let him in and find out why he was knocking so urgently.

'What's the matter?' she asked as soon as she pulled the bolts back. She felt scruffy, when he was as neat as if he had the valet she had twitted him about yesterday and had slept in a fine feather bed, not a stable.

'Good morning, Miss Defford,' he replied coolly, but shadows under his eyes said he hadn't slept as well as she first thought and she was fiercely glad. 'I can hear Jackson and his troops in the distance.'

'Oh, I see,' she said and supposed she did since his ordeal was nearly over. 'I will tidy myself,' she said and went to do so before joining him in the best kitchen.

'I'm sorry,' he said as she walked back in, looking as elegant as she could in his sister's old clothes.

'What for?' she replied distantly, hoping he wasn't going to propose again.

'Being alone here when you arrived so your good name isn't as spotless as it should be.'

'It wasn't spotless to start with, not after I crossed England on my own five years ago, but I never felt as lonely then as I do now.'

'Oh,' was all he said stiffly and they walked to the main house several yards apart. 'Is it my fault?' he asked at last.

'Is what your fault?'

'The loneliness?'

'No,' she lied. 'I expect most women of two and twenty are lonely now and again when they lack a husband or lover.'

'Never mind them—I'm interested in you.'

She shot him a sceptical look. 'So interested you left these shores five years ago and didn't bother to find out if I had married or not when you came home?'

Pard came running up to tell them strangers were on their way and he was here to protect her, so at least she could make a fuss of him and hope she and Nathaniel had nothing left to say to each other because she didn't want him to propose again. It was as cold in the main house as it was outside, but she agreed to wait in the ladies' withdrawing room as if she was only visiting while Nathaniel went to greet Jackson and the villagers and warn them a lady had been forced to take refuge here by the storm. She opened the shutters and uncovered a chair to sit in solitary splendour and wait for her audience like a stray princess.

Jackson turned out to be a small man who exuded energy and by the time it was dark Juno had a maid and mattresses were being aired for her and the master of the house and his man. Jackson had theirs carried up to Lord Grange's unsuitable quarters above the stables as soon as they had been swept and dusted and mopped to his satisfaction, as even he could not magic up a chimney sweep to make it safe for fires to be lit in the main house. As the capable man began to exert control over his master's kingdom, Juno wondered where Nathaniel was, but he turned up at twilight cold and weary and said he had walked down the hill and the lower he got the thinner the snow cover became so they could probably leave tomorrow if it didn't snow in the night.

'*We* can leave?' she asked him with haughty look to argue with that word.

'I can't let you ride on alone, so don't even think about doing so.'

'I am perfectly capable of getting home without your permission.'

'Just as you did the day you set out without any luggage in a blizzard?'

'As I would have if not for the freakish weather you have up here.'

'Of course, it must have been balmy and quite calm down on the Severn Plain and a magic carpet will waft you home without any need to worry about mud or changes of horses or your comfort and safety along the way.'

She wanted to argue her life would be wonderfully easy the moment she got away from here, but knew the roads would be muddy and busy when it was just over a week before Christmas, even if the snowfall was negligible elsewhere. Goods must be got where they were needed for the festive season, travellers would be on their way to family or friends for a solemn Christmas Day churchgoing and eager celebrations after and he was right about her disastrous journey here.

'I know it won't be easy,' she admitted. 'I intend to hire a coach at the next posting inn so there's no need to twit me about riding alone since I know it was folly.'

'True, but you did it for love,' he said as if he understood she loved her family even if he thought she was a fool to risk so much to get home.

Chapter Nine

'My uncle's carriages are still in the carriage house, imagine my surprise, but since all his horses have been sold, I can't lend you one of mine,' Nathaniel said with the bitterness of that loss in his deep voice so he must be really tired.

Juno hated the idea of Hedges getting away with such a heavy blow to Nathaniel's power and pride, but he wouldn't want a man to hang even after stealing the vast amounts the rogue must have taken when his back was turned.

'There's no need for you to worry about me when your house needs putting in order so badly. I'm glad the villagers know it was Hedges who closed it down and put them out of work so he could pocket their wages. You will now have plenty of willing hands to help you restore it back to its former glory.'

'The Grange waited so many years for me to come home that a few days won't make much difference and you're not leaving without me so you might as well re-sign yourself to my company,' he told her a bit too firmly.

'I can look after myself.'

'As you did on the way here? No, I'm coming with you even if you pretend we are strangers all the way home.'

'We *are* strangers.'

'Liar,' he said softly and, confound the man, he was right—he wouldn't feel like one of those if they lived apart for the rest of their lives and what a horrid idea.

'You don't want me,' she argued with him anyway.

'Not true.'

'Don't, Nathaniel,' she said, 'and don't you dare propose again.'

'Why not?'

'Because I won't marry you for less than love and you don't believe in it.'

'Don't you love me any more?' he said almost as if he was teasing, but she refused to be joked into the marriage bed even if she still did.

'Irrelevant,' she said stonily and refused to weaken.

'Pretend I'm a cousin or a hired escort, then, but I can't stay here while you battle snow and mud and everyone who will try to take advantage of a lady travelling alone.'

'Hmm, maybe you can be my coachman?' she said slyly and was shocked to see he was taking her flippant comment seriously.

'Excellent idea,' he said smugly. 'Then I can make sure you are not driven into a ditch by a hired one who has taken too much brandy to keep out the cold.'

'I wasn't serious. You're a lord; you can't drive a coach and four.'

'I can, you know; I'm a devil of a fellow. I can drive anything from mule cart to coach and six thanks to my travels and I doubt anyone will recognise me muffled up to the eyes on the box. The more I think about it, the more it looks like an excellent idea, so well done, Miss Defford.'

'Will you stop being so infuriating?'

'Sorry, I was born this way.'

'Indeed you were,' she said between gritted teeth and wondered if she could slip away before anyone was up to-morrow, but it was not the sort of weather for stumbling about in the dark and she didn't know the way. 'My uncle will know you are no coachman,' she cautioned.

'Therefore he will be on my side next time I propose to you.'

'Remember the stocks you said he would have put you in if he knew you had kissed me so often before I fled town five years ago?' He nodded. 'Well, he will throw those stones himself if he finds out you did it again and I won't marry you.'

'You won't tell him I kissed you, then or now,' he said confidently.

'No, I won't,' she admitted with a gusty sigh—he knew her too well.

'Then stop trying to evade my company. I shall stick to you like a burr until you're safely home and then we shall see.'

'Yes, you will see I managed perfectly last time I travelled alone and can do it again,' she muttered, but he must have heard since he frowned and shook his head.

'No, you didn't. You survived and you're not going alone this time,' he said as if that was it: Lord Grange had spoken.

'I won't marry you if you ask me in front of my uncle and half of Herefordshire.'

'That could hurt my lordly pride,' he said as if she might pity him and give in.

'I have told you no often enough for it to be your own fault.'

'Even if you turn me down in front of the entire county and this one as well, I intend to get you home safely, so stop wasting your breath.'

'You could be a complete whipster for all I know.'

'Luckily for you I'm not.'

'So you say,' she said, but he was irresistible in this mood and if only he had it more often they would already be lovers. Laughter fitted the young man he should be so much better than the morose mood he was in when she arrived and was it really only two days ago? It felt as if her whole life had changed since she set out in such a hurry, but it hadn't. Reminded how urgently she needed to get home to find out if Marianne and her baby had survived the birth, she decided to give in and cope with Nathaniel's proposals of marriage purely to stave off scandal when she got there.

'You are a very contrary woman,' Nathaniel told her

and it felt better to argue with him than dread bad news when she got home.

'Says the most contrary man I have ever encountered,' she said crossly.

'I will ride behind you and make you conspicuous if you don't accept my escort,' he carried on as if she hadn't spoken.

'My new maid says she can stand whatever the weather throws at us after working on the farms since the old lord died so I won't be alone.'

'She won't protect you from mud and bullies and greedy landlords, so give up, Juno. I'm coming with you even if you take half the village with us.'

'Why?'

'Because you are far too lovely to be safe on the roads. While a maid and a dog won't scare the wolves away, I can.'

'I suppose so,' she said reluctantly. He *was* big enough to put off any man thinking of taking advantage of her or Jessie. Riding to Chantry Old Hall over the hills was one thing, travelling main roads in the cold, mud and bustle was quite another.

'Be ready to leave at first light,' he said. Common sense argued get home as fast as she could and she didn't want to say goodbye to him yet anyway.

'Have I ever told you how infuriating you are?' she said.

'I think we were too busy kissing each other to spare enough breath last time.'

'Don't say that. Someone might hear you.'

'Someone is very welcome to.'

'That would suit you very well, wouldn't it, my lord?'

'It would, my Juno, it most definitely would,' he told her with a mock leer that made her want to laugh again, but she couldn't afford to.

'I was wrong. You're not infuriating, you're maddening, and I still won't marry you.'

'Shame,' he said as if he knew she wanted to, but couldn't trust her heart to him twice unless she knew he truly loved her back.

She wasn't sure she could live without him for the rest of her days anyway. Even if he never said *I love you* she could have his children to love. Maybe mutual interests could be enough as long as she had them with him. Or would it be torture to feel more, love more and always be disappointed when he didn't love her back? If she had never seen Uncle Alaric and Marianne so happily in love, she might accept half-measures, but she had so she must not. Yet the thought of spending the rest of her life without him hurt so much as she went to bed alone again that night to be haunted by those stupid dreams of what might have been if the Fates were kinder.

Jackson and Nathaniel were a formidable team. The newly appointed stable boys had walked Juno's horse to the village the night before, then set out as soon as it was light next morning to very carefully lead the horses down the hill. Juno tried not to be sad she was leaving a neglected old mansion that could easily have been home if Nathaniel truly wanted to marry her. Where the lads stopped to wait for them with the horses there was only a dusting of snow already melting, but it still took all day to reach Worcester, so they had to stay the night.

There hadn't been a carriage to hire on the way there— *'What with it being so near to Christmas and all, my lord*—so Juno had pulled her jockey cap down and kept her head bowed whenever Nathaniel claimed she was his sister. She just hoped none of her uncle's neighbours were on the roads to argue, but everyone seemed far too busy getting where they wanted to be for Christmas to bother much with strangers. She took dinner and breakfast in her bedchamber with Jessie and made sure they both stayed out of sight as much as they could.

Being lodged so close to the cathedral reminded her it was not very long to Christmas Day now and joy would soon break the austerity of Advent. If Marianne and Uncle Alaric's baby had not survived, it would be bleak for everyone at Prospect House. Juno was desperate to find out now they were so close to home.

By the next morning Nathaniel had managed to borrow a chaise and four from an old army friend who lived in a smart town mansion on the outskirts of the city, then he did as he had threatened to and tooled the horses himself, claiming he had promised his friend he would before he agreed to lend his prized team as well as his smart new carriage.

They changed horses in Broadley and Nathaniel took

one look at Juno's set face when he tried to suggest they stay the night and accepted her curt refusal. She was tense as a bowstring and trying so hard to be hopeful as they got closer to her home and all the reasons not to be piled on her shoulders.

By the time Nathaniel turned the team into the now-smooth drive twilight was falling. The instant he pulled up his team Juno wrenched the carriage door open and jumped down without waiting for the steps to be lowered. Nathaniel tossed Jackson the reins and leapt from his perch, almost beating Pard in the race to catch up with her.

'Hold up, my Juno,' Nathaniel whispered encouragingly as he put an arm round her waist when she stumbled in her hurry to get to her family. He must be so weary and cold after driving over muddy roads for so long, yet he was supporting *her*? No wonder she loved him, she thought hazily but never mind that now, she needed to know what had happened to Marianne and the baby.

Chapter Ten

'Oh, my goodness, Juno, here you are at last. Where on earth have you *been*?' Miss Donne stood on the steps, scolding as Juno dashed towards her with a complete stranger holding her up. 'We have been so worried about you,' her governess's own former governess said with a sharp look from Juno to her unlikely coachman and back to wonder if they had reason to be concerned.

The noise of their arrival brought grooms running from the stables to attend to their horses and Marianne and Uncle Alaric's latest group of waifs were peering out of the windows of a cosy sitting room where Miss Donne must have ordered them to stay or they would all be out here as well.

'It snowed. We were stuck,' Juno explained tersely. 'What happened?'

'Well—' Miss Donne said, then broke off when Jackson and Jessie appeared behind Juno. 'Maybe you should go first,' she said as if all sorts of mistaken ideas were scurrying about in her busy head.

'Lord Grange; this is Miss Donne, my former governess's former governess and a very dear friend of the family when she is not stalling.'

'How do you do, ma'am?' Nathaniel said with such an elegant bow Miss Donne looked pensive.

'Penelope, Percival and Persephone Parker, Angela Randal and Sophia Black are the ones watching us from that window as if we are exhibits at a fair,' Juno added impatiently. 'And now...?' she said to Miss Donne with a hard look to say stop drawing out the agony.

'Juno! At last.' Fliss Yelverton ran down the steps to hug her former pupil so Nathaniel finally had to let her go.

'Please, Fliss, just tell me what's happened,' Juno begged.

'You might not believe it, I'm still not sure I do,' her uncle's voice interrupted from the top of the steps and he didn't *sound* broken-hearted.

'Believe what?' Juno said impatiently.

'Two of them, Niece.'

'Two what?' she snapped before his words sank in and wonder took the place of acute anxiety at long last. 'Two *babies*?'

'No, ostriches,' Uncle Alaric said, then shrugged to let her know he was still in shock. 'Of course two babies—twins.'

'What sort?' she managed to say.

'Oh, you know, the usual,' her annoying uncle said with a broad grin. 'Two legs, two arms, the right bits in the right places.'

'Which bits?'

'Well, really, Juno! One of us should have taught you better than that,' Miss Donne scolded and chivvied them up the steps so they could start to get warm and at least see each other's faces in the brightly lit hall.

'One of each,' Viscount Stratford told Juno with a very proud smile as soon as the door was shut behind them. 'My Marianne has done it again; she has given us an instant family to go with our first proper home. She's a woman in a million,' he told Juno with a wide gesture at the fire burning in the hearth and polished panelling reflecting the candlelight where it wasn't covered in greenery or bright berries and China oranges and knots of ribbons in red and gold ready for the Christmas season.

'Oh, Uncle Alaric, I'm so pleased for you both! And now I have *two* little cousins to boss around, and a boy and a girl as well. Clever, clever Marianne.'

'It was a joint effort and you'll be more aunt than cousin, love, but if you think you're being introduced to them in that state and without an explanation of where you have been first you had best think again.'

Fliss just smiled as if she hadn't stopped since the Defford twins were born safely. Even the sight of her former pupil dressed in clothes a decade out of date and accompanied by a mysterious lord couldn't stop her delight that Alaric and Marianne had a family of their own to spoil now.

'We *do* need baths, a warm fire and something to eat,'

Juno said, hoping to put off the explanation her uncle demanded.

'You do,' her uncle said silkily and eyed Nathaniel frostily.

'Lord Grange was kind enough to drive me home after I was stranded at his house while trying to cross the hills to Chantry Old Hall in a snowstorm,' she said, hoping Nathaniel's travel-worn state would soften her uncle's stern gaze.

'Lord Stratford,' Nathaniel said with an elegant bow in return to her uncle's curt nod.

'I didn't know you were back in the country, Grange. I hope you will take your responsibilities more seriously now you are finally home.'

'I will, although I have hardly had time to get the full measure of them yet.'

'You were home in time to meet my niece though, weren't you?'

'Indeed, I had that privilege,' Nathaniel lied stiffly.

Juno wanted to bang their heads together for acting like a pair of stiff-legged dogs getting ready to fight for dominance. 'His Lordship rescued me from a blizzard and insisted on seeing me safely home as soon as it was safe to travel,' she said to try and stop them doing something stupid to one another.

'What the devil were you doing riding alone, Juno?' her uncle demanded sharply.

'Trying to get here as soon as I could after reading your dour letter and it was barely seven miles to Chantry Old Hall so it should not have taken long.'

'It might not in the summer, but you could have died from exposure in a storm as fierce as the one Harry and Viola described as they dashed down their hill ahead of it to get here in a hurry.'

'What did you expect me to do, sit in my godmother's house twiddling my thumbs while we waited for your next gloomy message? Begging a place in their carriage was the fastest way to get here.'

'I should never have sent one to you as well,' Uncle Alaric said, clearly embarrassed about his panicked despair for Marianne and their unborn child when he sent them.

'The babies were born a month early nevertheless,' she said, feeling anxious again as twins were usually smaller than single babies so premature ones must be tiny and so vulnerable.

'Probably not, according to the midwife; she thinks they were barely a fortnight less than full term and we are a pair of nodcocks who can't add up. Apparently twins often come early since there isn't enough room in there for both of them, if you see what I mean.'

Juno smiled and shook her head. 'Oddly enough I do, but you really aren't very good at explaining your instant family to the one you already have.'

'I'm not, am I?' he said, forgetting to be suspicious of Nathaniel in his overriding joy at being a father. 'Marianne wants to be up and about again, but the doctor forbade it for at least a week, although I'll lay you odds she won't stay there for Christmas.'

'I would not take them, but that's why I'm here. I can order a household nearly as well as she can now, so she has no excuse to be up and doing too soon,' Fliss said.

'You had best go and tell her so again, then, and explain why there is such a fuss down here before she gets up to find out for herself,' Uncle Alaric said with an anxious glance upstairs.

'I wish Darius was here,' Fliss said wistfully, 'she might listen to her brother.'

'She might,' Uncle Alaric said doubtfully.

'Where is he?' Juno asked.

'Playing host to Sir Harry and Viola at Owlet Manor since a houseful of guests would only make Marianne more likely to ignore the doctor's orders.'

'I will take my leave, then, Your Lordship, Mrs Yelverton, Ma'am,' Nathaniel said and Juno was amazed he had been a silent spectator for so long.

'As you have only just returned home you cannot have made arrangements for the Christmas season, Grange, so I hope you will come back and join us for ours,' her uncle said, sounding so smoothly chilly Juno shivered on Nathaniel's behalf. 'You have done us a great favour by giving my niece shelter in her hour of need, then seeing her safely home, so we really must insist on sharing our celebrations with you to say thank you.'

Nathaniel bowed silent assent and Juno shivered again at the manly glare the two men exchanged under cover of being painfully polite to one another. It made her feel furious with both of them, but Nathaniel was gone before she could tell him so and her uncle was far too pleased with himself to listen to her reproaches when he came back inside from seeing his unexpected visitor off in every sense of the words.

The twins were delightful, when they weren't crying, or hungry or smelly, which their doting mama accused one or the other of being most of the time. Marianne was so besotted with them she was even jealous when Fliss, Juno or their father whisked a twin off to be changed. Juno supposed it was the privilege of the wealthy to have nannies to do the bathing and changing and one she would gladly enjoy if she ever had a baby herself, but best not think about that now.

It promised to be the most joyous Christmas season the Defford family had experience in living memory, with two healthy and usually happy babies sleeping in Lord Stratford's dressing room, since their parents refused to banish them to the nursery. Yet Juno missed Nathaniel so badly it was hard to be as happy as she should be. She even missed him pretending to be immune to deeply felt emotions and every day had expected a letter to arrive saying Lord Grange would be unable to join them for Christmas after all.

By the day before Christmas Eve, it still had not arrived and she almost began to believe he would turn up as ordered.

'You're so sad, Juno,' Fliss said when she found her

in the still room where she was hiding from all the excitement.

'No, I have a headache.'

'It wasn't a question, my love. Something happened when you were lost in the snow and I know you don't want to talk about it, but I love you too much not to try to. Are you pining for Lord Grange?'

'Of course not—he's the most infuriating, stubborn, wrongheaded man I have ever met. I don't miss him and I never have.'

Oh, curse it, her tongue had run away with her and now Fliss knew more about Juno and Nathaniel Grange than she wanted her to.

'Ah, so I was right; you two *have* met before.'

'We were barely acquainted five years ago,' Juno said and what a loose tongue she had today.

'A few minutes can be long enough,' Fliss said and maybe they were for her and Darius, but there wasn't going to be a happy ending for Juno.

'Not for him.'

'Tell me,' Fliss urged quietly. 'You know I will keep your secrets and Darius has always understood that, so please don't accuse me of telling him in advance.'

It was a relief to shut the door on the rest of the world and tell someone who loved her the secret she had kept for so long.

'So you loved him five years ago?'

'Yes, I couldn't help myself. He lit up my world.'

'That's a hard feeling to lose and now I know why you

were so sad and quiet the year we three were busy finding our own particular Yelvertons to love. I thought there
was more to it than your grandmother's appalling behaviour and the shock of escaping from that awful old man
on your own.'

'I missed Nathaniel so much, Fliss. I hated thinking he
might be killed so far away and I would be the last one
to know.'

'No wonder you didn't want another Season in town
and were set on making a life alone, but why can't you be
happy with Lord Grange instead?'

'Because he wasn't here; he didn't come for me after
Waterloo or when his ex-wife died, so he can't have loved
me. He wouldn't make love to me last week either and that
proves it.' Juno didn't blush and Fliss didn't pretend to be
shocked. They were not pupil and governess any more,
but two adult women who knew too much about love and
life to bother with false modesty.

'Men are such stiff-necked idiots when they decide they
are not good enough—or rich enough—for us, as my daft
love convinced himself he wasn't for me; as if we care
about such things as long as they love us back and never
stop.'

'He doesn't want to, Fliss. He thinks I would grow
bored with him just as his late wife did, but she was a
fool and he's all I have ever wanted. I love the great gruff
idiot, but he doesn't even want to love me back.'

'Prove to him he's an idiot then, fight for him.'

'I already have, but she's won, Fliss. His late wife's

ghost whispered *Look what happened when we married for so-called love* and he listened to it. I hate her for making him doubt himself and he just won't see that I can't help loving him. I would have stopped long ago if willing it away would work.'

'What fools men can be, Juno, love,' Fliss said and held Juno when she finally let herself cry for the young love that she had kept a secret for so long.

'Oh, Fliss, why does love hurt so much?' she wailed for a desolate moment, then heard herself being melodramatic and gave a watery chuckle. 'Because it *is* love, I suppose, and that is always a risk.'

'Very young men can be hurt so badly, despite their manly defences, Juno,' Fliss said gently, 'and Lord Grange had to protect himself from his wife's infidelities at such a young age he must have been hurt more than most of them can imagine. I don't know him, but I can tell he feels something powerful for you and don't look at me as if I don't know what I'm talking about. He wasn't acting like a man who doesn't care when he brought you home. He hardly took his eyes off you the entire time he was here and Alaric tried very hard to capture his attention with his stiff-necked comments and suspicions.'

'Truly?'

'When he turns up in answer to your uncle's lordly summons, ask who else was here but you and your uncle that day. I'll lay you long odds he has no idea.'

'He only wanted to marry me to avoid a scandal when

news gets out that we were stuck in his snowbound old house for two days and nights without a chaperon.'

'He's made a fine mull of things, then, hasn't he? I know he has strong feelings for you, whether he wants to admit to them or not, Juno.'

'I won't marry him to silence the scandalmongers.'

'I don't think you will have to, but I shall cross my fingers and hope he has looked into his heart since he left you here to stew.'

'That's just what he has done, isn't it? The conniving wretch.'

'Now I think he's rather a clever wretch since it seems to be working.'

'It's all right for you to think so since you're not in love with him,' Juno said grumpily.

Chapter Eleven

Nathaniel arrived on Christmas Eve looking fine and fashionable and quite unlike the gruff bear she first met again at The Grange in the snow, or the weary travel-stained giant who drove here last week. Juno's heartbeat skipped at the sight of him looking as close to a model gentleman as he could manage in such a short time.

He also looked very serious and a little nervous when Uncle Alaric bade him welcome, almost looking as if he meant it. Nathaniel looked ominously like an honourable gentleman come to propose marriage to a lady he had compromised and somehow Juno had to stop him doing that again.

She had already weathered a thundering scold after confessing she had refused Nathaniel's dutiful offer of marriage to save her good name. She could tell she wasn't forgiven for that refusal yet when Uncle Alaric told Nathaniel he was very welcome with a sharp look in her direction. He had changed his tune, hadn't he?

Juno sighed when they went off together pretending

gentlemen didn't have time to eat between breakfast and dinner by way of the kitchen. She didn't eat much of her own luncheon since she couldn't force it past the tightness in her throat. Fliss had gone home to spend Christmas Day with her brood and Viola and Harry had done the same thing. Juno ate with the children and Miss Donne, who claimed someone must keep the children occupied, so she might as well stay and do so since everyone was so busy with the babies.

Miss Donne obviously didn't need her help, so Juno wandered out into the winter garden trying not to feel lonely and rather forlorn. Here and there faint signs of new life were showing—primroses and violets were starting to grow and a robin sang from the top of an ancient holly tree.

It had been dry all week so she sat on the steps in front of the summer house and wondered why it wasn't a winter house. With nothing else to distract her she let out a pent-up breath and tried to compose her thoughts. It was the Defford twins' first Christmas and she had to hide this edgy tension somehow, so maybe being still for a while might calm her enough to act as if Nathaniel was a chance-met acquaintance.

'What a heavy sigh,' the man himself said so close by she wondered how such a big man could move so silently. Her heart was beating so fast she couldn't think of anything to say when he swirled his heavy old army cloak off his shoulders and gestured for her to sit on it before he joined her. 'It's too cold for us to shiver on opposite sides of the garden,' he said with a smile in his eyes that made her heart threaten to turn over and it ought to know better by now.

'You will be cold without a cloak.'

'I hope not,' he said and looked as if he was the one with an attack of nerves this time. It softened her determination not to listen to his latest offer of marriage. 'For a man who hates to waste words, your uncle can be very eloquent,' he added ruefully.

'What has he been saying?' she said warily.

'Nothing I haven't told myself ever since I left last week and he's right: I am a coward for not risking being hurt again. You are the opposite of Dorinda in every way I can think of. I love you, Juno. I have loved you from the moment I first laid eyes on you pretending you were quite happy in your hiding place. My life had a purpose again and that was to persuade you it was safe to love me. No, please don't interrupt; Stratford says I need to clear my slate and he's far too terrifying to argue with when he's intent on protecting his beloved niece.'

'But you only ever needed to say you still love me, Nathaniel. It's all I ever needed you to say, but you didn't when it mattered, so why should I believe you now?'

'Because I have been a fool for such a long time?' he said wryly. She was so tempted to give in to the leap of joy in her heart, but she hardly dared trust her own ears when they were desperate for the words.

'That's true,' she said.

'I'm trying to be humble, Juno.'

'Oh, is that what it is?'

'I am a fool,' he said doggedly. 'I loved you, but I thought we needed to wait until the scandal of my divorce had died down so I could court you in form.'

'I would rather you had just loved me,' she said.

'Maybe later,' he said and his dear eyes were full of emotion at last and his pretending-not-to-be-sensitive mouth was smiling wickedly and this felt real.

'Maybe,' she whispered and her world had suddenly turned the right way up again. She saw love and heat openly in his darkest of green eyes at last. Had the daft great bear truly loved her all along? A cold and lonely place inside her warmed and settled, even if he was an honourable great fool to have stayed away so long.

'Where was I?' he said shakily, as if he could hardly believe happiness was within touching distance either and didn't want to risk ruining it.

'Being a fool,' she reminded him.

'Ah, yes, I dreamed of you all the way across the Atlantic Ocean and back. On the eve of the Battle of Waterloo I sat in the rain and mud and all I could think of was how much I missed you.'

'While I was nibbling my fingernails to the quick worrying about you and then you were wounded—' She stopped, because seeing his name among the wounded had been the worst moment of her life so far. Never mind having to flee her grandmother's wicked plans for her, that was the day she knew something important inside her would die if Nathaniel failed to recover. He silently reached for her hand as if he had needed her as much as she had him. 'I ached for you,' she said simply.

He gave her the wry grin that always made her heart race. 'Me, too,' he said, then seemed to go into himself as he recalled that terrible time again. 'I saw things at Waterloo I can never forget, Juno. My men fell around me before I took that bullet and I will only admit to you how glad I was to be excused from the slaughter. I could not come home to you when I had such nightmares and dark moods it would have been a kind of hell to live with me.'

'As if living without you was not,' she said. His emotions were so fiercely felt it must have hurt him to hold them inside and wander the Continent until some of the horror receded. 'I wish you had let me share it, Nathaniel; love isn't just for the good days, or it wouldn't be love.'

'How could I offer you shouts in the night and a husband who couldn't tell the difference between remembered horrors and his own wife if I had dared to sleep next to you and risk fighting the enemy again in my dreams?'

'Ah, my love, you have suffered so much, but I would have said yes to any and all of it. I would have gone with you on your travels if it helped you fight your demons. I would live anywhere with you rather than be so lonely again without you.'

'Oh, love, you humble me,' he said shakily. 'Did you really miss me so much?'

'Only as if I lost half of myself and nothing felt quite real without you.'

'Me, too, as if I had lost an arm or a leg.'

'Ah, my love, you are such an idiot to have left us both so lonely for so long and I'm not sure you deserve me, but I will love you until my dying day and don't you dare go away again.'

'What would my life be without you, love? I know I don't deserve you, but will you marry me anyway?'

'Oh, very well then, as we love one another I might as well.'

'Ah, at last—you are showing some common sense, my love. Tomorrow will suit me and the Reverend Yelverton assures me he has one more Christmas marriage left in him so it might as well be ours, since he and Mrs Yelverton are staying at Owlet Manor and I have a special licence burning a hole in my pocket, so will you marry me in haste, love?'

'I don't have a wedding gown or any of the things brides are supposed to have like guests and attendants and bride cakes.'

'You will have me and I'll have you. What else do we need?'

'Nothing,' she said blissfully and he kissed her until words faded away and only feelings mattered.

It was such a happy Christmas Day after all and Juno loved every minute of her scratch wedding. She wore the deep red velvet gown she had been keeping for the day without realising it was perfect for a Christmas wedding. Her uncle gave her away; Fliss and Darius were their witnesses and Jackson Nathaniel's groomsman.

'I love you, Juno Grange, so much I can't find words for how happy you have just made me,' her groom said as they walked down the aisle together as man and wife.

'And I love you, despite your poor vocabulary and shameful tardiness, my lord,' she teased and smiled blissfully back at him.

'You're never going to let me forget that, are you?'

'No, a wife needs some advantages, what with this being such an unfair world for us females.'

'You will never be less than my equal, Juno,' he promised solemnly and then his wonderful smile broke out again and he halted her for another kiss.

'It's all very well for you two billing and cooing like lovebirds, but the rest of us want to be in the warm again,' her uncle said from behind them, but everyone knew it wasn't the cold making him impatient; he wanted to be with his beloved family on this day of days. So Reverend and Mrs Yelverton, Darius and Fliss went back to their Christmas dinner and the bridal party sped off for Prospect House, where Marianne and the babies and their rescued waifs waited for their Christmas dinner and a wedding breakfast combined and Juno wondered if the dear old house had ever witnessed such a joyful Christmas as this one.

A year later

'Happy anniversary, Lady Grange.'

'It is, isn't it?' Juno felt so loved and contented when her husband's warm arms pulled her back against his great body as he caressed her baby bump, feeling their child kick, and his deep hum of happiness said more than words about his state of mind. 'I thought last Christmas could not be bettered, but I was wrong,' she added dreamily.

'Just over a year ago this house was cold as charity and so was I, but just look at us now, my love. Look what you did,' Nathaniel said.

'Look what we did,' she corrected and snuggled even closer into his warmth and strength. 'It is very fine now, though, isn't it?'

'Nowhere near as fine as you are, my lady,' he murmured in her ear and she snatched a quick look around them to see if anyone else had noticed, but amid the chaos and chatter of a large family Christmas everyone was too busy, or maybe too tactful, to watch their host and hostess very closely.

'I was cold, too, Nathaniel, cold and lost and now…' Words failed her for a moment as sheer happiness made tears threaten and that would have him in a fine tizzy now she was so big with child. 'Now I have you,' she said huskily, 'and the Bump,' she added with a rueful smile as her hand joined one of his on her great belly.

She felt dreamily content as she watched the children her family already rejoiced in chase the twins, who were determined to explore every inch of The Grange's spotless great hall decked out with evergreens and gilded fruits and warmed by the vast Yule log that was only the latest one to burn on the hearths to make sure it was warm enough for the babies.

'I feel even more of a fool for staying away and making you lonely as well now we have all this, love,' Nathaniel told her.

'Don't, we were too young to live well with this much love. We both needed to grow up a little to realise how precious it is.'

'I certainly did,' he said dourly.

'No, you needed to heal.'

'What I really needed was you, if only I had been clever enough to realise it.'

'And now you have me,' she said with a purr in her voice, 'in every sense.'

'Behave yourself, my Juno,' he said with his body telling her how happy it was about all those senses.

'I don't think it's me we should worry about right now,' she said.

'No, you will have to stay where you are to hide my delight in my wife and our coming child while we talk about snowstorms to cool my ardour.'

'I don't think that will help much,' she said, memory of the one that had forced them together again making her feel a little too delighted about him as well.

'I think it's time you had a nice rest, given your condition and the strain of playing the perfect hostess.'

'What's your excuse?'

'Love,' he said and it worked.

* * * * *

MILLS & BOON®

Coming next month

ONE WALTZ WITH THE VISCOUNT
Laura Martin

Sarah made the mistake of looking up and for a long moment she was lost in Lord Routledge's eyes. Of course she'd noticed them before—even in the semi-darkness it was impossible to ignore the man's good looks. His eyes were a wonderful deep brown, full of sadness and intrigue.

She swallowed, her pulse racing and heat rising through her body.

She knew she was passably attractive, and there had been offers from a couple of young men of her acquaintance to step out over the last couple of years. Never had she been tempted. But, right now, if Lord Routledge asked her to run away into the night with him, she would find it hard to refuse.

Silently she scoffed at the idea. As if the poised and eligible Lord Routledge would ask her that. No matter what he said, he probably had five or six elegant and well-bred young women waiting for him downstairs.

'You look sad,' he said, an expression of genuine curiosity on his face. 'The waltz isn't meant to be a melancholy experience. At least not if I'm doing it right.'

With a press of his fingers he spun her quickly, and somehow they ended up closer than they had begun, her body brushing against his. She inhaled sharply, and for a moment it felt as though time had stopped. Their eyes met. Ever so slowly, he raised a hand to her face, tucking a stray strand of hair behind her ear.

In that instant Sarah wanted to be kissed. She felt her lips part slightly, her breathing become shallow. She'd never been kissed before, but instinctively her body swayed towards Lord Routledge. Her heart thumped within her chest as he moved a fraction of an inch towards her, and then stopped.

Continue reading

ONE WALTZ WITH THE VISCOUNT
Laura Martin

Available next month
millsandboon.co.uk

COMING SOON!

We really hope you enjoyed reading this book.
If you're looking for more romance
be sure to head to the shops when
new books are available on

Thursday 19th December

To see which titles are coming soon, please visit
millsandboon.co.uk/nextmonth

MILLS & BOON

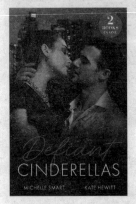

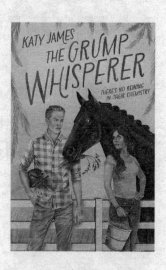
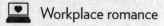
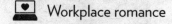
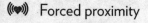
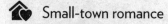

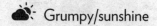

LET'S TALK
Romance

For exclusive extracts, competitions and special offers, find us online:

📘 MillsandBoon

𝕏 @MillsandBoon

📷 @MillsandBoonUK

♪ @MillsandBoonUK

Get in touch on 01413 063 232